Also by Micheal Maxwell

Cole Sage Mysteries

Diamonds and Cole
Cellar of Cole
Helix of Cole
Cole Dust
Cole Shoot
Cole Fire
Heart of Cole
Cole Mine
Soul of Cole
Cole Cuts

Logan Connor Thrillers

Clean Cut Kid
East of the Jordan

Adam Dupree Mysteries

Dupree's Rebirth
Dupree's Reward
Dupree's Resolve

Flynt and Steele Mysteries (Written with Warren Keith)

Dead Beat
Dead Duck
Dead on Arrival
Dead Hand
Dead Ringer

Copyright © 2020 by Micheal Maxwell

All rights reserved. No part of this book may be reproduced in any form or by any means, electronic or mechanical, including photocopying, recording, or by any information storage and retrieval system, without permission in writing from the publisher.

ISBN: 9798564238748

SOUL OF COLE

MICHEAL MAXWELL

Each of us is a book waiting to be written, and that book, if written, results in a person explained.
- Thomas M. Cirignano

Chapter One

"What is the hold-up?"

"I'm putting on my shoes!" He wasn't, he was reading the news on his computer. Russ Walker wanted to be sure he was up on all the latest before his morning debate session.

"For fifteen minutes?" Sharon was now standing in the archway outside Russ' office. "Get off the computer!"

"Oh, for heaven's sake. They're not going anywhere."

"Nine o'clock means nine o'clock. Not nine-fifteen or nine-thirty." Sharon stood hands on hips, head cocked to the left and a scowl that would make babies cry. "Let's go already."

Russ stood, yanked at the back of his running shorts through his warm-up pants. He felt like an idiot. Running shorts? He hadn't run more than ten paces in the last twenty years, and that was when a rattler was in the back yard flower bed. The outfit Sharon bought him for his sixty-fifth birthday was an embarrassment and the butt of endless jokes from his buddies.

"Let's get this done," Russ grumbled as he closed the front door.

"You'll thank me someday for getting you up off your duff and out for some exercise. 'Sides, I think you're just teasing. Once we get going, and you and Warren get arguing about whatever it is you two argue about, you don't even know you're walking."

"We don't argue, we have meaningful, spirited, discussions." Russ went down the steps and off they went.

"OK, as long as you are enjoying yourself, that's all that matters."

"Be more fun over a cup of coffee and a cinnamon roll." Russ finally laughed. It was a daily ritual that eventually showed that all his bluster was just an act.

Sharon gave him a swat on the butt and picked up the pace.

Warren and Judy Poore lived two blocks from Sharon and Russ. The two couples met over forty years ago and they have been friends ever since. The Poore's came to Orvin as young marrieds. Warren was the assistant pastor at the Calvary Methodist Church where Russ and Sharon attended.

Sharon and Judy were pregnant together. Their kids grew up together. Brownies, Cub Scouts, ballet, swimming, dance, t-ball, little league, softball, soccer, Pop Warner football, piano, practices and recitals, Judy and Sharon were there. Rain or shine they carpooled through activities and ten years of school. The Poore and Walker kids were often confused for each other, the wrong boys matched with the wrong sister. It was like one large cooperative family. That is until they reached Jr. High, then hormones, cooties, and peer pressure drove a wedge between the kids, and that was that.

The men bonded over their love of music. They traded recordings of their favorites, some of which, without a doubt, the members of Calvary Methodist would have raised their collective eyebrows at. They started with cassettes, moved to mini-discs (short-lived), then to CDs. With the purchase of their first computers, they entered the digital world. They learned to burn CDs, then DVDs. The ocean of music available to them on MP3s they found on the World Wide Web was a King Solomon's Mine to the Musicaholics. Now they pass flash drives in the foyer of the church, red for Warren and black for Russ. Like an info drop between spies, they were sly and silent, transferring their stash of new tracks with a quick handshake.

As Sharon and Russ made their way the last few yards to the Poore's, Russ couldn't help but admire the beauty of the morning. "Makes you glad to be alive!"

"Now there is a change of spirits!" Sharon grinned. All it took was to get Russ outside in the fresh air and he was a new man. She knew how much he hated exercise, but she was bound and determined to get him up and moving.

The Poore's house was like a photo from *House Beautiful;* the all-American white picket fence, manicured lawn, gigantic front porch with a swing on each end; Truly a dream home. Judy had a knack for decorating that Sharon could only dream of.

Sharon went up to the door first. After forty years, the formality of knocking was neither observed nor expected.

"Good Mornin'!" Sharon called out as she went through the front door. The house seemed unusually quiet. She moved to the bottom of the stairs and called up, "Let's get a move on, you two!"

"And you were rushing me!" Russ teased.

The faint sound of a radio announcer came from the kitchen/family room end of the house. Sharon turned and gave Russ what he would later recall as a concerned look. He moved toward the kitchen.

"Hey, are you guys here?" Sharon called, with a bit less enthusiasm than before.

As Russ entered the kitchen he noticed that the usual mess of breakfast dishes and coffee cups was nowhere to be seen. Walking past the snack bar, the first thing he saw was the family room wall and a three-foot splattering of blood, tissue and what appeared to be hair. Russ' eyes seemed locked on the circle. He was unable to process the nova of crimson that was spread across family photos and the *God Bless Our Home* stitchery.

"Russ? Whatcha doin' in there?" She peered across the kitchen, and out a back window to see if their friends had stepped outside.

Sharon's voice thawed Russ' frozen muscles. His eyes slowly moved down, fully aware of the carnage he would find.

Slumped on the sofa Warren Poore sat, head leaning in an odd, unnatural, position. A clotted, dangling, drip of blood hung from his bottom lip. The top of his head was an open mass of red and pink tissue. Warren's white Sooners t-shirt was a solid red from neck to waist.

"Russ!" Sharon was getting closer.

"Go home!" Russ shouted.

"What?"

"Leave, get out! Go home, call 911!"

Her voice was drawing ever closer.

"Damn you woman, do as you're told!" Russ screamed.

In all their years of marriage, Russ Walker never swore at his wife. He seldom, if ever, raised his voice. The combination of the two sent a wave of shock and nausea though Sharon. Not understanding or knowing the cause of the outburst she turned and ran all the way home. With each step, her tears grew. Her mind was grabbing at every memory, replaying every moment in the house, and every synapse searching for what just happened.

The reality of what he found began to sink in and Russ shifted his gaze from his friend's lifeless body and around the room. On the floor near the end of the sofa Judy was slouched, her head resting against a cushion. Her mouth was wide open. She stared with dead eyes at the ceiling. A large hole was surrounded by blood on the front of her white Cancun sweatshirt.

There was no blood behind Judy. Russ let his eyes slowly move from her head to her feet. She wasn't wearing shoes. Her bare feet were a strange hue of purplish blue. At her feet was a trail of blood. Russ followed the blood as its path led into the kitchen.

There were several partial footprints from where he stepped in her blood. On the back side of the snack bar was a large pool of cordovan liquid, an ever-narrowing, ever thinning trail of her blood leading to where she leaned.

Russ felt his neck with two fingers. As the space in front of him began to twinkle and shift to black and white he realized he wasn't breathing. His heart was rapidly beating out the pounding in his head. He took a deep breath and held it. The vein on the side of his neck was thumping hard against his fingers. His heart was pounding.

Far away and in another world, the sound of sirens pulsed. As they grew ever louder Russ felt his hands tingle and his legs began to quiver and shake. He backed up from where he stood and collapsed in a thick leather recliner. Across the room, the circle of Warren's life matter was in Russ' direct line of vision. He closed his eyes.

With his eyes closed his memory took over and he saw an image of Warren and Judy sitting on the couch with brightly colored packages on their laps and surrounding them on the sofa. In his mind, he heard the laughter of a hundred gatherings. He heard Happy Birthday being sung accompanied with visions of Warren, Judy, Sharon, the children of both families at various ages, all surrounding the couch, all different seasons, all different years, all different ages.

Time was no longer a thing Russ was aware of so he couldn't determine how long he was in the chair when he heard a loud, deep voice come from the front of the house.

"Police!"

"In here!" Russ's voice broke with emotion.

Seconds later two police officers with guns drawn entered the room. From somewhere down the hall the booming voice of another officer yelled, "Clear."

"Mister Walker?"

Russ did not respond.

"Are you okay sir? Mister Walker?"

"Russ felt his head nod and his voice say, "Yeah, I'm okay."

"Let's get you out of here, alright?"

Russ felt the strong hand of the officer take his arm and help him to his feet. Out on the street a siren slowly wound down. He heard doors slamming shut with metallic thuds.

"We have some folks who are going to check you over. You've had a pretty bad shock this morning. Can you do that for me?"

Russ nodded the affirmative.

As the officer half led, half carried Russ to the front door and the waiting paramedics his eyes landed on something that looked strangely out of place. Not that he hadn't seen it before, and not that it wasn't something normal for the Poore home, but on the counter by the sink was Warren's open Bible.

"I wonder what he was reading," His voice was lost in the crackling chatter of police radios.

"What's that?"

Russ didn't respond.

Chapter Two

"Good morning everybody!" Kelly approached the door of the *Love, Laugh, and Learn Indian Children's Center*. "Nobody has a key?"

"No, Warren isn't here yet." One of the six people waiting at the door volunteered.

"Well, that's kind of weird." Kelly scanned the group hoping for more information. "I have one. Let me open the door."

Kelly unlocked the door and the group of four women and two men filed in. They spread out to their various work areas and began the morning tasks. Ray Chandler, the older of the two men, went to the back and turned on all the lights. It seemed strange to be in the building without Warren.

Maryann Kopek approached Kelly with a concerned look. "You think we should give him a call?"

"Yeah, it's kind of weird that he just wouldn't show up." Kelly went into the office and Maryann followed. Just as she was about to dial the number, she heard a man's voice coming from the front doors.

"Anybody home?"

Maryann stuck her head out of the office door, then turned and whispered, "Kelly, it's a policeman."

"Good morning officer, something we can help you with?" From the look on the officer's face, this was not a community service visit.

"Are you in charge, ma'am?"

"For today she is." Maryann took a small step back.

"I guess so, I'm Kelly Sage." She extended her hand to the ruddy-faced officer.

"Is there a place we can talk privately?" The policeman shifted his hat from one hand to the other and back again.

"Is something wrong?" Kelly glanced at Maryann as uneasiness began to come over her.

"Better we didn't talk out here." He looked past Maryann into the large open room of the Center. "How many other folks are here?"

"About seven, counting us." Maryann came a little closer.

"Okay." The officer looked toward the office door.

"Let's go in here," Kelly suggested, re-entering the office.

"My name is Hawke." Maryann looked at him suspiciously. "Short for Whitehawke." He looked at Maryann and ran his hand through his jet black hair defiantly.

She smiled. "Thought so. I know your sister."

"So, what's this about?" Kelly braced herself for what must surely be bad news.

"You ladies might want to have a seat. I'm afraid I have some bad news." Kelly and Maryann sat. Kelly's heart raced knowing something must have happened to Warren Poore. "It seems, well, the thing is Pastor Poore and his wife were found dead this morning." Officer Hawke found himself unable to take his eyes off the floor.

"Oh, my Lord." Kelly threw her hand over her mouth feeling her heart skip a beat.

Maryann gasped. "What happened?"

"Well, it appears to be a murder/suicide. One of the fellows at the scene was familiar with your work here and thought somebody should come down and let you know, in case you want to lock up, or I don't know. I'm really sorry ma'am. It's a terrible thing to have to break to you." The young officer was plainly out of his depth, as he stumbled for what he felt was the right thing to say.

Kelly stood and crossed her arms across her chest. "I can't believe it. Why? We just, he was just, he worked here yesterday and was happy as could be." She looked from Maryann to the policeman and back, completely stunned.

"I don't know ma'am. The investigation will be ongoing. Is there anything I can do for you ladies?"

"Have their daughters been contacted?"

"I don't know ma'am. I was told to come here and tell whoever was in charge." As far as Officer Hawke was concerned his task was accomplished. He moved almost unnoticed toward the door.

Maryann sobbed and pleaded through her tears. "Will you tell the others, Kelly? I couldn't possibly."

"Yes, sweetie, I'll take care of it. Thank you, Officer. Is there anything we need to do, should we lock up and go home, or..."

"Just a second, ma'am." The young officer took his radio and spoke, "Lt. Bishop, Hawke here."

"Go ahead," the radio squawked.

"Sir, do the folks here need to lock up and leave?"

"I'm on my way there. Please keep anybody there out of the office." Hawke's eyes met Kelly's and they led Maryann out of the room.

"Will do."

"See you in a few minutes." The voice on the other end of the radio was firm but with a hint of regard for the rookie policeman.

"Yes, sir." Officer Hawke stepped out into the entry, closing the office door behind him. "I guess you heard that."

"Yes, I understand." Kelly looked out to the great room. The staff of volunteers busily vacuumed, straightened, and prepared for the day as usual, completely unaware.

In an hour, a group of fifteen to twenty kindergarteners would come through the door, most accompanied by their mothers, some alone. As was the tradition of the people from the reservation, they all looked out for each other's children. To hug, scold, help, and nurture was the duty and responsibility of all.

"Is she going to be okay?" Officer Hawke observed Maryann now facing the windows in the front of the building.

"I think so. This is such a shock. She lost her daughter not long ago. Her emotions are still pretty raw." Kelly suddenly felt the need to reassure the young policeman that things were under control.

"Yes, ma'am." Officer Hawke bowed his head for a long moment. "Please keep everybody out of the office until Lt. Bishop gets here."

"No problem."

"I'll be outside." Hawke moved toward the door. "I'm sorry I had to bring you such bad news."

"I imagine it's never easy." Kelly gave Hawke a reassuring smile.

"This was my first time." Hawke turned and quickly exited the building.

Kelly went to the center of the play area and called out, "Everyone, everyone, can we all gather here for a minute?" From the various stations in the large open space, the staff of the Center made their way to where Kelly stood.

"What's going on?" Ray Chandler spoke first.

"Let's wait till we're all here." Kelly breathed a prayer. As she watched the group of friends and long-time members of Warren Poore's congregation, Kelly felt a wave of emotion sweep over her. You can do this Kelly, she thought to herself.

Emma Connor was the last one to the circle. Kelly looked at the group and one by one made eye contact. "I'm afraid I have some terrible news. Before I say anything, can we just stop and have a word of prayer?" Several of the people answered in the affirmative. "Lord, please prepare our hearts for the sorrow that we all will share. I ask your guidance in helping me choose my words and I pray that we will all hold each other close. Amen."

"What on earth is the matter, Kelly?" Nellie Swanson, the oldest member of the group, was a particular favorite of Warren Poore.

"Yeah, what's going on?"

Kelly sensed the tension mounting in the small group and fought back tears.

"A police officer just informed us that Warren and Judy were found dead this morning." There were gasps from the group and two of the women burst into tears.

"What happened?" Ray asked.

"I don't know much, but a Lt. Bishop will be here in a couple of minutes. But, my understanding is that it was a murder-suicide." Esther Jacobs dropped to her knees and sobbed. Two of the other ladies turned and held each other in their arms. Ray stood one arm across his chest and his hand over his mouth. Otto Desmond turned and walked away from the group. Kelly turned, and seeing a chair, went and sat down.

Lt. Marty Bishop arrived with another detective and the Chaplain.

"Kelly!" Maryann called from the front of the building. Kelly's feet felt like lead as she made her way to join the three men.

"I'm Detective Bishop, this is Detective Finlay and I think you may know Pastor Cunningham, our Chaplain, already."

Kelly extended her hand to the detective. "I'm Kelly Sage." She reached a hand out to the tall, gray-haired man to the right. "Hello, Pastor Cunningham."

"I'm so sorry to meet you under these circumstances, but we really need to get as much information as quickly as possible. Is that the office?" Bishop was kind, but all business.

"Yes, sir."

"Has anybody been in there this morning?"

"Just Maryann and myself. I went in to use the phone to call…" Kelly choked with emotion.

"I understand." Bishop wondered if that was before or after he ordered Hawke to not let anyone in the office. "We're going to need to have a look around in there."

Kelly stepped back and the two men entered the office and closed the door behind them. Through the door, she could hear their muffled voices.

"What on earth has happened, Pastor?"

Cunningham wore an expression that Kelly found hard to read. "From the looks of things, Warren killed Judy and then turned the gun on himself."

"How can that be?" Kelly could hardly process the words.

"I can't begin to understand how such a thing could be possible. Warren and I have known each other and served on the Orvin Ministerial Association for over forty years. This goes against everything he believed, and everything he stood for. He loved Judy more than anything in this world. This just can't be. I am completely lost." Cunningham's words were no longer for Kelly, but the thoughts and concerns that flooded his heart.

"What about the girls? Have they been contacted? Do they know?"

"One of our female community service officers and a detective has gone to Cassie's. We thought it would be better if a woman was with him. I came here because I knew there would be a gathering of the staff."

"I can't think, my head just can't take this all in." Kelly shuddered and fought back emotion.

"What is going to happen to this place? Warren was the heart and soul of the organization. It was his baby." Cunningham shook his head.

"Somebody will step up." The future of the center didn't even enter Kelly's mind.

"You're a member of the board, right? Can you notify the other board members?"

"I guess so." Kelly was still trying to process the news. *I need some time*, she thought. *I need to talk to Cole. I can't make the calls.* She looked around the room and the others were still in a state of shock.

"What's the appropriate thing to do here, Pastor? We have all those kids coming in when school gets out."

"Do you think these folks are going to be able to handle that?"

"I don't think so." Kelly knew that the last thing she wanted to do was play with a room full of kids.

"I tell you what. I will stay here and meet whoever shows up. Let's send the rest of the folks home, whoever wants to leave."

"OK, I'll stay here with you." Kelly breathed a sigh of relief knowing the Chaplain would have the words to say, and she would be happy to let him.

"That's fine; it would be way better coming from us, rather than the television or radio. I know this town and the news is going around, already spreading like wildfire."

It was almost ten minutes before the two detectives came out of the office. Bishop held a stack of file folders and Finlay carried the computer.

"We'll be taking this stuff with us. I don't expect it will interfere with your operation." There was no question whether it mattered if it did. The two men were in full investigative mode, and they were not about to be deterred.

"No, take what you need." Warren is, was, the only person who used the office."

"I'll be back in a minute and get the contact information from you and the rest of the folks."

"How about I do that for you, Lieutenant?"

"That would be a great help, thank you, Pastor. We'll be in touch Miss…"

"Mrs., Mrs. Kelly Sage."

The detective nodded and left the building.

Shortly after 12:15 the children and the mothers began arriving at the center. All of the other staff left except for Ray and Maryann. Pastor Cunningham gathered everyone in the center of the open area and gently, kindly, explained the situation in words that the children would understand without going into a lot of detail. He asked the mothers if they wouldn't mind if he prayed for the group.

"That would be wonderful." Several of the mothers agreed. It was then decided amongst the mothers that, out of respect, they should all take their children home for the day.

Kelly felt a need as the lead staff member to offer a word of hope to the families. "Let's start fresh on Monday. Thank you all for your concern and please be praying for the Center and Warren's family. I know the Poore girls will be devastated."

The children and mothers quietly and solemnly left. A few stopped to have a word with Kelly or Pastor Cunningham and said they would be back with their children on Monday. Several volunteered to work next week to lend support to the center.

As the last of the mothers and children left, Pastor Cunningham said his good-bye. Standing in the front of the darkened building, Kelly finally broke down and cried. Her sobs seemed to echo in the cavernous space as they came back to her again and again. A while later Kelly locked the door and went home.

As Kelly pulled into her driveway she could see Cole and Ernie sitting on the front porch. Cole's feet were up on the railing and looked the picture of relaxation.

"What are you doing home so early?" Cole lowered his feet from the rail and stood.

"I'm afraid we got some bad news today."

"Oh yeah? What's that?"

"Warren and Judy Poore were found dead this morning."

"The hell you say!" Ernie now stood, too. "The fellow that runs that Indian Center where you work?"

"That's the one. It appears that he killed his wife and then shot himself."

"You've got to be kidding." Cole descended the step and moved toward Kelly. "Why on earth would he do that?"

"I don't know, it runs contrary to everything I know about Warren Poore. I saw him yesterday. He talked about giving special treats to the kids today. It just makes no sense."

Cole wrapped his arms around his trembling wife. She buried her face in his chest. For a long moment, they stood in the front yard holding each other.

"How did you find out?" Cole waited for Kelly to step back before he spoke.

"When I got there the place was locked up and Warren hadn't arrived. Shortly after that, a young policeman came. He gave us the news. A few minutes later two detectives came along with Roy Cunningham, the Chaplain."

"Cunningham is the pastor at Georgia's church. I mean our church," The pastor's name seemed to bring an urgency of the news for Ernie.

"Ray and I, along with Pastor Cunningham, stayed until the kids and some of the moms arrived. The pastor, bless his heart, broke the news and gave the sweetest little talk to the kids about death and heaven and being sure you're ready. Then he prayed with everyone and we all went home."

"So, is that the end of the Center?" Cole found himself at a loss for words. He wanted to show his concern and interest, but hardly knew Warren and only met his wife once or twice at fundraisers.

"We told everyone we would reopen on Monday, but I have no idea what the future brings."

"As a board member, don't you have some say in that?"

"I suppose." Kelly went up the steps to take a seat on the porch. "But I'm a volunteer. It's not my program and I certainly have no intention of working there full time, or being responsible for the daily operations."

"Doesn't he have a couple of kids?" asked Ernie. "Seems to me, I recall one of them was a pretty good soccer player back in the day."

"Yes, there are two girls. Cassie works in the Center part-time. The other sister is a missionary in Guatemala. I've never met her."

"That's right, I remember that now. Whew." Ernie began to process the news. "We catered a fundraiser there not too long ago. There's a lot of money tied up in that building with the improvements and all. It would seem a shame if it shut down." Ernie recalled preparing food for the event. It was one of the largest catering jobs they had done.

"I'm just stunned that Warren would kill himself." Cole shook his head. "The thing that's even weirder is that he would kill his wife. I don't get it. They've been married forever, right?"

"Forty-some years. They just celebrated an anniversary not long ago."

"Just goes to show you, you never know people as well as you think you do. I knew a fellow one time that had a big, old birthday party for his wife. They sang and danced, ate barbecue, had twenty or thirty friends over. And danged if he didn't go in the bathroom, crawl in the bathtub, lay down and blow his brains out. You'd have thought he was the happiest guy in the world." Ernie shook his head in wonder.

Cole looked at Ernie, who instantly recognized his story was poorly timed.

"Would you guys like something to eat? I didn't have lunch and I'm suddenly starving." Kelly moved toward the door.

"Yeah, I could stand to eat something, too." The offer of food brought Cole to his feet. "I was working on my new project and completely forgot about eating. Then Ernie came over. We've been sitting out here for awhile."

"I betcha you got some cookies in there somewhere, don't you?"

"You know I always have cookies, Ernie."

"The hell you say. I thought that was just a once in a while deal."

"Liar," said Cole. The two men laughed, then thought better of it. They went into the house sheepishly.

After Ernie ate three or four cookies, Kelly wasn't sure how many because she thought he snuck another when she wasn't looking; he wiped his place at the table with his napkin. "I better get home and get some of my chores done before Georgia gets home or she'll skin me. I'm sure sorry to hear about your friend, Kelly."

"Let Georgia know, will you please?" Kelly asked.

"I sure will, see you guys later."

Kelly picked at her lunch, misreading the hunger pangs for just an overall feeling of sorrow. She was sick at heart.

"Are you okay, Sweetheart?" Cole reached over and took her hand. "I know how much you cared for Warren and Judy."

"They were some of my first friends when we moved here. Remember, we went with Ernie to that retirement party for his hunting buddy, Russ? That was really the first thing we went to. I remember Warren telling me about the Children's Center and how excited he was about getting matching funds from the city for some renovations on the building."

"That's been a while." Cole sighed. "How long have you been volunteering?"

"Almost two and a half years now."

"It would really be a shame if the place closed up, but you know, sometimes the vision of the founder is hard to transfer to someone else. It reminds me of a neighborhood afterschool program in Chicago. A lady named Luellen Kaiser started babysitting for a couple of women in the neighborhood after school. She knew they didn't have any money and so she did it for free. You know how people are; sometimes they kind of take advantage of a good situation? She ended up with four or five kids in her little apartment every day after school.

"On the ground floor of her building there had been a little shoe repair shop. The old guy who ran it died and the landlord cleaned out the building. Luellen went to the landlord and asked him if she could use it as a space for kids when they got out of school. At first, the landlord wanted nothing to do with it, but when Luellen pointed out it would make a nice tax write-off, he jumped on it. Within six months it grew to over twenty-five kids. The kids helped her paint and build tables. The guy down the block, at the second-hand furniture store, donated a bunch of mismatched chairs and some throw rugs. Luellen won several awards from the city for volunteer work and the little center gained support and ran for nearly ten years before she died of cancer."

"She sounds like a wonderful lady."

"Yeah, she was a sweetheart. I wrote a couple of pieces on her over the years because a couple of kids from the center went on to live very successful lives and they credited Miss Luellen for keeping them out of trouble. The thing is, the point of the story is when she died nobody stepped up to take over. The little center was boarded up and a while later became a consignment shop for women's clothing."

"I would hate to see the kids at the center have no place to go. The facilities and opportunities for Indian kids in our county are almost nonexistent. The reservation pretty much has nothing."

"Well, it will be interesting to see what happens. This might sound selfish, but I would sure hate to see you tied down to it."

"You're right, that does sound selfish, and I'm a bit disappointed in you."

"I guess it was a bit premature, but there are things we want to do, like go to see the kids and do some traveling. I'm sorry, I guess I was insensitive."

"You're right, it is a bit premature. Let's see what the girls have to say. The daughter from Guatemala will be here in a couple of days. Maybe after the funeral, some decisions can be reached."

Chapter Three

Michael Blackbear was a popular figure in Orvin in his youth. He played football and ran track at Orvin High. He led the team to the district championship his senior year, rushing for nearly 3,000 yards and beating all school records. For his two varsity years, he was in the paper almost as often as the President. In order to not have to attend the schools on the reservation, he walked over two miles every morning, rain, snow or clear skies to the nearest bus stop to take him to school. After football practice, he walked home, often in the dark. He was a big man on campus.

His football hero status, however, only took him so far. It was rumored that he won Homecoming King by a landslide, but the honor went to the blue-eyed, blonde son of the town's biggest building contractor. After all, you couldn't have an Indian walking out to face the hometown crowd with the granddaughter of a bona fide Vietnam War hero, and three-time mayor, on his arm.

Michael was offered a scholarship at OU, but being a big fish from a very small pond, he barely made the first round cut for the football team. The final cut left him without a place on the team, and no scholarship. He sought financial aid, but with his grades not being as stellar as his sports record, he was advised to enroll at the community college on an Indian enrollment program.

Three weeks into the school year, when two airliners slammed into the World Trade Center, a third into the Pentagon and another nosedived into a field in Pennsylvania, Michael Blackbear enlisted in the army. His alcoholic, single mother and already married and divorced younger sister, and her two children, barely noticed his change of direction.

During his two tours in Iraq Michael was often in daily contact with locals as part of his assigned duties. A frequent visitor to the food distribution center that Michael oversaw was an Iraqi girl named Miriam.

Miriam was different than the other girls and women that came for rations. She walked head held high and with defiance in her step. Most days she wore a veil across her face, leaving only her sparkling dark eyes exposed. That was enough for Michael Blackbear. He missed the girls of high school with their breezy flirtatious ways. Even though he had neither the means nor transportation to date them, everyone knew where the invisible line was, and few, if any of the pretty girls who teased and returned his attention, dared cross it.

As he watched the dark-eyed beauty come each day to get a package of rice, lentils, and a gallon of clean water, Michael couldn't help but notice the way the other women seemed to shun her. Over the course of several weeks, Michael began putting an extra packet of flour, a can of meat, or a small package of sugar into her basket. The first time he offered the little extra Miriam's eyes flashed and seemed to reproach him. He just smiled and continued the practice.

He began to greet her when she arrived and bid her a good day when she left. The Wednesday of the fourth week, Miriam slipped Michael a small cloth bundle tied in a knot. Inside were three small, cinnamon raisin cakes. She became so flustered and embarrassed she left without her food.

At first, the shy, young woman never spoke to the handsome American soldier. As they continued to exchange small gifts they seemed to reach an understanding simply from their speechless communications.

When she finally spoke he was surprised to find that her English was better than almost any of the people in the area. She explained that her father was educated in the United States and, before the conflict, worked as an interpreter. This was the reason her family was suspect in the village. When her mother died they moved back to the village of his parents. A year later the war broke out, and he was suspected of being a CIA informant. Nothing could be farther from the truth, she explained.

Soon they found themselves going for walks and having long talks about America, Oklahoma and the traditions of the Cheyenne people. She explained the difference between Shiite and Sunni Muslims, and how it was political, not religious. Michael listened intently, not because he was interested, but because Miriam was speaking. He could have happily listened to her talk about anything for hours. He held no religious beliefs and hers had no bearing at all on his growing love for her.

During the eighteen months he served in the town, they fell deeper and deeper in love. They would find the time and places to steal away and talk, laugh, eat, and eventually make love.

Shortly before the anniversary of his first year in Iraq, Miriam came to him with the news that she was pregnant. He went to his commanding officer and requested the paperwork for them to be wed. Michael would bring her back to the United States.

"Don't be a fool." His commanding officer laughed off his request. "Find some nice Indian girl back in Oklahoma, and leave these people be."

Try as he may, and even going over the head of his commanding officer, he found the army to be unwilling, uninterested, and frequently hostile toward his desire to make an Iraqi his wife and claim the child as his son.

As the time grew nearer for him to return to the U.S. and a different post, the couple panicked. Miriam grew larger by the day. The women of the village went from the shun of silence, to open disdain for her. Some went as far as to throw rocks and rotten vegetables at her when she walked down the street. If she were left behind, life would be intolerable for her and their child.

They could no longer go for their walks due to Miriam's condition. Her father, though enraged at her pregnancy, and even more so of her relationship with an American, allowed them to meet in his home.

It was on one of these visits Michael suggested he desert the Army and go into hiding in Iraq to be with her. Miriam was steadfast in her refusal. She knew far better than he that it would be a death sentence for them both. Instead, she put her faith in his ability to work things out. He insisted they be married, and tried to find a magistrate in the town to perform a civil ceremony.

The law prohibited the union of a Muslim woman to a non-Muslim man. Michael's anger grew hotter towards the army prompting his decision to abandon his plans for a military career. As his time for reenlistment neared he refused all offers, counsel, and pleading from his peers, as well as superior officers.

One evening he took Miriam to the outskirts of the small town. Beneath a cobalt sky filled with a million stars, he performed as much of the Cheyenne wedding ceremony as he could remember, sprinkled with the words of preachers at the few Christian weddings he attended. Miriam spoke in Arabic, quoted the Koran, and translated the verses for Michael.

That night, before Allah, the Christian God, and the Great Spirit of the Cheyenne people, Michael Blackbear took Miriam as his wife.

When the baby was born, Miriam refused to name the little boy, saying that he would have an American name and they should wait until they were all together to give him the correct name. She found great honor in knowing her son would be a member of the Cheyenne tribe and would be given a name by the chiefs and elders.

Arriving back in the U.S., Michael tried many different channels to get Miriam and the boy a visa into the U.S. Because of the conflict in Iraq, and the quotient for Iraqi immigrants, his request was denied time after time. Back in Orvin, a friend suggested he go to Warren Poore, the Methodist pastor and founder of the Love, Laugh, Learn - Indian Children's Center, to see if there was some way for him to help.

Pastor Poore's first reaction as a Minister was to suggest that marrying a woman of another faith was a recipe for conflict in the marriage.

"Religion was for each one to choose," Michael told Poore he cared nothing for religion. "I don't care what she believes."

"Does she wear Muslim headdress?" Poore went straight to the heart of his objection.

"Yes, but..."

"Can you imagine a woman walking the streets of Orvin looking as she did at home? In this town where we have lost so many young men to wars in the Middle East? Her presence would be far from welcome."

"It would be almost as bad as being an Indian." Michael Blackbear was losing his patience with the prejudice he was seeing. The people of the United States were willing to give the lives of their sons and daughters for the Iraqis, but unwilling to have them in their country.

"That's not fair. We have made great strides in the coming together of our communities." All Michael heard was an air of 'look what I've done' in Warren

Poore's response. Unfair or not, Michael was blinded by frustration and anger.

"So, are you saying that as an Indian?" Michael scoffed at Poore's words. "No. You are still the kindly white man, still trying to teach little red children and their mothers the ways of the white world. Nothing has changed in two hundred years."

Michael Blackbear's words burned with the reality of growing up Indian in Orvin. Good enough to win football games, but not good enough to date white girls. The poverty and substance abuse of the reservation drove him from his home only to find a different kind of prejudice in the army for the people he fought for.

Michael left his first meeting with Warren Poore angry, confused and longing for a return to his life in Iraq. He would go home, calm down and write him a letter. Maybe that would convince Poore he was serious about bringing them home, Michael thought driving home.

"Descanso! Tomemos un descanso!" There were so many Mexicans and Central Americans working the construction job sites that the foreman no longer bothered to make announcements or call a "break time" in English.

Michael Blackbear walked to the west side of the house they were working on. It felt good to get out of the hot sun for a few minutes. He opened his large, yellow, insulated jug and took a long, slow drink of cold water. Several of his new co-workers came and sat around him on boxes and empty five-gallon paint buckets.

"Eres Indio?" Jesús, the unofficial leader of the group asked.

Michael Blackbear knew enough Spanish to answer "Cheyenne. Do you speak English?" he asked the man.

"A little." Jesús nodded.

"Tell me something." Michael began. "How did you get here?" The four men sitting with Michael all looked at each other. Finally, one nodded his head toward Jesús.

"Through the desert into Texas."

"How did you know where to go?"

"Why you want to know?"

"I want to get someone into the U.S." Michael looked the man in the eyes. He wanted his trust. He needed his help.

Jesús turned and spoke to his three comrades in Spanish. Again, they looked at each other trying to decide whether they could trust Michael Blackbear.

"You know Coyote?"

"I have heard of such people." The ice was broken. Michael knew what a Coyote was, and he needed to find one.

"You need Coyote."

"How do I find one?" Michael asked.

"Tomorrow, Mañana."

"Is it expensive?"

"Mañana."

An uncomfortable silence fell over the group. For the first time since he began working at the site,

Michael felt alienated and not part of the crew. He wondered as he sipped his cool water if this was his answer to getting his family into the United States.

The rest of the afternoon the crew worked hard but, other than instructions or questions about what they were doing, there was little of the usual chatter and good-hearted teasing. As they knocked off for the day, Jesús walked past Michael and without stopping or turning his head, again said, "Mañana."

Michael's night was filled with restless sleep, dreams, and tossing. As he drove to the work site, he wondered if his crew would actually help him, or were they just using Mañana to put him off? As he pulled up to the house they were currently working on, the sound of Tejano music blasted from one of the cars and the four members of the crew were standing around talking. As Michael approached the group they all separated. There was no longer a feeling of camaraderie and he wished he never mentioned their legal status.

"Good morning." Jesús approached Michael.

"Buenos Dias." Michael smiled. Maybe all is not lost, he thought.

"They are going to work on the roof. Me and you, we work on the siding." Michael Blackbear did not question and followed Jesús to a stack of plywood. They worked without talking for more than an hour.

A white Chevy pickup pulled up onto the empty lot next to the house, stirring up a cloud of dust near where they were working. Two men sat in the truck and scowled out the window at Michael and

Jesús. As if to give himself courage or a sense of well being, Michael put his hand on top of his hammer in his tool belt, like the hero in an old cowboy movie.

The passenger door of the truck opened and a small, thin man dressed in jeans, a white western shirt, a cowboy hat, and very pointy, lizard-skinned, cowboy boots got out.

"Jesús!" It wasn't a greeting. It was a command to join the man.

The two men walked out of hearing distance of Michael and chatted for a minute or two. Then Jesús disappeared around the end of the building. A man approached Michael, and he gave an uneasy, soulless smile.

"So, I hear you need a friend." He was not friendly and his words held the feeling of a veiled threat.

"I understand you are someone who can help me."

"Help is expensive." The words lost any hint of cordialness. "Where does a man who works here building a house get money for such help?"

"You let me worry about that. I can get the money."

"So, who is this person you want to bring across the border?"

"My wife and my son. But, they are not Hispanic."

"What do you mean?" The man gave an inquisitive look.

"They are from Iraq."

"Chingada ese. Where the war is? You crazy?" The Mexican's swearing showed a crack in his tough guy posturing.

"Yes. Can you help me?"

"This is totally new to me. I've never done such a thing."

"Can you put me in touch with someone who can?"

The Mexican studied Michael Blackbear. Michael worried that his request was so far out of the ordinary that a small fish in the food chain like this guy, in his beat-up pickup, might not want to swim in these waters.

"I didn't say I couldn't do it, I said I *hadn't* done it. Let me talk to my people and see how it could be done. But, I can only get them across the border. You will have to get them into Mexico."

"I'm not sure I know how to do that," Michael said.

"Anything can be done for a price. Let me get back to you in a day or two. I'll see what I can find out."

"Thank you, I'm Michael Blackbear." Michael offered his hand.

"No names. I will see you in a couple days." The man did not shake his hand and returned to the passenger side of the pickup. The other man took the wheel dutifully.

The next two days and nights were spent thinking, planning and worrying if he had done something stupid. He was desperate to have Miriam and his boy with him, so it didn't matter.

The morning of the third day it was nearing lunchtime when the white Chevy reappeared. This time it parked across the street and down the block. There were three short blasts on the horn and Jesús called out to Michael. "That's for you".

This time the small man was driving and the passenger side was empty. As Michael approached the truck, the small man said, "Get in".

Michael's heart pounded as he rounded the truck and opened the passenger side door. An automatic pistol lay across the man's lap as Michael got into the truck.

"So, what did you find out?"

"It can be done, but it will cost $40,000. $20,000 now and $20,000 when I bring them to you."

"That's a lot of money, much more than I thought."

"I thought you wanted them out of their country." The man shrugged.

"I do, I do. I just…"

The Coyote reached up on the dashboard and took a card that was stuck into the air conditioning vent. "Call these people and they will help you with the money. When you have the money, call me again. My number is the red one."

Michael took the card and read the number. The card was for a heating and air conditioning company. The words were scribbled through. The sight of the gun and phrase, 'help you get the money' written on the back made him very uneasy, but he was committed to having his son and Miriam back again.

"I'll call you."

"If you do, you do." The man started the pickup.

Michael shoved the card deep into the pocket of his jeans and went back to work.

The plate of leftover chicken and potatoes held no interest for Michael. He sat and stared at the card on the table and the telephone number with no name. He somehow knew he was about to make a deal with the devil. He put the number into his cell phone twice before he worked up the nerve to hit the green dial button.

The phone rang three times before a man's voice said, "Hello".

"I was told you can help me raise the money to get my wife and son into the U.S."

"Who gave you this number?"

"He didn't give his name. He's a Coyote. White pick up, he wears lizard skin boots."

"I don't care what you do with the money, but yeah, I can help. Do you know the Chew'n'Chat just outside of Orvin? Meet me there tomorrow at 3:30. We will discuss the details."

"How will I know who you are?"

"Don't worry about it, I will figure out who you are." With that, the line went dead.

In the late afternoon of the third day, Cole went with Kelly to pay a visit to Cassie Poore, the daughter of the murdered couple, to show their respect and offer condolences.

"My father has been depressed lately because the finances and the backing for the Center have been drying up." The young woman sat on the couch in Russ and Sharon Walker's living room. "People, who for many years were an integral part of my father's ministry at his church, just aren't interested in his new Indian charity. A lot of them, because of recent problems with the Indian community, were openly hostile towards dad. Old friends, people who have known him for years."

Cole watched the girl closely as she directed most of her words at Kelly. She seems very together, he thought.

"Listen, I don't know what people are saying but my father would never kill himself. He believes that suicide is the one sin you can't ask forgiveness for. You go straight to hell. And the thought of him killing my mom? That is absurd. He loved her more than anything. Forty-one years they were married, no way, there is just no way."

"I can't imagine him doing it either." When Kelly replied, Cassie looked down into her lap.

Cole spoke for the first time. "When was the last time you spoke to your folks?"

"The night before, they were..." Cassie glanced up at Cole for a brief moment then down to her lap. "They were all excited about my party. They were throwing me a twenty-first birthday party at the Center. My birthday is in three weeks."

"I'm sorry." Cole tried to sound more compassionate than he felt. He didn't like the girl. Everything she said seemed to have an underlying selfishness in it.

"For what?"

"For your party being canceled."

"Who said it was canceled? You're only twenty-one once. It might sound harsh but I want that party. I have been waiting since I was sixteen. That other great landmark birthday, Sweet Sixteen, I didn't get either. My sister got appendicitis, so my party got canceled and then forgotten."

"Then I'm doubly sorry." Cole was right; he really didn't like this girl.

"Speaking of my sister, she's flying in tomorrow. She's a missionary you know, in Guatemala."

"That's wonderful." Kelly was trying to distract from the obvious tension between Cole and the young woman glaring at him.

"That's part of the problem with the lack of funds. I'm sure it was part of my dad's worry and depression. All their money was going to support Rebecca as a missionary."

On the way home, Kelly and Cole discussed the girl's response to their questions and inquiries.

Cole asked, "Don't you think the discussion of her sister was kinda weird? I think I detected a real resentment towards her."

Kelly answered, "I don't think at a time like this you can read much into a person's responses. She's obviously very upset right now at the loss of her parents."

"Yeah." Cole tasted his words. "But I didn't get the impression that she was particularly excited about her sister's arrival."

Chapter Four

"Have you got the barbecue lit? They'll be here any minute."

"Yes ma'am, I did it about twenty minutes ago."

"I'm excited to see what everybody thinks of this new recipe." Kelly manically flew about the kitchen seeing to every detail, even the ones no one would notice. When she was in full-on hostess mode Cole tended to stay out of the way.

"It smells wonderful."

Yakety-yak, Don't talk back, Yakety-yak, Don't talk back. Cole's phone rang with the old Coasters hit to warn of an incoming call from someone *not* in his address book.

As the refrain repeated Kelly reminded him of the obvious. "Are you gonna get that?"

"I guess I have to." Cole teased as he picked up his phone. "Hello."

"Is this Cole Sage?"

"Yes, it is. Who's this?"

"This is Michael Blackbear."

Cole realized it was the young, angry veteran he met at the Center. It took a moment for Cole to put the name with a face. It was several weeks since they met. Blackbear was having a shouting match with

Warren that ended when he stomped out. Cole went into his, "let's see what we can do" mode, and probably got more involved than he needed to. Cole thought back to that first meeting.

"I had to return home and tried to resign from the army. My commanding officer refused my resignation, said I was a fool, and that I would lose my benefits and regret my decision for the rest of my life. Last month my enlistment ended. Since then, I have talked to our congressman, the state department and the INS. No one recognizes our civil ceremony. They've all either stalled or pushed the responsibility on to someone else. I've talked to anybody who was anybody, what makes you think you could possibly help?"

The voice on the other end of the line snapped Cole from his recollection. "You don't remember me, do you?"

"Of course I do, how are you, Michael?"

"You said you were going to help me but I haven't heard back from you. It's been almost three weeks. I got another denial letter in the mail. You want to hear it?"

"Does it say anything beyond no?"

"Not really, same old BS."

"Let me tell you where we are on my end. I called my old friend that worked in the State Department. He's retired. My other guy passed away a few months ago. I'm kind of starting over, dropping their names as a way of getting my foot in the door. I did find one sympathetic guy in the INS that deals with refugees with asylum issues."

"She's not a refugee, neither is my son! She is my wife!" Blackbear was nearly shouting. His anger was quite obvious, born of the resentment of getting nowhere for months on end.

"Whoa. Take a deep breath. I'm on your side, remember?"

"Sorry. I'm just at the end of my rope with all this."

"Okay, here's the deal. We have a far better shot of getting her to the United States if she is declared political asylum status. Showing that she and the boy are in danger works way better than wife status when you have no paperwork. By the way, what is the boy's name?" Cole thought the mention of the boy might lower Blackbear's blood pressure.

"We haven't named him yet. We're waiting for them to get here to give him a real American name."

"Would you be willing to write out a sworn affidavit that she and your son are in physical danger and are in a hostile environment due to her relationship with you and the United States Army?"

"Of course, of course, how do I do that?"

"You just need to see an attorney and tell them." Cole thought for a moment. "I tell you what, how about we go together? I have the names, departments, and address where it needs to go. You have a case number, right?"

"I have everything that anybody, anywhere, has ever sent me. That is after I realized I would need them and stopped tearing them up."

"Okay, that's fine. How 'bout this, you make the appointment and let me know when and where and we'll get this done. I know you've been at this a long while, but you're going to attract a lot more bees with honey than vinegar. If we're going to be successful in this you need to mellow out. Do you understand what I'm saying?"

"Yes, it's just that…"

"It's just that nothing. If I'm going to work with you we're going to have to do it as friends, not like I'm the enemy. Otherwise, I don't have time for this."

"I'm very sorry, sir. Truly, it won't happen again."

"I'll take you at your word. Alright, let me know when you have the appointment set up."

"I'll get right on it, thank you again. And, sorry I was a jerk."

"All is forgiven. We'll just start anew. Talk to you later."

Cole set the phone down on his desk and walked back towards the kitchen.

"What on earth was that about?" Kelly was standing in the kitchen door wearing an expression that was a combination of amazement and anger.

"That was your buddy, Michael Blackbear."

"He's not my buddy. What did he want?" Kelly was not amused by Cole's attempt at transferring his relationship with Michael Blackbear to her. "That guy is a ticking time bomb."

"He is so angry and frustrated at how slow and ineffective the wheels of government are that he lashes out, even at the people who are trying to help him."

Kelly wiped her hands on her apron. "I think you should cut him loose. He was a real problem at the Center. Every time he would come in it would end up with him shouting and screaming at Warren and stomping out. It wouldn't surprise me one bit if he was the one that killed him."

"Okay, hold on. It's your turn to take a deep breath. Just 'cause you don't like the guy and he has a short temper doesn't mean he's a killer."

"I've seen far too many of the men who come off the reservation wearing a huge chip on their shoulder and angry at anyone trying to break the cycle of poverty and dependency on the government. I've seen it time and again. The husbands and fathers come in half drunk, ranting about how we are brainwashing their children and destroying their culture. I've called the police more than once when they got physical with their wives."

"Okay, you have some valid arguments for why an Indian would be suspect. But, you know as well as I do, you can't throw a blanket of generalization over a whole group of people based upon the actions of a small group. Aren't you the one who is always telling me how wonderful the Cheyenne people are?"

Kelly went back into the kitchen, clanged pans, closed a few cupboard doors a little too hard, and mumbled and grumbled just loud enough for Cole to not be able to understand what she was saying.

Cole waited nearly five minutes before he followed her into the kitchen. "I hope all of that steam you're letting off isn't directed at me." He gave a sheepish smile thinking that maybe his mini-lecture went a bit too far.

"No Professor, I'm angry at myself because you're right. I love the people I work with at the Center. Most of the fathers are very supportive of our work. But, I am angry and frustrated too, at the death of my friend Warren. Say what you will about the Center's history of hostility from fathers, I won't be surprised at all if one of them killed him."

Kelly crossed the kitchen, took Cole's face in her hands. "I could never be angry at you for being right." She kissed him gently.

"Thank you, that's very kind."

"Actually, you're right so seldom that it's not a big threat." Kelly laughed merrily and slapped Cole on the butt.

The sound of car doors slamming announced the arrival of their guests.

"They're here." Cole looked out the front window at Brooke and Randy Callen coming up the front walk.

"Cole, I am serious about one thing." Kelly was now standing behind him and slipped her arms around his waist. "I want you to be very careful getting involved with Michael Blackbear. I don't have a good feeling about that guy."

"I promise." Cole went out onto the porch and greeted Randy and Brooke as they approached the steps.

The young married couple was more like a second set of kids than just friends. The newlyweds had gone through some rough water with Brooke's dad. In a moment of sentiment or guilt, he pledged to build them a house. He had since changed his mind. After an angry, tear-filled confrontation with Brooke, they are now estranged, making her bond with Kelly even stronger.

Randy's computer sales and repair business was doing very well. Brooke came into the business after they married to run the front counter. She was a real hit with customers and her bookkeeping experience kept her young entrepreneur husband in the black.

They rented a cute little house in a new subdivision not far from the shop. Kelly saw to it that they came over at least twice a month for dinner. It was a nice way for them to get away and have people to talk to.

Randy did a Boy Scout salute and called up to Cole, "Is the back of the house on fire?"

"It's the barbecue, funny guy." Cole shook his head in mock disgust. Brooke giggled and made her way up the stairs. She gave Cole a hug and a peck on the cheek.

"It's always so nice to get to come out to the country." She looked over Cole's shoulder. "Is Kelly in the kitchen?"

"Yep, ever since about three o'clock. You know how she is." Brooke went inside. Cole and Randy followed her. They went straight through the house heading for the backyard.

They stopped at the newly screened in porch. "Wow, this looks amazing, did you do this, Cole?"

"Yeah, right. I had a friend of Ernie's do it. Actually, Ernie used to work with this guy's dad at the sewer plant. Like it, huh?"

"Yeah, it looks awesome." They continued on through to the backyard. "Did he do the gazebo, too?" Randy walked across the yard to the new addition. He knelt and examined the newly sprouting Sweet Peas.

"Yeah, I think he could build just about anything." Cole raised the hood on the Weber and poked the coals with a stick that was leaning against the handle. This looks about ready. "Kelly, you got that meat ready?" He heard footsteps on the porch.

"Yes, it's on its way." She came through the back door with a large, blue, plastic tray. Neatly laid out on it were four steaks, four chicken thighs, four pork chops, and four pale, nearly white, bratwurst sausages.

"Is there somebody joining us?" Randy asked.

"No, I just thought since the coals were fired up we'd do a little of everything." She handed over the tray to Grill Master Cole.

"Kelly's under the foolish impression there will be leftovers." Cole laughed and winked at Randy.

Randy came back to where Cole worked at the grill. Taking a chair, he looked around the yard. "Man is this a nice place. Someday I'd like to live out in the country. I grew up kind of out in the country."

"That must be why you turned to computers." Cole laughed at his joke. Randy just gave him a sarcastic courtesy grin. "It gets pretty boring at times."

Cole placed all the meat out on the grill, adjusted the air vents, and took a seat across from Randy.

"So, how are you guys doing? Feels like I haven't seen you in ages."

"Brooke is pretty upset about the Poore's being killed. You've probably heard all about it, right? Kelly must be really upset."

"Yeah, she's putting on a brave face, but she worked really close with Warren. It's a weird deal. Everybody seems to have loved the guy, except for a handful of Indians who *really* didn't like him or, probably better said, his Center."

"Brooke's mom went to Calvary Methodist before she died. You know Sharon and Russ are good friends of her dad. I can't imagine what it must have been like to have found them."

Cole kind of let the talk of Warren drift into the air along with the smoke from the grill for a while.

"You know, I've never been the one to find a body, but I've been there shortly after and it's something you can't wash from your mind very easily. I really hope those folks have the good sense to get some counseling. Kelly has worked there over two years now and I've been down to the Center a bunch of times and Warren was a real sweet guy. He really seemed to love those kids. I don't know why anyone would want to do him any harm. Or his wife. That's really a weird one. The strange thing is it wasn't a robbery. Nothing was missing, the house wasn't torn up, the cop told Kelly they were just sitting in the family room with bullets in them."

"How did they know it was suicide?" Randy leaned forward in his chair and lowered his voice. "Could it have been murder?"

Cole smiled. "You don't have to be Sherlock Holmes to figure out somebody didn't kill themselves if there's no gun to be found."

"That's true! So, which is it really?"

"That, my boy, is the $64,000 question."

"I liked it better when we used to know what was going on in an investigation."

Cole let that comment pass but knew exactly how Randy felt. "So, how's business?" Cole again tried to deflect away from the Poore's.

"We're doing really well. I guess putting Brooke at the front counter was a smart idea."

"Yeah," Cole said. "She's way prettier than you are. I bet that didn't sit well with her dad."

"It really doesn't seem to matter anymore. They had such a blow out he may never speak to her again."

"That's too bad. What now?"

"It's still all about the stupid house. I wish he'd never mentioned it. I think he was just caught up in the moment, feeling generous and briefly sentimental."

"I'm really sorry, buddy. You know, like they say, 'can a leopard change its spots?'"

"You know, I never liked him in the first place. It's really hard on Brooke, though, because he's the only family she has. She tries to put up a good front too, but there are times I can see she's really hurting."

"That's rough." The two stood silently as Cole took the cover off the grill. The smoke wafted through the back yard. Cole poked one of the sausages. "You're going to have to be her family. If anybody knows what it's like to be alone, it's you. So, you just have to be there. We're here, too. Don't forget that. We've got your back."

Randy smiled. His gratefulness didn't need to be spoken between the old friends. "So what have you been doing to keep yourself busy?"

"I started another book."

"Oh, yeah? What's this one about?"

"Well, I thought I might try my hand at writing a historical novel. Seems like I always gravitate to history, biographies, stuff like that. What do you think about a book about World War II?"

"Yeah, I love books based in history. The background makes for good fiction and you know the old saying, truth is stranger than fiction."

"Right?" Cole agreed.

"But you know what I think would make a great book? Some of the stuff that happened in San Francisco. You couldn't make that stuff up, either. Besides, if you need help with your fading memory, you can give me a call. Believe it or not, I kept all our stuff from the Chronicle. All the research notes, pictures, police reports…"

"Police reports?" Cole was surprised that Randy would have kept, better yet, got his hands on, police records.

"Yeah, well, sometimes you just can't help yourself."

"You mean *you* can't help yourself!" Cole turned the steaks.

"Isn't that what I said?"

"Very funny."

"So, this book you've started, what's it going to be about?"

"Actually, I'm kind of excited about it."

"Your war idea?"

"Yeah, it starts at the beginning of WWII. It's about a diamond, and concentration camps, and a girl who goes through the whole thing." Cole's tone changed and a thread of seriousness entered the conversation. "I want it to show the horrors of war and how the diamond kept the girl dreaming of a better life. It kind of symbolizes hope."

Cole watched Randy closely, trying to read his response.

"Does it have a happy ending?"

"Yeah. It works out."

"In that case, I can't wait to read it."

"What is that wonderful smell?" Brooke washed her hands in the sink and sniffed the air.

Kelly turned and smiled at her. "A new recipe I have been wanting to try; bacon, apricot, jalapeño jelly. I thought it would be amazing on the chicken."

"It smells incredible."

"Good." Kelly gave the pan a stir and moved to the counter.

Kelly looked over at Brooke and she was staring out the window, the water just running over her hands. "You look troubled. Anything I can do?"

Brooke welled up with tears. "You can start by giving me a hug. This has been the worst three or four days ever." Kelly stepped forward and put her arms around Brooke. "I've known the Poore's my whole life. Anytime I saw them, they always had a nice memory of my mom. They really were one of the few links I had to her. Judy taught my Sunday School Class when I was little. Who would want to hurt them, Kelly? I just don't understand." Brooke willed herself not to cry.

Kelly stepped back, reached down and took both of Brooke's hands. "There are some things, sweetie, that just aren't explainable. I've worked with Warren for about two years. He was one of the kindest, gentlest people I've ever known. The older I get, the harder these pointless acts of violence are to understand, and they seem to haunt me."

"What will happen to the Center now?"

"It was Warren's life dream to help the Indian community. I don't know what will happen without him there. I'm not sure how much of a commitment Cassie has to the work there. I've never met the other daughter, Rebecca. Do you know her very well?"

"She's a couple of years older than I was in school, so I didn't know her all that well either. She's a missionary, you know."

"I know, her father was so proud of her. I hear she is supposed to arrive tomorrow."

"What a horrible thing to have to come home to."

"Oh, heavens." Kelly sighed deeply. "Let's not let this horrible news throw a damper on our dinner. Let's think of something happy. What have you got, anything? How is working in the shop going?"

Brooke opened the refrigerator. "Goodness Kelly, you've got everything done." Brooke shook her head and gave Kelly a faint smile. "I can't believe I'm working the front counter in our own business. I'm the one who had a hard time just answering the phones when I worked for my dad. Now, I really get a kick out of meeting and talking to people and seeing Randy turn their bad situation into something good. I think that guy could fix anything!"

"That's wonderful, I'm so proud of you. I wasn't going to bring it up but have you talked to your dad lately?"

Brooke giggled. "Gee, Kelly, out of the frying pan and into the fire. I thought we were going to talk about happy stuff."

"I take that as a no?"

"Yeah."

Kelly ran the spatula around the edge of the big glass bowl and turned the potato salad one last time. "This looks like it's ready to go. Can you get the fruit bowl out of the fridge? I think we're ready. I wonder how much longer Cole will take with the meat. You take this," Kelly handed her a tray with the plates, utensils, and drinks.

"What's this?" Brooke pointed at a bowl covered with plastic wrap.

"That? Another new recipe, Mango Ginger Chutney."

"What do you do with it?" Brooke looked down into the bowl filled with chunks of yellow mango in a shiny brown sauce.

"I'm thinking the place for it is on the pork chops, maybe even the chicken. I can't wait for you to try it." Kelly smiled at the thought of chutney being completely foreign to Brooke.

"I'm game." Brooke headed out to the patio with the tray. "Why do you two look so guilty?"

"Because we are." Cole shook the barbecue fork at her.

Kelly stuck her head out the door. "How much longer?"

"Just a couple of minutes."

"Okay, we'll bring everything out to the table. I've sautéed some vegetables; I think they need another minute or two."

"These are looking like they're done," Cole announced with pride.

"Good, I'm starving." Randy moved to where Brooke was setting the table and kissed her on the cheek. He picked up a stack of napkins off the table and placed one at each setting.

The four gathered and were seated at the table. With the table set, the food ready and waiting, Cole asked Kelly to say grace.

After everyone was served, Randy suddenly stood and cleared his throat. "There's something we've been wanting to talk to you guys about. Well, umm… I think that since I, or we have been, that is…"

"Oh, let me do it, silly!" Brooke was smiling from ear to ear. "We're going to have a baby!"

"Oh, Brooke!" Kelly's eyes filled with tears. She jumped up from her chair and gave the startled girl a hug. Randy looked at Cole and they gave each other a high five.

Kelly took her seat, wiped her eyes and took a deep breath. "Oh, my. How long have you known?"

"Umm, well, actually for a couple of months. But, the doctor said he was a bit concerned with, oh I don't know, so we didn't want to say anything in case something happened."

"Here's the thing." Randy looked down at the table and his voice cracked. "I don't have any parents, and you know the story with Brooke. What would you guys think of being the honorary grandparents?"

"That's the most wonderful thing anyone has ever asked me." Kelly teared up again. "We would love it."

"How about you, Cole? You haven't said anything." Brooke looked at Cole with a bit of concern.

"I'm still kind of in shock." Cole smiled. "I don't know what to say other than, I would be honored."

"We have this idea. We kind of wanted to run it past you." Randy turned slightly and looked directly at Cole.

Kelly leaned forward in anticipation.

"What would you think if we were to name the baby Hanna? If it's a girl, I mean."

"Wow." Cole was taken completely off guard. "I think that would be amazing. She would be so proud if she knew."

"We know she meant a lot to you, Cole, and you know how much she meant to Randy. We thought it would be a nice way to honor her memory."

Brooke reached over and took Randy by the arm. "If both of you loved her she must really have been something."

"I think that is very thoughtful. Just wonderful." Kelly looked around the table with a warm smile. "I just love you all so much."

"Okay, Okay. Don't start me crying. Can we eat now?" Randy poked a bratwurst with his fork.

The two couples laughed merrily.

Chapter Five

The large, glass sliding doors slid open onto the sidewalk at Will Rogers International Airport. Rebecca Poore came through the door dressed in a colorful, native Guatemala skirt that reached nearly to her ankles. On her feet, she wore handmade leather sandals. She wore a heavy, green sweater over a white peasant blouse. Over her shoulder was slung a large, khaki green duffle bag. Her dark brown hair was pulled back in a single braid, reaching the middle of her back.

She stood for a long moment scanning the area when she heard the blast of a horn. In front of her on the curb was her sister, Cassie, in a silver Dodge Durango. The passenger side window rolled down and Cassie called out, "Hop in!"

Rebecca opened the back door and tossed her duffle bag inside with the small purse she draped around her neck.

"Have you been waiting long?" Cassie asked.

"I just walked out the door." Rebecca looked thin and tired. "How are you, sis?"

"Not good," Cassie responded. Rebecca buckled her seatbelt as Cassie pulled away from the curb. Neither sister spoke as the car moved through the crowded lanes leading out of the airport and back to the highway. "How was your flight?"

"Well between the motion sickness and crying, not the best. I'm so sorry, Cassie. This is the worst thing that has ever happened." Cassie didn't respond.

She just stared forward and drove. Several miles went by before Cassie spoke. "How long are you here for?"

"As long as I need to be." Rebecca tried to be reassuring. "I imagine there are things to do and affairs to be settled, not to speak of the house and all the stuff in it. Do you want to live there?" Rebecca asked softly.

"I don't want anything to do with Orvin, now, in the future, or ever. I hate that place and I always have."

Rebecca was shocked by her sister's hurtful response. She showed no signs of grief or mourning. Her open hostility toward their hometown was a side of her Rebecca had never seen.

"I'm sure you don't mean that. This is a terrible shock and a terrible thing to have to go through. We mustn't rush into any decisions that you might come to regret." Rebecca sighed and continued. "What in the world is going to happen to the Children's Center?"

"I don't know and I don't care. I hate that place, I hate those kids and I hate working there."

"Cassandra, how can you say such a terrible thing?"

"Easy. I didn't want to work there. I never wanted to work there."

"Then why did you?"

"Because I didn't want to be the only one in the family who wasn't serving people in some way. You might say I was shamed into it. This whole ministry thing might be your thing and daddy's thing, but it was never mine. I just wanted to go to school and have a career and get out of Oklahoma." Cassie's voice broke with emotion. "Forgive me. You're right. Too much has happened. Feelings I have suppressed are bursting out of me. I feel like a snake must feel shedding its skin."

Rebecca sat staring straight out the window, tears streaming down her cheeks. Her emotions were so raw and her heart so broken she couldn't respond. She leaned over and rested her head on the window. As the car gently moved along the highway the vibration and humming of the road rocked her to sleep.

A hard bump jostled Rebecca awake as they pulled into a self-serve gas station. "You want something to eat or drink?" Cassie asked as she opened the door.

"Yes, some water would be really nice."

"I'll be right back."

Rebecca decided to get out and stretch her legs. The wind blew hard into her face, dry and warm. It was good to be home, she thought. But, what is home? Her thoughts drifted to what she would face when she got to Orvin. The dread of a funeral, and all the planning without her parents there to help and guide, was unthinkable. Her mother sang at a thousand funerals since she was young. Her father gave funeral services, both grandiose and simple, graveyard prayers. I don't think I can do it, Rebecca thought. She paced next to the car until Cassie returned.

"Here," Cassie said with no feeling, handing her a bottled water.

"Thank you."

Cassie got back into the car after pumping the gas. Rebecca joined her a moment later. "Cassie, please don't be upset with me. I didn't mean to upset you and I certainly didn't understand how you felt. This is hard enough with us together; I couldn't bear it if I had to face it all alone."

"I'm not mad at you. And I'm sorry if I just blurted out my feelings, but I've had it bottled up for so long it just came out. I'm sorry."

"I love you, Cassie."

"I love you too, Becca."

As they pulled back into traffic on the highway, Rebecca asked, "If you went back to school what would you study?"

"I think I would like to study accounting. Work on being a CPA."

"Really? That's an interesting field."

"No it isn't, it's boring as hell and you know it. But, I wouldn't have to deal with people. The idea of having my own little space, even one of those cubicles in an office with my work to do, seems like Paradise to me."

"You always did seem to have a knack for math. I remember you helping me with mine in high school and you were still in Junior High."

"How long do you think you're going to stay in Guatemala? You look like a native already."

"It's funny, most of the clothes I took with me are either worn out or I gave them to somebody. So, in the villages, I dress like this." Rebecca pulled at her skirt and flopped it back and forth. "These things are cheap and they wear like iron. Not exactly a Kardashian look, is it?"

"No, but nobody would ever say it makes your butt look big." The sisters laughed which seemed to ease the tension and release some of their anxiety and sorrow.

"We will be staying with Sharon and Russ. I couldn't face going back to my apartment yet. They have been so kind and Sharon is taking care of a lot of the preparations for the service. Daddy's friend, Roy Cunningham, will be doing the service. They will have closed coffins, of course. Daddy's would have to be." Cassie fell silent.

They rode for a way before Rebecca said, "I don't think mom would want people staring down at her, either."

"Seth called yesterday."

"Booth?"

"You know another? He wanted to know if you'd be coming home."

"Why would he call? I thought he was engaged to that Calhoun girl."

"I heard they broke up a long time ago. Something about her fooling around with one of the Epperson boys."

"Huh," was Rebecca's only response as she seemed to drift into her own thoughts.

Cassie reached over and turned on the radio. The sound of country music blasting through the Durango seemed a bit much as she reached back down to lower the volume. She hummed softly along with the girl singer, occasionally singing a lyric or two as the landscape changed to the familiar, dry, rolling hills toward Orvin.

"There it is." She pointed to a green highway sign stating 'Orvin next exit', complete with a dozen bullet holes.

"I haven't gotten a letter from Molly Kopek in over a year. Is she still in town?"

"Oh, I'm so sorry, Becca. I forgot to tell you, Molly passed away last year. She had some kind of tumor or growth, or something on her spine, that by the time they found it, it had spread until she had only weeks to live. I'm so sorry."

Becca put both hands over her face and rocked back and forth in the seat.

"I'm sorry," Cassie said, "I shouldn't have told you right now."

"How could you not tell me? She was my best friend. I intended to call her as soon as we got home. I have to go see Maryann."

Cassie flicked the turn signal, merging off the highway at the Orvin exit.

"I suddenly don't want to do this, Cass. I don't know how much sorrow I can take."

Cassie reached over and patted her sister's leg. "Don't worry; we'll get through this together. It's just a few more days."

But it won't be, Rebecca thought, looking out the window as they slowed for the turnoff. "Nothing has changed. Everything looks the same, but everything will be different." Rebecca turned to look at Cassie for a long moment and then back out the window at her hometown.

Russ Walker stood in his front window staring out at the street. The dull ache in his chest, since finding his best friend sprayed across the wall, had receded little. The sense of dread of seeing Warren's daughter Rebecca, the funeral to come, and life without his best buddy seemed almost too much to bear.

"They're here!"

Sharon entered the room drying her hands on her apron, scurried past Russ and out the front door across the lawn to the sidewalk. Cassie and Rebecca got out of the car. Cassie stood next to her closed door as Rebecca eagerly ran around the front of the car to embrace Sharon.

"Oh Becca, I'm so sorry," Sharon said as she began to sob. Rebecca couldn't speak, just stood holding onto her mother's dearest friend.

"Thank you so much for taking care of things. I don't know what we would have done without you."

"Where are your bags?"

"Oh, my bag is in the back." Cassie moved to the back and popped the lid.

"Russ, come get the bag." Russ moved from the porch to where the three women stood. He almost made it to the girls before breaking down into heavy sobs.

"Oh, Uncle Russ," Rebecca called out as she ran across the lawn to meet him and gave him a warm embrace. They both stood crying and holding each other tightly. Finally, Rebecca said, "I thought I was all cried out."

"I'm sorry Becca, my blubbering doesn't help, I'm sure." Rebecca placed her hands on his cheeks and pulled him down and gave him a gentle kiss on the forehead.

Russ wiped his eyes looking down at the grass. "I'll get your bag."

Sharon reached out and took Cassie's hand and said, "Let's go in." As they passed Rebecca, she looped her arm through hers.

As they entered the house Rebecca said, "Thank you so much for allowing us to stay with you. I couldn't face going home just yet."

"You must be terribly tired from your trip. I put you in Matt's old room. Cassie is in Jessica's. I hope that will be alright."

"It's fine," Rebecca said with a faint smile. "It's so good to be home and to see you again."

"Are you hungry? Would you like a sandwich or coffee, anything?"

"A cup of tea sounds wonderful if you have any."

"Come on in the kitchen." The two girls took a seat at the table as Sharon put a kettle on to boil. Cassie sat silently, still having not said a word since they arrived. This did not go unnoticed by Rebecca.

"Cass, you've had a long drive. Do you want to go lie down?"

"No, I've laid around too much."

"Is there any coffee left?" Russ asked entering the kitchen.

"Coming right up, I'm making some more."

"Cassie, would you like something, hon?"

"Coffee sounds good."

The three sat quietly, Russ drew circles on the kitchen table with his index finger. The kettle was working up its way to a whistle as Sharon took it off the heat. "I have some cookies here I made yesterday. Let's see if we can't finish those off." She brought cups and teabags to the table and returned to get the coffee pot. "I spoke with Jeannie at the church and everything is arranged for the service and the social hall. Several ladies have volunteered to prepare a light lunch just after the service."

A knock on the door came as a shock as the four sat in silence drinking their coffee. "I'll get that." Russ quickly rose. To his surprise, when he opened the door there were two police detectives standing on his porch.

"Mr. Walker, I'm not sure if you remember me. We met under pretty unpleasant circumstances. I'm Detective Bishop. This is my partner, Detective Finlay."

"Yes, I remember," said Russ. "How can I help?"

"I understand that Cassie Poore is staying with you."

"That's right, and her sister just arrived today."

"Good," Bishop said. "We have some information we need to share with the daughters. I understand you were very close to the Poore's."

"Yes, lifetime friends," answered Russ. "Please, come in." Russ led the two detectives into the kitchen.

"This is Detective Bishop and Detective Finlay. They have some information to share. I think you know Cassie already. This is her sister, Rebecca, who just got into town." The two girls nodded toward the detectives. Rebecca stood and crossed the room to shake hands with the detectives.

"Do you know who did this horrible thing? There is no way my father could have done it. No way on earth he would be capable."

"That's kind of why we're here. It's our opinion, and that of the forensics team, that you are correct. This was not a murder-suicide. We are formally declaring it a double murder."

Sharon threw her hand over her mouth, "Oh my! But, who?"

Cassie stared at the two detectives and was speechless.

"I just don't understand." Rebecca's voice quaked with emotion. "If it wasn't a robbery, and there was no break-in, what happened? How can this be?"

"I know your father and mother were well loved in the community. Even my family has a connection with your dad. He officiated at my sister's wedding and did the funeral for my uncle. Times like these, it's hard to imagine someone doing such fine people harm. But, we have to try and think of things that, maybe on the surface, don't seem so apparent."

Sharon stood and said, "Please, please sit down. Coffee?"

"That would be nice. Thank you." Both detectives took a seat at the table. "Do any of you know anyone who may have harbored bad feelings toward your father? Going back, can you think of anyone he may have had a run-in with at the Center, or maybe a counseling session that ended badly? Sometime there may have been a conflict? This was not a random act, and the person, whoever it was, was welcomed into the home. There was no sign of a fight and no indication of a struggle, which leads us to believe it was someone familiar to both the pastor and his wife."

"I've been in Guatemala for over two years. This is my first trip home in three. I really have no sense of my parents' relationships other than Russ and Sharon. Since my dad retired from the ministry, the Center has been the focus of his life."

"Most of the people who come to the Center are mothers and children and the occasional father. It is supposed to be a place of safety, learning, and fun." Cassie tapped the top of the table lightly with her index finger.

Bishop turned to Russ and Sharon. "You were their closest friends. Did either one of them ever mention a problem with anyone, an angry neighbor, anything?"

Sharon spoke first. "Other than old ladies with complaints about the church service, loud music, the ushers, the parking, or some other silly thing, I've never heard Warren mention any kind of an issue."

Russ took a sip of his coffee. You could almost hear the wheels turning as he thought of some possible time when anyone could be angry with him. "You know, I can't think of anyone at any time that Warren had words with, except me, maybe. And arguing was our favorite sport. But it was all good natured and in good fun."

"Have the funeral arrangements all been made?" Bishop was drawn to Rebecca, and it didn't go unnoticed by anyone at the table.

"We've kind of been discussing that this morning." Rebecca offered.

"I don't mean to sound crass or invasive, but we'll need to have a couple of plainclothes officers at the service."

"You think the person would cause trouble at the funeral?" Sharon looked at Bishop in disbelief.

"No ma'am, but it is not unusual, or unheard of, for the perpetrator to attend their victim's funeral. We will be looking for any kind of strange or unusual behavior of those in attendance."

"I saw that on TV once." Russ injected his thoughts into the conversation. "The killer showed up at the funeral and was so twitchy and weird that the cops were suspicious of him."

"It's usually not that easy." Bishop gave a faint smile. "But yeah, that's kind of the gist of it."

"I have no problem with that." Rebecca nodded at the detective. "Cassie, what do you think?"

"So long as they don't look like they're on guard duty. I would hate for their presence to be distracting or disruptive."

"You have my word, you won't even know who they are."

"Then I guess it's okay."

"When is the funeral?"

"Friday at 2:00 at Calvary Methodist," Sharon explained.

Bishop reached in his pocket and pulled out a cardholder. He placed his card on the table and said, "If you think of anything, no matter how trivial it may seem, it can trigger other memories that can be very important, so, don't feel funny about letting us know. If you can think of anything, anything at all, call me."

"You guys don't seem to be looking in the right place."

"What do you mean?" Bishop's head jerked toward Cassie who suddenly appeared to be angry.

"I mean, have you looked at guys like Tommy Running Dog? He's threatened my father on more than one occasion. Have you talked to him? How about Richard Armendez? He tore the Center apart once screaming and yelling. He shoved his wife to the ground and scared the kids half to death. And how about Samson Knight? He swept everything off my dad's desk and told him to watch his back. Seems to me those three are pretty good suspects. Have you talked with any of them?" Cassie stood and glared at the detective.

"That's what I mean about pieces of information. No, we haven't spoken to them. Nobody had mentioned them up until this moment. Thank you for your cooperation."

What happened to the 'place of safety, learning, and fun'? Bishop glanced down at his notes. Marty Bishop was trying to remain calm in the face of Cassie's outburst, but he could feel redness creeping up his neck and into his cheeks. He motioned to his partner and both men took their leave and exited the house.

"Why has no one ever told me about these kinds of problems? Are there any others? How often does this sort of thing happen?" Rebecca looked at everyone in turn around the table.

Cassie turned from the window and stood to face Becca. "Why would we bother? You're 3,000 miles away. That's just a small part of why I've had it with this place. Imagine how those guys would behave if it were just women in charge."

"I feel like I'm so out of the loop on everything. Is there anything else I need to know?" Becca was on the verge of tears and stunned by her sister's revelations.

"I'm not in the mood for this." Cassie left the kitchen, a few moments later the sound of the bedroom door slamming jarred the silent house.

"Are you okay, sweetheart?" Sharon was quick to tend to Becca's emotions.

Becca looked up, tears streaming down her face. "I just don't know her anymore."

"You know," Russ took a deep breath and reached over and patted Rebecca's forearm. "People all react differently to tragedy. Some people roll up in a ball and lay in the dark. Some people break things. And some people go on as if nothing has happened. Everybody is different. Cassie's lashing out at everybody and everything around her."

"I just don't know what to say around her because everything sets her off. I'm still trying to get my head wrapped around the idea my parents have been murdered, while at the same time I feel like I'm in a boxing ring with my sister."

Sharon set her cup by the kitchen sink. "I think it would be best for everybody if we just gave Cassie some space for a while. You must be exhausted. Why don't you go into your room and take a nice long nap? I will go walk the dog. Where are you, boy? Come here, Ratchet." Within seconds the dog came running into the living room. "Wanna go for a walk?" The dog jumped up and barked at the door.

"You know, I think I'll go with you. Maybe the air, sunshine and some exercise will make me feel better." Becca stood.

"Ol' Ratchet and I would love the company. I'll get his leash."

Chapter Six

Michael Blackbear knew of The Chew'n'Chat. He'd never eaten there. He realized that he'd never even been in it. It is such a nasty little redneck place that to call it a greasy spoon would be a compliment. The building was badly in need of paint, the sign on the street was faded on one side. The other side was broken when some drunk probably threw a bottle through it years ago. There were four cars in front as Michael pulled up to park. One was a shiny, black Escalade. The others were old, dirty, and missing a bumper, chrome, or large patches of paint.

Michael opened the door and entered just far enough for the door to close behind him. He glanced around the small restaurant. There was a man sitting at the counter drinking coffee. Two men were at a booth, old wrinkled cowboys a decade past their prime. A third man in a Harley Davidson t-shirt stood hovering over an old jukebox. On the opposite side of the small space sat three men in a booth.

The man facing the door waved. He then motioned to one of the men across the table to move next to him. Michael made his way across the room to the booth.

As he walked toward the far end of the restaurant he remembered the words of a gunnery sergeant he served with in Iraq. "Be careful who you trust," he told a young Blackbear on his first tour, "The devil was once an angel." At the time Michael had no idea what the reference meant. Now, the beguiling offer of money and the illegal crossing of Miriam and his son seemed to speak clearly of the temptations of things that shone a bit too brightly. You still have a chance to leave, he thought to himself. But he didn't pay his thoughts any mind.

"Have a seat." Michael reluctantly sat down next to a large man wearing dark glasses. "So, you're in need of funds."

"I am." Michael tried hard to appear relaxed.

"Well, my friends and I can, and will, buy anything you can bring to us."

Michael studied the man sitting across from him. He was average in every way. It would be difficult to describe him. Must be a real benefit for a criminal, Michael thought. The man sitting next to him, on the other hand, would be easy to pick out in a crowd. He possessed the face of a killer. Michael knew the look; he saw it often in Iraq. Men who, having lost all hope, turned off their conscience. They were devoid of morals and cared nothing for the feelings, well being, or lives of anyone else. Pulling a trigger was of the same importance as scratching their nose. Crossing one of these men could result in a letter being sent home explaining you somehow died from friendly fire.

"I'm not sure I follow." Michael wanted, no needed, a clearer picture of what these men did.

"Anything of value that would fit on top of this table, we'll buy from you." The man beside Michael laughed and rested his forearms across the table.

Michael did not speak. He observed the man who spoke, his eyes showed no sign of humor or irony.

"You mean you're a fence?"

"I'm not *a fence*. I fence things, meaning I buy things from people. You've watched too much TV." The man next to Michael chuckled again. "Nobody says that anymore, but just so you know we are clear, I'm a fence of barbed wire."

This time no one laughed. The tone of this unremarkable man left no doubt the muscle he surrounded himself with was not to be trifled with.

"So are you suggesting—,"

"I'm not suggesting anything. I'm simply saying we will buy shiny, sparkly things that you lay on this table."

The conversation was moving dangerously close to Michael wanting nothing to do with these people. He owned nothing of value. Truth be told, he didn't know anyone who did. His only possession of any value was his car, and it wasn't worth much, and certainly wouldn't fit on the table.

"And where do I find these things?" Michael asked, still not allowing himself to accept what they were suggesting.

"That's not my concern. When you have something for us to buy, call that same number. Until then, I don't want to hear from you."

Michael sat silently and looked at the three men sitting at the table for a long moment. He wanted to get up and run, but he knew that they were Miriam's ticket.

There were things he wanted to know, needed to know, but just as he began to speak the man sitting next to him gave a hard nudge with his elbow. Michael turned to look at him and he jerked his head toward the door. The conversation was over.

Out in his car, he replayed the conversation. He was to steal things for them to buy. "I'm no thief." Michael's words came out in gasps. How could he trust such people? What would stop them from just taking whatever he brought? Who would he report it to? 'Hey, they stole my stolen stuff.' In the army, he knew of thieves and guys who would loan you money. They required collateral. They didn't ask where it came from.

The drive home was filled with an ongoing conversation, both in his head and aloud. In the end, it was Miriam and the boy that mattered. It would only last long enough to get the money. Then it would be over. She would join him. They would raise the boy in the safety of the reservation, Federal laws, Federal protection, and a community that doesn't ask questions. His people would be her people and his son would be a proud member of the tribe. He would figure out a way to do what they wanted.

The following morning when Michael arrived at the job site, his crew was nowhere to be found. Instead, the job foreman sat on an upturned bucket in the garage. The glare he gave Michael left no doubt there was a problem.

"Where's everybody at?" Michael asked.

"Gone." The foreman stood.

"What do you mean, gone?"

"I mean not here. They didn't show up. They didn't show up yesterday, either. Then again, neither did you." The foreman walked out to the driveway.

"I was sick."

"Uh huh." The foreman turned to face Michael. "So, do you want to work here or not?"

"Yes sir, I need this job."

"Alright, join the guys down at #1607, they'll tell you what to do. But if you pull a disappearing act again, you're finished. Understood?"

"Understood."

The foreman walked to the next house. Michael walked back to his car and instead of joining the new crew, he headed for the reservation.

It felt strange to enter his house at this time of day. The light was all wrong. Michael went into the bedroom and pulled a small suitcase from the closet. He opened the case and saw the things Miriam sent with him to America. 'These will make it feel like I'm coming home.' This was the first time he opened the bag since she gave it to him on the day that he left Iraq. 'When I join you in America.'

He reached in and took a scarf and held it to his face and breathed deeply. The sweet smell of her jasmine perfume still lived in the scarf. He pulled several articles of clothing from the small case before he found what he was looking for. Picking up a burka he held it up in front of him. Turning, he walked to the mirror above the dresser and placed the hooded veil over his head. As he stared out of the small, mesh square he realized that no one in the world would ever know who he was. He opened the top dresser drawer and took out a pair of thin, goatskin gloves that Miriam gave him as a gift. He remembered saying to her. 'These are very nice, but where would I wear such a wonderful thing?'

'In America when you drive your fancy car.' Her voice seemed to float melodically.

There was no fancy car, but he knew they were just what he needed for his intended purpose. Taking the gloves and burka, Michael went to his car.

There was an uneasy feeling about the drive to Enid. The churning in his guts reminded him of the first time he was in a firefight in Iraq. He turned on the air conditioner to combat the sweat rolling down his face. The blast of the cold air did not remedy his nervous perspiration. It simply gave him a chill.

He drove around for nearly an hour before he spotted *Town and Country Jewelers*. There were other jewelry stores, but they were always in a crowded shopping center. The small store sat in a strip mall between a carpet store and a consignment shop. Michael parked his truck sideways, taking two parking spaces parallel to the store. He slipped on the gloves that were waiting in the seat and took the rolled burka and wadded it tightly. There were few other cars in the parking lot as he made his way to the door. The six feet of bricks between the stores hid him as he pulled the burka over his head. He pulled his service 45 from the waistband of his pants, took a deep breath and burst into the door.

"Do as I say and no one will get hurt." Michael's growl left no room for misunderstanding.

"Please." The woman's eyes bulged behind the counter as she stared at the strange figure before her.

"Is there anyone in the back?" Michael stepped into the small space between the counter and the glass showcases.

"No, my husband has gone to the bank."

"Then take a bag and fill it as quickly as you can. I would hate to put a bullet in your head and have to fill it myself."

"Don't shoot, I'll do it, I'll do it." The woman grabbed a bag and began dumping trays into the bag. She worked methodically right to left, dumping rings, bracelets, earrings, necklaces and watches into the waiting bag.

"Other side." The barrel of Michael's gun jerked hard in the direction of the opposite showcase. "Now!"

She moved around the counter and repeated the actions along the length of the other showcase. As she reached the end nearest the door, he snatched the bag from her.

"On the floor, hands on your head!" She obeyed without a word and he ran from the store, yanking the burka off his head as he went.

He was nearly a block away before Michael could breathe again. Careful to not exceed the speed limit or do anything to draw suspicion, he headed for the highway and home.

As he drove, he shoved the burka and the gloves into the bag and stowed it under the seat between his legs. A few miles from Orvin he pulled into a shopping center. There was a pay phone on the corner of the small café. Approaching it, Michael took a handful of change from one pocket and the card the man gave him at Chew'n'Chat in the other. He dialed the number on the card. It took four rings before a familiar voice answered.

"So soon?" The man seemed amused at the call.

"I have some sparkly things for you to see." The sound of his voice sent a shudder through Michael. His pact with the devil was sealed. He stepped across a line so unnatural to him it was as if someone else was speaking.

"7:00." The line went dead. Michael stood motionless, staring at the names and phrases scratched onto every surface in the phone booth. "What have I done?" His voice seemed completely lost in the wind as he stepped from the phone booth.

The hours moved so slowly that Michael forced himself to not look at the clock. In order to calm his nerves and pass the time he decided to take a nap. As he laid on his bed, the woman's face in the jewelry store came to him again and again. He felt ashamed, and even embarrassed, at what he did. He lay on the bed for what seemed an eternity before he opened one eye and looked at the digital clock on the nightstand.

Only forty-five minutes had passed. He got up and decided to drive to town.

Cole sat on the porch staring out at the yard. His phone rested in his lap. He picked it up, started to tap in a number, then stopped, and turned it off. He turned the phone end over end several times. He wanted to make the call, he was just hesitant. If this were a case in the old days he would have been on top of it, already in the middle of gathering information. Now just a civilian with no reason, right, or willing ally to put him in the middle of the case, he just felt old and out of place.

He looked at the phone. There was an ache within him for an outside connection; someone who knew him, not as that author guy from California that inherited that little place out by Ernie the Greek, but someone who knew his worth, his value in a tight spot, as a fact finder, interviewer, decipherer of clues. He turned the phone around and punched in the numbers.

"Hello, Leonard?" Cole felt hesitant, even embarrassed, to be making the call.

"Hey!" Detective Leonard Chin sounded both surprised and pleased to hear his old friend on the other end of the line. "I thought you died."

"No, it just feels like it. What's new?"

"Well, you should be thankful you don't live here anymore. This whole city has turned into a giant outhouse. When you're not stepping over human waste on the sidewalk, you're dodging homeless carts, junkies and crunching needles under your feet. I'm really beginning to hate this place." Leonard spoke with no humor in his voice. "What's going on with you?"

"We've got a case here that I wish you and I were working."

"I miss doing that." Leonard's chair screeched when he leaned back. "You're the best partner I ever had, and you weren't even a cop." Both men chuckled. "So, what's the story?"

Cole's spirits lifted. Just being acknowledged was the balm he needed for his emotional aches and pains. It was as Sherlock Holmes used to say, the game was afoot, if just for the next few minutes.

"Okay, let me tell you. We have a minister and his wife shot dead in their home, the rumor is nothing missing, no suspects, no enemies, and no traces of forced entry."

"That sounds more like a mystery novel to me," Leonard said. "Speaking of which, I read your book. I liked it, are you going to write any more?"

"Yeah, I got some ideas."

"So, these dead people. You say it was a minister?" Chin brought the subject back around.

"Yeah, he had been the pastor of a big church here, but in recent years he ran a center for Indian kids and their mothers, part after-school program, part parenting program, with some free nutrition thrown in the mix. Kelly has been volunteering there almost since we moved here. She can't imagine who would want to harm those people."

"How old are they?" Chin seemed genuinely interested.

"I'm guessing mid to late sixties. They have two kids, one that was out of the country and one works in the Children's Center."

"Who found them?"

"Their lifelong friends. They all went walking together every morning."

"Oh, that's rough."

"Yeah, they're not taking it real well." Cole could see his old friend pondering the information as if they were drinking coffee across the table from each other.

"So how would you rate the police there?"

"The Sheriff's Department is okay, but unfortunately this is the Police and they're a pretty snotty bunch. Kelly seems to like the lead Detective. She said he was kind to the daughter and the people at the Center." Cole paused. He was starting to feel homesick and the call was not helping. "To tell you the truth, I really called just to hear your voice. I can't remember the last time I had an intelligent conversation with somebody. This town is not what you would call a pinnacle of cultural, gastronomic, or literary activity."

Chin laughed. "My wife keeps bugging me for us to move to Vancouver."

"Washington?" Cole was shocked by the idea of Chin leaving San Francisco.

"No, British Columbia. She's got three or four cousins that have come over from China. She says we should move there to be near them. I don't have anybody left here and I'm really considering it."

"How many years do you have left before you retire?" Cole asked.

"Too many. Once my daughter goes off to college we really have no reason to stay here."

"It sounds like you've got your mind made up."

"I don't know about made up, but I'm certainly leaning in that direction. I had a case last month where we found five kids locked in an apartment with a dead dog and an empty bag of dog food. Nobody knows how long they had been there, but the M.E. said they all starved to death. We don't know where they came from, who they belonged to, or why they were in there. Who the hell does something like that, Cole? What kind of animal lets children starve to death?"

"You and I both know starving to death is way better than what could have happened to them."

"Yeah, you're right. I think I've just seen too much and it's getting harder and harder to shake the images in my head. Why don't you and Kelly fly out and maybe we can all take one of those cruises to Alaska?"

"I'm sorry, who am I talking to?" Cole couldn't believe his ears. Leonard Chin, in all the time he'd known him, never took a vacation. A long weekend here and there, or a couple of days either side of a holiday, but real honest to goodness downtime with no threat of being called in on a case was unheard of.

Chin laughed. "My wife has been bugging me to take her on a real vacation, not just a weekend trip to Carmel. I hear they don't have internet on those ships unless you pay a hundred bucks an hour or something. And no phone service either."

Cole smiled broadly at this new Leonard, and he liked him even more. "Remember that time I was planning a railroad trip through the Canadian Rockies?"

"Yeah, you never did get to go. We could do that, too. But I really like the idea of the big boat. I think the ladies would like it too. What do you think?"

"I'll talk to Kelly; it sounds like a great idea to me. I really need a break from all this peace, quiet, dust, and flat."

"Boy, aren't we a pair." Leonard's remark was meant to be funny, but the melancholy in his voice crushed any irony. Cole heard the sound of a squawking police radio in the background. "I hate to cut this short, but I've got a call. Think about the cruise. I've got a couple of links I'll send you. I really need to take some time off."

"Alright, good talking to you, buddy, be safe." Cole felt like the call ended in the middle of his sentence.

Cole set the phone back in his lap. He knew he missed his friend, but he didn't realize how much. His thoughts drifted to the view from the Bay Bridge. He wondered if Kelly would agree to a ten-day trip to Alaska. He wouldn't care if the boat never left San Francisco Bay. It would be like heaven to see the skyline and Alcatraz again.

Cole got lost in thought of all the times he rode across the Golden Gate Bridge when he and Kelly were first dating. He remembered his bike tires were flat. They had been for over a year. The bumpy, poorly paved road that ran in front of the house was not very good for riding. Cole smiled as he remembered the Marina and his long bike rides. For a moment he pondered getting up and going to pump up his tire but realized it probably had a goat head sticker in it and it would be a totally pointless exercise. Maybe he should go get a new tube, but he didn't feel like a trip to town. He would just run over another one on his next ride anyway. He put the thought out of his mind.

Standing, he walked to the end of the porch and gazed at Ernie and Georgia's house. Now that's a lovely little place, he thought. Lots of flowers and green stuff surrounding it. He looked at his lawn and wondered what the patches of golden, dead grass were from. He walked down the porch steps and picked up the hose and turned the faucet on full blast. Turning to face the lawn, he began to spray the dead spots on his lawn.

"Maybe that's what I need!" he said out loud. And he turned the hose and squirted himself in the face.

Chapter Seven

"Becca," Sharon called from the kitchen. "I'm gonna fix something for lunch, would you like something?"

Becca was sitting, her legs tucked under her, in a recliner in the family room. The curtains were pulled apart on the sliding glass door to the backyard. Russ was scooping leaves out of the pool. Without really reading any articles, Becca was thumbing through an old copy of *Better Homes and Gardens* just looking at the pictures and reading the occasional caption. Cassie left earlier in the morning with one of her girlfriends. Becca wasn't invited and it was obvious she wasn't welcome. She put the magazine back in the holder next to the chair and entered the kitchen.

"I think we need some comfort food," Sharon was standing with the cupboard open. "How about a grilled cheese sandwich and a bowl of tomato soup?"

"I haven't had any since I left for Guatemala. You know it's my favorite. You are so sweet, Sharon, to remember."

"Do you still dip the sandwich in the soup?" Sharon smiled holding up a can of soup.

"Just watch me!" Becca smiled. "I have an idea. I think I'd like to go see Maryann Kopek."

"I think that would be very nice." Sharon nodded reassuringly as she prepared the food. "She's kind of been at loose ends since Molly died."

"I know she volunteers at the Children's Center but I'd really like to go to the house and just reminisce about Molly. Do you think that would be okay?"

"I think it might do both of you a lot of good. Why don't you take my car after lunch and you can spend as much time as you want."

"Thank you. I think I'll do that."

When lunch was over Becca put her bowl and plate in the sink. She gave Sharon a hug. "Thank you, that's just what I needed."

"Let me get you the keys to my car. Remember, she's just driven by a little old lady to the grocery store and to Bible study on Wednesdays, so don't go hot-rodding around." Sharon laughed as she searched for her keys at the bottom of her purse.

"I don't see any little old ladies around here." Becca grabbed her sweater and purse.

"Here you go, now get out of here. See if you can't cheer Maryann up."

The drive to the Kopek home was as if Sharon's car was on autopilot and knew the route by heart. As kids, Becca and Molly were best friends. They spent hours together; had slumber parties, went to the roller rink, and shared every lunch hour at school from Kindergarten through senior year of high school. In a way, Becca always felt guilty that she was closer to Molly than her own sister.

Now that the initial shock of losing her parents was subsiding somewhat, the full weight of Molly's death pressed down on her. She pulled up and stopped in front of the house that held so many memories. She sat for several minutes and almost decided to not go in but she felt a tugging at her heart and a need to see her best friend's mother again. As she looked up, she saw movement in her peripheral vision and Maryann was walking across the lawn toward the car.

Maryann seemed to have aged twenty years since the last time she saw her. Her hair was nearly white and she had lost a lot of weight. Becca got out of the car, and before she could get to the sidewalk Maryann took her in her arms and buried her head in Becca's shoulder and began to weep. "It's so nice to see you." Her words squeezed out between her tears.

Becca was unable to speak, her emotions were welling up and she decided to just take the comfort offered. Maryann reached down and took her hand. "Let's go in the house."

As Becca entered the home she spent so many hours as a girl, the familiar smell embraced her. Funny, she thought, how homes held their own special scent. The lives lived, the cookies baked, the candles that burned, the holiday meals, all seemed to infuse the soul of the house. It wasn't so much that there were identifiable scents, it was more like a perfume that lingers when someone you love has left the room.

"Maryann, would it be okay if I went to Molly's room?"

"Of course, sweetheart, I'll be in the kitchen."

Becca went down the familiar hall to the second door on the right. The door was closed, but the small woven basket they made at church camp still hung on the door with a small bouquet of purple, silk violets resting inside. Becca took a deep breath and opened the door. Everything was exactly as she remembered it, except it felt older and void of Molly's essence. She flicked on the light switch and moved across the room and sat on the edge of the bed.

She glanced around at the posters, old soccer trophies, picture collages and the tree of necklaces that sat on the dresser. Nothing had changed, but everything had changed. She ran her hand across the top of the quilt that Molly made when they were seniors in high school. So many memories, so many hours shared sitting on this bed after school and on weekends, as they went from girls to young women full of hopes and dreams. Becca stood and looked in the mirror above the dresser. She, too, had changed, seeing her frazzled reflection. She looked thin, and the look of grief showed heavy in her eyes.

She was home, but there really was no home. She had no parents and she had no Molly. "I miss you Moll", she turned and looked back towards the bed. "I really need you here." Becca left the room and closed the door behind her.

"Would you like a cup of tea? I have some of your favorite, chamomile."

"Yes, please. Becca took a seat at the snack bar. I wish I had a dollar for every page of homework I worked on here."

"It always amazed me how you girls could chat and giggle as much as you did and still get good grades."

"We cheated." Becca giggled.

"Oh, you did not."

Becca smiled seeing a glimpse of the Maryann she remembered.

"Did you know that your dad was with Molly at the end?"

"No. I know almost nothing of her being sick. Did Cassie come to see her?"

"No."

"How about my mom?"

"Just once."

"I'm so sorry I wasn't here. Do you mind talking about it?"

"It's been very hard, Becca."

"Cassie said she had cancer?"

"It was the strangest thing." Maryann took the whistling teapot from the stove. "I think I noticed it before she did. She was dropping things. She'd go to pick up her fork and it would dangle in a weird way. It was little things, she complained once about the remote for the TV not working right. Then one day she came in the kitchen while I was fixing dinner and she said, 'Mom I think there's something wrong with me'." Maryann handed Becca a cup of tea.

"And what was it?"

"The way the doctor explained it, she had a tumor on her spine that sent out runners, almost like ivy or something. By the time it reached her motor functions, it was so embedded and entwined, it was inoperable. Three months later she was gone."

Becca stared down at her tea. She knew if she looked up she would burst into tears. She couldn't, wouldn't let herself. She needed to be strong for Maryann. "You said my dad was with her?"

"Yes, he came to visit her several times in the hospital and then the doctor sent her home. Your dad came nearly every day for three weeks. They would sit and talk about you, he would pray with her; sometimes he would just hold her hand. Your father is a very dear man. Oh, Becca, I'm so sorry. We've been talking all about Molly. How are *you* doing, dear?"

"I'm still kind of in a daze. The sixteen hours it took to get home was kind of a decompression chamber, you might say. There was no one around me I knew, and I could bury my face in the pillow and sob. I got a lot of my grieving done on that plane. Now jet lag has kicked in and I feel almost numb. Russ and Sharon have been so kind."

"Those poor things. I can't imagine what it must have been like for them finding your folks."

"You know, we really haven't talked about it. I have a strange feeling we never will. I think it's been far harder on Russ. He spends a lot of time in the garage or in the backyard. A couple of times I've caught him choking up looking at me from across the room. I feel so bad."

"Do you remember that dog we had, oh what was its silly name…Daisy?"

Becca gave a chuckle. "You mean that mutt that Molly brought home from the pound?" Both women laughed.

"She rode her bike to the pound without telling anyone and brought that silly dog home. Can you imagine those people giving a child a dog?"

Maryann took a sip of her tea. "That was the third grade, right?"

"Yes, nobody gave her permission and she just took it upon herself to go and rescue a dog. We had that thing for almost six years."

"That's right. We were in the tenth grade when it died. I remember it upset Molly terribly."

"The thing you don't know, it was hit by a car."

"You're right, I didn't know that."

"Molly was the one who heard it and ran out into the street. The car drove off leaving that poor little dog crushed, broken and dead. I remember looking out the window and seeing Molly holding the dog, and rocking it gently in her arms. I was thinking about poor Russ and that image of Molly came back to me. That poor man. Oh, Becca, I'm so sorry, that must sound awful."

Becca looked up, tears streaming down her cheeks. "Who would do that? Who would kill my daddy? Who would hurt my mom? I just don't understand." Becca's shoulders shook as she sobbed. Maryann came around the end of the snack bar and held her in her arms. It was several minutes before either woman was able to speak.

Maryann kissed Becca on the top of her head and patted her cheek softly. "We're kind of alike, you and I." Maryann cleared her throat and took a step back. "First I lost my Doyle and you lost your folks. And we both lost our Molly. So, it feels like we've both been cast adrift. The big difference is you've still got Cassie."

Becca sighed deeply. "We've never been close. She's changed a lot since I've been gone and now I feel like we're further apart than ever before."

"I'm sorry to hear that."

"Molly was always more like my sister. When Molly went away to college I felt all alone in the world. Then I went on my first mission trip. El Salvador was very dangerous for us. Once we were threatened by gangsters in the town and we had to go into hiding. While hiding in the house I knew we were going to be killed. I knew I probably would not survive the night. I found myself wishing I could talk to Molly just one more time.

"Strangely, it wasn't my parents or my sister I worried about receiving the news of my death. It grieved me to think of Molly hurting, and now it's me who has been left alone. My dad always told us that God has a plan for everything. But, I swear I wish He'd give us a hint why all this has happened to us."

"I don't have an answer for that. I do know I need to ask your forgiveness for not letting you know that Molly was sick. But I just didn't know how to do it."

"There's no need to apologize. You know, we exchanged letters many times while Molly was at college, but when my mission moved to Guatemala, sending and receiving mail from my small village was nearly impossible. Once I received a packet of twelve letters from Molly, tied in a bundle. They had gotten wet and molded, and for the most part, were illegible. It was one of the few times that I cried on the mission field. I'm glad I didn't know she was sick. I probably would have dropped everything and came home. Maybe that's part of God's plan. He knew I couldn't bear to see her so ill."

"When do you think you'll go back?"

Maryann's words were like a shot through the heart. Up until this point, Becca had not considered what the future would hold. What would become of the Children's Center? Then there was the estate of her parents to deal with. She dreaded the thought of having to deal with Cassie. For her part, Becca didn't really care about the money, but she knew that Cassie would scratch and claw for every cent she saw as her share. Becca felt her face flush. What a horrible thing to think of her sister that way. But, she knew down deep that it was true.

"To tell you the truth, it hadn't even occurred to me. I somehow feel I need to stay here. There is the ministry my father started here with the Children's Center. What will happen to it? I know Cassie wants nothing to do with it. It would seem a shame if it were to just close up. Oh, Maryann. What am I going to do?"

"There's plenty of time to worry about that. When Doyle died it took me nearly a year to sort out all the loose ends, benefits and details that I was completely ignorant of. He took care of everything, paid the bills, deposited his checks, I didn't even know what the house payment was. If I can be of any help at all I hope you'll feel comfortable asking me. I've certainly learned a lot in the last three years."

"What do people in town think of the Center?"

"Oh, you know how people are, you've got the ones that see the need and are thrilled someone else is doing it. You've got the people who volunteer and donate money to support the ministry. Then you've got the haters that think the government should have to take care of anything and everything having to do with Indians, as long as it's on the reservation."

"My sister thinks we should just shut it down."

"I think that would be a tragic mistake. But you know, I've heard, and I'm not saying it's true, that even the Indians can't decide whether they like it or not. We've had some of the fathers of the kids come and really raise Cain. They've complained that we are trying to destroy their culture. They don't want their kids bringing home Christian teaching. More than once I had to call the police because this crazy father was threatening your dad."

"Was that a common occurrence?"

"I wouldn't say common, but it was frequent enough to where it was a concern."

"You don't think one of them could have, could have--"

"I don't know, I don't think so. I think we shouldn't think like that."

"But what if it were one of them?"

"We need to let the police do their job and we need to concern ourselves with just getting through this tragedy. The law and God will see that justice is served in the end. Jumping to conclusions and speculating will just turn you bitter and resentful of the very people your dad was trying to help."

"I'm sorry. I shouldn't have said that. That makes me just as bad as the haters."

Maryann replenished their tea. "Have you met Kelly Sage yet?"

"No, who is she?"

"She and her husband came to town shortly before you left. She's been volunteering at the Center. I think you'd really like her. The day your parents died and the police came I went all to pieces. Kelly stepped up, took charge, and was a real blessing. If anybody would be a good sounding board for the future of the Center it would be her. Maybe we should all have lunch together after things settle down."

"I would like that. The thing I worry about most with my dad gone is raising support for the Center. He had all the connections, all the old friends, and all the people from the church. People my age don't have money. It really worries me."

"Well, if it's meant to be, the needs of the Center will be provided for. Maybe it could take a new direction."

"Maybe so."

"I promise you if you stay and take over the operation of the Center you can count on me to be behind you every step of the way."

"That's very kind of you, but I don't know that I'll be staying to run it. Oh, Maryann, there are so many things pulling me this way and that. How will I know what to do?"

"I think God has led you and protected you this far, I'm pretty sure He'll see you through this and you'll know just what to do. What do you say we go into the family room where it's a little more comfortable?"

"Yeah, I'm a little bonier than when I used to sit in these barstools all afternoon." They both laughed and moved to the other room. Becca stopped when her eyes caught a collection of family pictures on the wall. Her eyes were drawn to an 8X10 toward the edge of the grouping.

"I remember this. This is when we all went to Arrowhead Lake. Remember how sunburnt I got? You were right there with the Aloe lotion. Thank you, Maryann. Thank you for all the things you've done for me. You've been just like a second mom. I don't think I've ever told you how much I appreciate you."

"Stop it or I'm gonna start crying again. Let's change the subject, but, thank you. What did you bring with you from Guatemala?"

"Just my backpack."

"Do you have something to wear to the Memorial Service?"

"Oh, gosh, no. I'm going to have to go shopping."

"I don't know how you would feel about this, but I want you to feel free to go see if there's anything in Molly's closet that you could use. I know the dress she wore to Doyle's funeral is still in the closet."

Becca looked at Maryann for a long moment. "I think that would be a wonderful thing. It would be as if I'm honoring Molly, too. Oh, thank you, I wonder if it would fit."

"Well, there's only one way to find out. Let's go have a look."

As they walked down the hall to Molly's room, Maryann stopped. "I haven't been in here since-"

"You don't have to come with me if you don't want to."

"No, I think it's time, and there's no one I'd feel more comfortable doing it with."

It was nearly two hours later when they left Molly's bedroom. They spent the time reminiscing, laughing, crying and telling Molly stories. The time together seemed to comfort them both and was healing to their broken hearts. Becca ended up with not only a lovely, navy blue dress for the service, but Maryann insisted she take two pairs of jeans and several tops to get her through till she could go shopping.

To Becca's surprise, Maryann opened the top drawer of the dresser. From it, she took a long, blue, velvet box. "Here's something I would like you to have. I don't want you to refuse because it would mean the world to me for you to have this."

Becca turned from the closet to face Maryann. "Oh Maryann, I know what this is. Are you sure you want me to have it?"

"Without a doubt." Maryann extended the box to Becca.

She opened the box and looked down on the simple, but elegant, string of pearls. "I remember the night you gave these to her. It was her eighteenth birthday and we all went out to dinner at the Carriage

House. They are so beautiful. It's funny, I was so jealous. They seemed so grown up and so beautiful."

"Well, now you're grown up, you're beautiful, and they're yours."

Becca put her arms around Maryann's neck and gave her a hug. "Thank you so much, this means the world to me." The whisper was for Maryann's ears alone.

As Becca prepared to leave she felt a great burden was lifted. Her love for Maryann was no longer just that of her best friend's mom, but moving forward she felt that they would grow even closer. As she waved from her car, she realized that the greatest gift of all was their time of bonding.

Chapter Eight

As Michael Blackbear entered the Chew'n'Chat, it looked almost frozen in time. One man at the counter, two men at a booth on the left side of the restaurant, and in the back booth on the right side were the same three men in the same position as they were several days before. He walked passed the waitress at the register and she made no acknowledgment of his presence. The man with his back to the wall in the far booth looked up with an expressionless glance at Michael. There was no sign of welcome or recognition. He immediately went back to his conversation. The backpack that Michael carried suddenly felt like it carried the weight of the world.

"Back again." The man against the wall finally looked up.

Michael set his backpack on top of the empty table and sat down at the booth with his back to the door.

"What have we got here?" A second man with his back to the wall pulled the backpack closer. He lifted his black Rayban sunglasses and propped them up on top of his head. Unzipping the top of the backpack, he pulled the two sides apart and gazed down at the fruits of Michael's first robbery.

He looked at Michael. "You've been busy."

"How much?" Michael tried to not let his nerves show.

The man holding the backpack looked at his two compatriots. "Five grand."

"You've got to be kidding." Michael's nerves shot from fear to anger. "That stuff is worth a fortune."

The man lowered the Rayban's, zipped the bag closed, and fiercely shoved it towards Michael. "Then take it somewhere else."

Michael glared at the pair sitting across from him. He could feel the man to his right bristle and tense like a coiled snake.

"Ten."

"This isn't *Let's Make A Deal*." Rayban wasn't backing down. "Take your crap and leave."

After a brief pause, Michael pushed the bag towards the center of the table. "Alright."

Rayban nodded at the man at Michael's elbow, and he nudged him signaling to get up. He left the booth and the restaurant. Michael and the other men waited in silence. After about five minutes the man returned with a small manila envelope and placed it on the table in front of Michael. "Now get lost." The boss gave a jerk of his head toward the door.

Michael picked up the packet. "I'll see you in a few days and I'll expect more." None of the men responded or even acknowledged that Michael spoke.

As he got back to his car Michael slammed the roof with his fist. "It's not worth it!" His rage boiled over. The car felt like an oven as he drove back toward town. He turned the air conditioner on full blast but soon realized the heat was from his anger. He drove around Orvin for about fifteen minutes, cursing and talking to himself, and gazing at the storefronts that he passed. Without thinking, without emotion, and without a plan he headed for the highway.

Arapaho Wells was a thirty-minute drive from Orvin and the opposite direction of Enid. He cruised the small, but fairly modern, main drag of the town. There was nothing that stood out or seemed like a good target. He turned down a cross street and within a couple of blocks came to a strip mall. Without signaling or barely breaking, he turned into the parking lot. He passed a Baskin Robbins, a Greek Gyros shop, and a comic book and baseball card store before he spotted Marco's Discount Jewelry. There were no cars in either direction for several spaces.

He reached in the back seat and retrieved the blue burka head covering that was tucked in the pocket behind the passenger seat. A canvas Wal-Mart shopping bag was on the seat next to him. Michael folded the bag into a small square, then bent and reached under his seat for the gun he hid there.

Without hesitation he left the car, bag in hand, the gun tucked in his belt at his back. He approached the door and there was no buzzer for entry. He stopped and turned from the door. It only took a second to put on the Burka. In just a matter of seconds, he was in the door. Four steps into the store he pointed his gun at the man standing behind the counter looking down at a newspaper. "Both hands on the counter."

The man complied. "Don't do anything stupid."

"I already have." Michael thrust out the Wal-Mart bag as he reached the counter. "Is there anyone in the back?"

"No." Marco's voice quaked with fear as he shot a look at the back room door.

"Is lying worth taking a bullet for?"

"I'm not lying. I'm here by myself right now."

Michael rounded the corner, gun still pointed at Marco. "Let's go in the back."

Marco led the way, receiving gentle nudges with the barrel of the gun poking him in his lower back. In the back room against the left wall was a large safe. It was standing ajar as if Marco recently opened it to stock the display cases. "We'll start here," he ordered, "Open it wide. Scrape the contents into the bag."

Little boxes and trays were clumsily put into the bag. "Dump the trays," Michael demanded. Marco complied and tossed the empty tray onto the floor. On the third shelf was a black box. "Open it and dump it." Michael poked Marco in the neck with his gun as he took the lid from the box. Dozens of small paper packets filled the box. It was apparent this was where they filed their stones.

Michael glanced around the back room seeing only a workbench and a desk. He looked back in the safe. He was satisfied most of its contents were in the bag. He stood for a moment considering if slamming Marco in the back of the head with the gun, or simply tying him up, was best. He decided that knocking him out would be the easiest, fastest course of action. Michael slammed Marco at the base of his skull with a tremendous blow.

Marco made a grunting noise and dropped to the floor. Michael turned to leave when he saw what must be the alarm system recorder. Yanking the cables from the back, he untwisted a coax camera line and shoved the unit in his bag with the valuables and left the store.

Carefully, slowly, and deliberately, he made his way back to the highway. He pulled over just before he reached the onramp. The burka and gun were already in the canvas bag. He got out of the car and put it in the trunk. Driving home he was careful not to exceed the speed limit or change lanes without signaling.

A half-hour later Michael pulled into the driveway of his small house. As he stood at the back of the car, he looked around the dusty row of small houses in lots with no grass, no trees, no flowers, no fences, just despair. Opening the trunk, he removed the bag and went into the house.

The idea of committing two robberies and a serious assault sent a shiver through Michael. Did he hit the man in the jewelry store too hard? What if he killed him? He wondered as he set the bag on the small kitchen table. Placing the security recorder on the table, he set his gun on top of it and covered them with the burka. He determined he would later take a hammer to the recorder, destroying it and the hard drive inside. He looked down in the bag at the packets, rings, necklaces, watches, and gold ingots.

He got up from the table and went to a drawer next to the sink. He fished around until he found a ziplock bag. He returned to the table and began to pull the packets from the bag. In his frustration that it was taking too long, he turned the bag upside down on the table. Taking the little paper packets he dumped their contents into the ziplock bag. Dozens and dozens of diamonds fell into the bag over the next few minutes. He meticulously laid the paper wrappers on the table and flattened them with his hand. Next, he sorted the watches, the rings, and necklaces into separate piles. One by one he tore off the identifying price tag from each item and placed them with the tissue papers from the diamonds. As his adrenaline began to subside, his hands began to tremble as he was having more and more difficulty removing the price tags. When he completed the task, he stood and got the small, plastic garbage can standing next to the refrigerator.

    He brought it back to the table and scooped the price tags and tissues into the garbage can. He retrieved a packet of matches from the drawer next to the sink. He took the can in hand, went to the back door and out into the backyard. Near the center of his hard, dusty, dirt lot sat a rusting 55-gallon metal drum. He dumped the pail into the drum that was already half full of trash. He reached in his pocket and took the packet of matches, struck one and then lit the remaining matches in the pack. Holding for a long moment to ensure they were all sufficiently alight, he dropped the flaming packet into the barrel. Within moments flames were leaping out of the top of the barrel. That should do it, Michael said, gazing at the fire.

"Hey, neighbor." Michael's head snapped to see Mary Wilson, the old lady who lived next door.

"Hi Mary, how are you today?"

"I'm still poor. I'm still drunk, I'm still an Indian, and this stupid dog has to pee a hundred times a day."

"You need one of those doggy doors."

"Maybe Santa will bring me one next Christmas." Mary's speech was slurred.

"I tell you what, you let me store a couple of boxes in your shed and I'll put one in for you."

"You can do that anyway. I ain't been in that thing since my Charlie died."

"Then it's a deal. How about tomorrow?"

"Just not before noon, I like to sleep late. How'd you like to join me for a drink?"

"I'm good, thanks." Michael chuckled and looked back at the burning barrel.

Mary called the dog. It ignored her until she yelled its name in a harsh angry rasp. Only then did they both go back in the house.

Michael walked over to her shed. There was no padlock on the bolt. He slid the bolt, pulled the door back with a rusty creak and looked inside. There were boxes, tools, and an inch of dust on everything. This will be perfect, he thought. He returned to the house.

He reached around under the sink for a plastic garbage bag and found just what he needed in a damp box of rags and brushes. He pulled out two drawers before he found the one with a small stack of dishtowels. Using one of the more faded towels he wrapped up his gun tightly and put it in the garbage bag. Michael returned to the waiting shed, moved one of the boxes and slipped the bag into the box below, replacing the dusty top box.

"Can't tell I've ever been here." He latched the shed closed and rubbed out his footprints in front of the shed. Shuffling and zigzagging back to his house, he felt confident that his path was completely gone. The next strong wind will finish the job, he thought.

"Thank you for coming with me." Kelly and Cole got out of the car at the Children's Center. Kelly was thankful, and very grateful, for his support.

"My pleasure, it's my hot date for the week." Cole's sarcasm was showing.

"Very funny. I just need you here for moral support."

"I'm always good for that." Cole smiled reassuringly.

They approached the door and found it unlocked. "Hello!" Kelly called out as they entered the center.

"In here!" A voice came from the office.

In the office, Cassie was sitting at her father's desk. There were papers and folders spread out everywhere. The normally neat desk was in complete disarray. She stood as Kelly entered the office. "This is my sister, Rebecca."

A pretty, dark-haired girl sat in a chair against the wall.

"Yes, I recognize her from the funeral. I'm so sorry we have to meet under these circumstances.

Your father was a wonderful man and he will be greatly missed. It was a lovely service."

"Thank you." Rebecca stood to shake hands with Kelly and Cole.

"I'm Kelly and this is my husband, Cole."

"Nice to meet you. I've heard a lot of nice things about you."

"Cole, you want to grab another chair from the entry?" Cole turned and left the room.

"So, let's get to it." Cassie left no doubt she intended to run this impromptu meeting. "I really want to get all this sorted out. Since you're on the board, and Becca and I are our parent's only heirs, you seemed like the obvious choice to help us figure out the direction we need to take."

"We hoped that you could help us make a decision, then present our findings to the board." Rebecca was the polar opposite of her sister. Her voice was kind, and her words carefully chosen to show she was asking for help and guidance. "Cassie tells me that the board is really just a means of reaching the legal responsibilities of a nonprofit. Is that true?"

"That's pretty much the case. The board is used more for fundraising and community outreach than any real decision making." Kelly gave a slightly embarrassed shrug.

"Here we go," Cole reentered the room.

The four sat and there was a brief moment of silence before Cassie spoke. "Becca and I do not agree on what should be done with this place. With my father gone, I have absolutely no desire to continue to work here. Or have anything to do with it, for that matter."

Kelly glanced over at Cole without expression. Nothing like cutting to the chase, she thought. "Okay, that's one side of the coin. Becca, what are your thoughts?"

"I have been committed to my mission ministry in Guatemala for nearly three years now. The work there is strong, well staffed, and well organized. My departure would not be a detriment to the program. I must confess I would miss it desperately if I didn't go back, but I'm beginning to understand that the Center needs me far more than the work in Guatemala. I would like to see things continue here, as much to honor my father's memory as the needs continue for the Cheyenne and Arapahoe community in our area.

"My understanding is, Kelly, that you know the staff here as well as anyone. Do you think the other volunteers will continue without my father's leadership?" It was Rebecca's turn to be the assertive member of the family. Her gentle demeanor was a covering for a strong, determined young woman who was no pushover.

"I believe wholeheartedly in the mission of the center." Kelly looked intently at each sister in turn. "However, at this point in my life, I cannot commit to a continued active role in the running of the Center's daily activities. Cole and I would like to do some traveling. Our kids are in Paris, our grandkids are growing up, and we really need to spend some time with them in the very near future. I'm not saying I'll abandon the Center completely, but I want you both to be aware that I will be cutting back on the hours that I work each week."

"I told you, Becca, this is a perfect opportunity for people to pull back or leave the Center. Daddy was the backbone, and without him, there's no reason anyone would feel they were abandoning him if they decided to not continue working." It was clear Cassie wanted out of there yesterday.

"Well." Kelly sat a little straighter. "This is quite a turn of events. I didn't realize how unhappy you were working here. From what you say, your heart isn't in it. It is pretty apparent it's become a burden. It sounds like you are beginning to resent its control over your life. Am I reading you right?"

"It's not beginning. I do resent it keeping me from continuing my education. You know my dad. My parents browbeat me into making their dream mine as well. I don't mean to sound ungrateful, but it is far from my dream job."

"And that's not fair to you, the kids, or the other volunteers, so I get it. I am curious though, if that was your feeling why didn't you do something else?" Kelly was not overly fond of Cassie and always felt she gave just as little as she thought she could get away with.

Cassie looked up with fire in her eyes. "Because, in my family, to not serve others is unthinkable. I couldn't be the only one to not be a martyr to the cause."

"Cassie! That's unfair, unkind, and untrue." Becca nearly came out of her chair.

"You know," said Cole, entering the conversation for the first time. "Death is a funny thing. It brings emotions and truth, that can be buried for years, painfully up to the surface. Sometimes the truth comes out in ways that aren't expressed the best way they should be. I'm speaking from personal experience here. I know I'm not on the board or a volunteer, but if I'm being perfectly honest, I've never been that interested in this place, either. But I've spent my entire professional career as a keen observer of the human condition and people's truer selves.

"So, here's my two cents: Cassie, you have to follow your heart. You can't let the dreams of others drag you along behind them. You have to find your own path or you will grow more angry, resentful, and bitter.

"Becca, I know you must be disappointed to hear how Cassie feels. But, you have to accept that she is sharing a painful harbored truth. You have to be able to let her go and go her own way. Both of you, I know, loved your father and must feel that letting anything happen to this place would be turning your back on his great love and mission. But, and this is hard to hear, it was *his*, not yours. You didn't start it, it wasn't your dream, and it doesn't have to be. Family businesses, and that is essentially what this is, often do not work into the second generation. Perhaps we would be better served here today if you two realized the feelings and needs of the other and came to peace with that between yourselves."

Cassie looked at Cole with what could only be described as wonderment. His words said what she struggled with so clearly, and she prayed Becca would take it to heart.

"Thank you." Becca smiled at Cole. "Sometimes it takes an outsider looking in to see through the window the clearest. I want my decision to be made from the love of this organization, not guilt or a sentimental longing to somehow stay in touch with my dad and his feelings." She turned to face Cassie.

"Maybe we should go for a long drive and decide what we need to do. I would hate for this to come between us. You're the only family I have left and I love you. I don't want to lose you."

"I think you girls are on the same page, you're just a couple paragraphs apart. Do you think this is going to help?" Kelly glanced at Cole with a 'thank you' in her eyes.

"I do." Becca nodded.

Kelly turned to the girl behind the desk. "Cassie?"

"It will only help if I am free of this place."

"That's pretty clear." Cole looked at Becca. "Feels to me like the future of this place is in your hands, but you need to make the decision that is best for you."

"As a board member, and I guess the primary board member, I feel it's my responsibility to get things in order for the transition, whatever the case may be."

"I've already done that." Cassie's words were sharp and final.

"Okay, then give me what you've got, and I'll take care of the rest."

"Fine." Cassie gave the mess on the desk a wave of her palm up hand. "So are we done here?"

"I am." Cole picked up the chair and took it back to the entry.

"Okay, Becca, it looks like it will be you and me determining how, or if, we will proceed. I just want both of you to know I understand how hard this is and I really hope you won't let this come between you. I respect the decisions you've made."

"Thank you, Kelly." Becca stood.

Cassie began to flip folders closed and stacked them. "Then, I'm out of here." Cassie picked up her purse. "See you later, Becca." Cassie walked past Kelly and out the door without another word.

"I'm so sorry, Kelly. I didn't see this going the way it has. It's not your fault and it appears it is no longer your problem. We'll get this all straightened out, don't worry."

"I know we will. You can count on my help too, don't worry."

Becca looked over at the desk and the stack of file folders. "Looks like I have some work to do." It was then she realized that Cassie left her key to the Center on top of the stack.

"Geez, no wonder you wanted my moral support." Cole started the car. "That was a tough room."

"I had no idea Cassie held so much resentment."

"I think it goes a lot deeper than that, I think that kid has some serious issues." Cole put the car in reverse.

"Well, I think whichever way the pendulum swings, I'm going to ease my way out."

"That's the best news I've heard all day. How about we hit Ernie's for a sandwich before we go home?"

"Seriously, you go straight to the food?" Kelly laughed. "You are a wonder, Cole Sage."

Chapter Nine

Cole pulled into Big Pete's Cafeteria parking lot just a little before noon, and it felt like going home. Cole realized as he got out of the car it was over a month since he'd been to his favorite restaurant. As he approached the door an elderly couple was coming up the walk. The man used a walker and his wife was several steps behind. Cole opened the door and smiled, letting the couple go in first.

The sounds and smells of Big Pete's lifted Cole's spirits, and he looked forward to chatting with Betty Cranfill. Inside the restaurant, a pretty young girl with a name tag that read Chloe approached Cole with a big smile.

"Good afternoon, sir. Are you by yourself today?" She tilted her head to the right and her naturally red ponytail fell over her shoulder.

Cole took a long moment to answer, wondering where Betty was and why she hired a hostess. "No, I'm meeting a friend. He's probably here already."

"Okay, follow me; we'll see if we can spot him." Chloe was cute and cheerful. Betty picked a winner. She spun about grabbing two menus and headed across the restaurant. "There he is." She pointed to the only person in the place wearing a suit.

"How'd you know?"

"He's the only person in the place that keeps looking at the door."

"Good job, Sherlock." Cole was still curious. "Is Betty here?"

"Yes, she's in the office."

"Ahh, well nice to meet you, Chloe."

Cole looked down and greeted Rowan Jensen, his publisher's representative. He couldn't have looked more out of place if he were wearing a clown suit. His $2,000 Brooks Bros. suit among the pearl button western shirts, t-shirts, and jeans of Big Pete's clientele was almost laughable. This man was so buttoned up he would probably feel naked without a tie. Jensen flew into Oklahoma City from New York and drove to Orvin just to meet Cole, a trip that Cole thought was a waste of time, and any business could have easily been done over the phone. To say he was flattered was an embarrassing truth.

"Welcome to Orvin, Rowan." Cole extended his hand. "Sorry I'm late. Have you been waiting long?"

"I just sat down." It wasn't exactly true. He already took the time to clean every inch of his seat. Jensen slid the menu toward the window, wiping down the top of the table with a handkerchief from his pocket, and then slid it back to get the other side.

Cole nearly laughed watching this germ phobic process. "I had an appointment with an attorney."

"Nothing serious, I hope?"

"It seems I can't let go of my crusading, journalist, do-gooder mentality." Cole smiled at Rowan.

"I've gotten myself tangled up in this fellow's immigration problem."

"An illegal alien?" Rowan looked astonished and Cole laughed.

"No, kind of the opposite. A local member of the Cheyenne tribe wants to bring an Iraqi woman and their child to the United States. He's got the door slammed in his face everywhere he's turned, so I was trying to help. But, it seems everybody I know is my age, or older, and they're either retiring or have died. Anyway, we went to the attorney for him to swear out an affidavit showing that she needs to be granted political asylum because of her relationship with him and the Army."

"Well, how is that going to work out? Doesn't seem that difficult."

"You know, I'm not really sure. With the war and anti-Muslim sentiment, frankly, I wouldn't want to bring her here. But that's not my call, it's his."

Rowan looked across the table at Cole and smiled. "No, my friend, your job is to write some more books. We need to come up with a timetable."

"You're right, but first, let's have something to eat, I'm starving."

"Is this the Oklahoma version of haute cuisine?"

Cole was not sure if Jensen was serious or making use of a gift of humor he didn't possess. "This is my favorite place in Orvin, I can recommend just about anything on the menu, but if you miss the ribs or brisket, you'll be missing something there are no words to describe."

Without speaking, Rowan picked up the menu and began to peruse the offerings.

"So, what brings you all the way to Oklahoma? Surely it isn't just to see me." Cole still couldn't believe his publisher would incur the expense of this trip just for him.

"Actually it is." Rowan didn't lift his eyes from the menu. "We see you as one of our most valuable assets in our stable of authors. I came here to discuss our future relationship and to find out what you have planned for your next book."

"Well, I'm certainly flattered. I hardly see the sales of *The Sages* warranting so much of your time."

"If I can be completely transparent, I also come with a bit of a concern. Our marketing research has uncovered a couple of things we weren't expecting."

"Really," Cole said.

Rowan finally looked up from the menu. "I'm not quite sure how to put this to you, Mr. Sage."

"First off, call me Cole. Secondly, there's nothing I hate worse than people who pussyfoot around bad news. Just spit it out." As Cole looked across the table, he realized that this trip was not going to be good news. Although his book sold well, it didn't crack the top ten on the New York Times' Bestseller List. He was sure that his publisher spent a lot of money in anticipation of a far greater return.

"Let me just put this frankly, Cole. The name recognition we anticipated when we signed your publishing agreement, based on your work as one of America's great journalists of the 20th century, is far lower than we anticipated. It seems in the years since you won your Pulitzer and left your positions with major publications, you're farther removed from today's audience than was first believed."

"So what you're saying if I'm hearing you right, is that an over the hill newspaperman isn't selling books like you thought he would, thus, dashing all of your expectations on the rocks."

"That's a little harsher than I think I would have put it." Jensen didn't change expression. "Even so, it's true just the same."

"I suppose it is. So, this future you see, does it still include you representing me and publishing my books?"

"Yes, yes, yes. My purpose here today is simply to re-evaluate our relationship and future projects in light of a revised marketing strategy."

"I guess I've been in Oklahoma too long. Your boilerplate B.S. is starting to sound like a foreign language to me. Why don't you just spit out what you're trying to say and we'll go from there?"

Rowan Jensen pursed his lips and squinted his eyes. For several seconds he just stared at Cole. "Okay, here it is plain and simple, black and white. We do not feel that your place in the market is stand-alone novels. It is our feeling, and that of our marketing department, that both of our interests would be better served if you were to write a series of some sort."

"You mean like Jack Reacher, or Harry Bosch, or somebody?"

"Exactly. You're a very talented writer. You have years of experience reporting and observations that you should be putting to work in a highly marketable, highly profitable series. You could use Cole Sage, though not by name, as the main character, a journalist who gets thrown into situations, investigations, and crimes and solves them."

"Are you serious?" Cole asked.

"Absolutely. You have a wealth of material that could easily be shaped into an amazing series of books."

"I'm not sure if I am capable of doing that."

"I was expecting that response. Here's what I would like to propose. We have a stable full of talented, young writers who can, and will, take your outline, draft, or whatever you feel comfortable in providing, and flesh it out and hone it into a very marketable product."

"A ghostwriter?" Cole stared in amazement. "Are you suggesting I put my name on a book written by somebody else?"

"This concept is nothing new; it is done and has been done for years, by names you are familiar with."

Cole interlaced his fingers and set them on the table. "I'm really not sure how I feel about that idea. I think we need to---"

"When did you sneak in?" Betty Cranfill was standing at the end of the table. She slapped Cole on the back. "Who is your handsome friend?"

Cole slipped out and stood next to Betty, giving her a hug. "This is my friend and agent, Rowan Jensen. He's come all the way here to suggest I can't write a book."

Betty looked down at Jensen with a look that would have taken the husk off a coconut. "Is that right?"

Cole put his hand on Betty's arm and laughed. "But that shouldn't concern your pretty little head. We're here to eat first and foremost."

"You never have been a very good liar, but I'll let it go. What are we having today Mr. Jensen?"

"I will have a simple green salad, and do you have any kind of oil and vinaigrette dressing?" He ordered with a condescending lifted eyebrow.

"I think Pete can rustle something up."

"Then I'll have it on the side, just in case."

Betty now raised her eyebrows and turned to Cole. "Pete's trying out a new pulled pork rub. I think you should give it a try and let him know what you think."

"That's an offer I can't refuse. I'll have that, and I'd like some of those sweet potato tots."

"Seems people really like those. Pete's pretty proud."

"Alright, that will do it. I know you want a diet coke. What would you like to drink, sir?"

"Do you have bottled water?"

"Yes, I think the mule train brought a case in today." Betty winked at Cole. "Coming right up." Betty made her way back to the kitchen pass through.

"Mr. Sage, I detect an underlying hostility in your response to my suggestion."

"Please don't misinterpret anything. I have *open* hostility toward your suggestion. If you want a series I will take that into consideration. If you want me to use a ghostwriter, consider that matter closed. It's not going to happen. Let's get something straight. Straight out, no hesitancy, no dancing around the room, if I should choose not to do a series, will I be dropped?" Cole looked across the table at Jensen, who he could swear had little drops of perspiration forming on his upper lip. Behind his eyes, Cole could tell that this was not the response he planned on.

"I don't think drop is the word I would use."

"Ok," Cole said, "How is this one? Put on the bottom of the list of people you're interested in."

"Let's just say we question the feasibility of another free-standing book without a strong anchor. That anchor being a series."

"Ok." Cole nodded. "That's fair. So, if I produce this series you would still publish novels that I would write, that by far would be more in keeping with what I want to do artistically."

"I think we could guarantee that."

"Well, I must say, Mr. Jensen, that this is not what I was anticipating. I will take your proposition into consideration. I will truthfully and sincerely respond by week's end. Is that fair?"

"That would be more than amicable."

"Good, then it's settled." Cole gave a nod. "But, I'm telling you, you were standing at the fork of one of life's great choices, and you have made the wrong decision. "

"How's that?" Jensen was truly baffled at Cole's comment.

"You are sitting in a restaurant with the best barbecue on the planet and you chose rabbit food.

That, Mr. Jensen, shows a lack of gastronomic intelligence, taste, and experience."

An hour later Cole Sage and Rowan Jensen parted company. There was little doubt in Cole's mind he, too, reached a fork in life's journey, where choosing the best decision for him personally, may be the worst decision professionally.

The Chew'n'Chat was empty, except for the two men sitting in the back booth. Michael Blackbear approached the table, canvas bag in hand. He set the bag on the table and slid into the booth as the man with his back to the door slid over.

"There's a lot more this time, a lot more. This should take care of all the money I need."

"We'll see about that." The man with his back to the wall nodded to the man next to Michael and he took the bag, leaning the open end toward himself. Michael's neat and tidy baggies of raw diamonds, gold necklaces, pendants, rings, and watches made it very clear there were five times more goods this time than the last. The man next to Michael looked at his boss and nodded.

"You did well. Ten thousand."

Michael reached over and pulled the bag towards him. "Twenty, or I walk."

There was a long silence at the table. Michael took the opened end of the bag and rolled it, and set it in his lap and crossed his arms over it.

"Thirteen." The boss, for the first time, showed a hint of emotion.

Michael stood up.

"Alright, Fifteen, that's as high as I go." The boss nodded and the man who was sitting next to Michael slid from the booth and left the Chew'n'Chat.

"I'm only doing this one more time," said Michael. "I just need to get the money to get my wife and son here."

"We'll see." The boss looked up without changing expression.

Michael backed away from the table and sat at a stool at the counter. He turned and looked at the waitress who was obviously used to the transactions made in the booth and she completely ignored him.

Less than five minutes later the man returned, envelope in hand, and handed it to Michael.

Michael opened the envelope and flipped the bills. Satisfied, he handed the man the bag. The man reached out and took it and before Michael released it he gave the bag a slight tug. "*One* more time."

The man didn't respond.

"Oh, thank goodness you're awake." Kelly stood next to the couch hovering over Cole.

"What's going on?" Cole stretched and rubbed his eyes.

"I can't figure out how this stupid Skype thing works."

Cole walked over, stood behind Kelly, and put his hands on her shoulders. He gently massaged her shoulders while looking at her laptop. "Well, first of all, you're in Dropbox."

"What do you mean?"

"Skype is this one." He reached over her and tapped the screen and the Skype window opened up. "Are you calling the kids?"

"What time is it in Paris?"

"Should be around 3:00 in the afternoon."

"That's what I was hoping. Are you ready?"

"I have been for over an hour and a half."

"Okay, hit that button." The screen changed colors, added a square in the center and the familiar ring tone filled the room. It took six rings before Erin's face came onto the screen.

"Hi, guys! This is an unexpected surprise. Is everything okay?"

"Everything is fine. We just miss you terribly. How is everybody?" Kelly tilted the screen slightly.

"Ben is still at the hospital working. Jenny just went to her room to take off her dreaded school uniform and little man Cole is down for his nap."

"That must run in the family." Cole leaned into the frame. "So are you getting any more accustomed to your new life in France?"

"Well, my French still sucks. The good news is Jenny speaks French like a native and acts as my interpreter. Ben absolutely loves his job. English being the international language of medicine, he's had little trouble adapting and there are several Brits and Australians at the hospital, too."

"Turn the camera around, I want to see your place," Kelly said.

"Oh, it's a mess."

"I've seen messes before, believe me. I just want to see what you've done."

Erin picked up her laptop and her face disappeared from the screen. It took a moment for her to re-balance the roller coaster ride visuals. She slowly panned the room in silence. The space was larger than Kelly remembered from the pictures Erin sent. The light from the windows momentarily whited out the screen. "Let me get a little closer to the window." As she moved across the room, the window came into focus and the view outside appeared.

"Oh, Erin, how do you stand it?" Cole was nearly speechless with the view.

"Pretty cool, huh dad? Who'd ever dream I'd have the Eiffel Tower right outside my window!"

"You're certainly living my dream."

"What are you doing mom?" Jenny's voice announced her arrival into the room.

"I'm talking to Grandpa and Grandma. You want to say hi?"

"Oui, oui, oui!" She squealed in delight.

"Hey, kiddo, did you do that all the way home?" Cole teased.

"Oh Grandpa, you and your silly jokes."

"Hi, sweetie." Kelly's voice rose in excitement.

"Hi Grandma, I miss you."

"Oh, I miss you too. I wish I could reach through this screen and give you a big hug."

Jenny moved toward the screen and her face became huge on the monitor. "Muah," she smacked the screen. "How's that?"

Kelly kissed her fingertips and blew at the screen.

Jenny giggled happily. "I wish you could see my school. It's really cool. Mademoiselle Fleurot, my teacher, is just the best!"

"Have you made a lot of friends?"

"Yes, Suzette, Juliet, and Anna are just my besties ever."

"Your mom says your French is coming along really well."

"Somebody in this house has to speak French; otherwise, we'd starve to death." Jenny turned to give her mother a big grin.

"So, what are you doing for your birthday?"

"I'm gonna have a sleepover with my friends and mom said she would make Mexican food. My friends have never had any."

"You think they'll like it?" Cole leaned back in as he spoke.

"I hope so. If they don't, there will be more for me and dad."

"How is Cole doing?"

"He's okay, but he sure can be a pain at times."

"Kind of like me." Cole jabbed his thumb toward his chest.

Jenny giggled merrily. "Not quite that bad, Grandpa. He thinks my iPad is his."

"Have your dad buy him one."

"Yeah, right. When are you gonna come see us?"

"We've been talking about that lately, maybe for Christmas."

"Oh no, that's too far away. Can't you come sooner?"

"There are a couple of things happening here that we sort of have to take care of first. That's why we were thinking of Christmas."

"But it's cold then. We couldn't go to the park. Grandpa and I have to go to the park!"

"Ok, we'll see, maybe we can come a little sooner."

"Ok, here's mom."

Suddenly all they saw was the back of Jenny running away from the computer. From across the room, they could see Erin approaching. In her arms, she held young Cole.

"Somebody else to say hello to."

"He's a monster. Look how much he's grown!" Cole teased.

"Can you say hi to Grandpa and Grandma?"

"Hi." The curly headed blond boy sitting in front of Erin smiled shyly.

"Move back a little, Cole." Kelly was tilting her head as if that would change the view.

"He's kind of grumpy when he first wakes up. Like somebody else I know."

"I'm not that bad."

"I was talking about Ben." Erin laughed and stood up so little Cole could back up a ways.

"Hi, buddy. You are getting tall." Kelly waved at the camera.

The boy put his hand over his head and jumped in an effort to touch his palm with the top of his head. "I'm going to be this tall!"

"Just keep jumping and one of these days you'll get there." Cole made a funny face toward the screen.

"Hey, Cole?"

"Yeah."

"Tell your dad I said you should get an iPad for your birthday."

"Yeah! That's what I want. Jenny always hits me when I take hers."

"Then don't take hers, silly!" Cole laughed.

"Bye!" The backside of the little boy disappeared from view.

With the kids out of the way, Erin filled Cole and Kelly in on all the news. After about fifteen minutes the phone rang. "I better take that."

"Okay, we just wanted to hear your voice and see your face. Glad to know everything is going so well. We'll talk to you again soon. Love you!" Kelly volunteered an end to the call.

"I love you too, guys. Muah! Big kiss from me." She waved it toward the screen. "Bye Bye!" The screen went dark.

"I'm not sure if that helps or makes things worse." Kelly wiped tears from her eyes.

"I know what you mean. Maybe we can push our trip up some."

"That would be wonderful, but there's so much going on. I feel so much pressure regarding the Center. I'm just not sure what's going to happen there."

"You know, sweetie, it's not really your responsibility. You're just a volunteer."

"I know. I just feel such a burden being the one left to consult on the future of Warren's dream. Cassie is very clear about wanting nothing to do with it. She's always been less than enthusiastic about working there. Maybe Rebecca will step up. But, she has her life to live too, and her missionary work means so much to her."

"Like I said, it's really not your responsibility."

"Let's change the subject. What are you going to do about this book thing?"

"That my dear will require a bagel and mocha, and a lot of discussion."

Chapter Ten

Kelly stepped out onto the porch. "Okay, one tuna sandwich, extra lettuce, on sourdough toast, and Fritos for the gentleman."

"You're the prettiest waitress I've seen in a while." Cole smiled and set his plate on the top step next to him.

"Just be sure you leave a big tip." As Kelly turned to go back in the house Cole's cell phone rang. "Great." Cole grumbled something about 'inconsiderate people calling at lunchtime'.

"I'll get it." Kelly went to retrieve Cole's phone from his desk, where he somehow always seemed to leave it. "Hello. Yes, he's right here. May I say who's calling? Okay, hold on." Kelly put her hand over the phone. "It's Michael Blackbear. Do you want to talk to him?"

"Mmmm, yeah." Kelly handed Cole his phone. "Hey there, what's going on?" Cole asked. He looked up at Kelly and frowned. "Really? When did that happen?" Cole stood and began walking to the far end of the porch. He stood peering over the edge for nearly a minute. "Umm, wow, I don't know. Let me make a couple of calls. Okay, I'll be down as soon as I can get there." Cole pushed the off button.

"What was that all about?" Kelly stood her arms across her chest. Cole knew this posture well. It was the *this-better-be-good* stance and always signaled concern. In the years they have been married she seldom showed displeasure with him or his activities. It seemed she possessed a gift for knowing when he was about to do something that probably would not turn out for the best.

"He's been arrested." Cole looked at Kelly and shrugged.

"For what!?"

"For killing Warren Poore."

"I knew it. I told you so." Kelly, in uncharacteristic fashion, shook her index finger at Cole.

"Whoa, Whoa, Whoa. Don't be jumping to conclusions."

"Well, why would they arrest him if he didn't have something to do with it?"

"It happens all the time, Kelly."

"Why'd he call you?"

"I'm not quite sure, but he asked me if I could help."

"And you said yes? I told you not to get involved with the guy." Kelly was clearly growing angry.

"I know, I know but this makes no sense. Hold on a second. Your getting upset with me isn't going to help. Let me make a couple of calls, then you can yell at me."

"I am not yelling. I don't yell. I am upset. I don't like that guy, and I am worried you will get involved and something bad will happen."

"We'll burn that bridge when we come to it." Cole smiled and winked at Kelly. "Let's just see what is what."

"Don't think turning on your Cole Sage charm will work on me!"

"It got me this far."

Kelly turned and went to sit down.

Cole scanned the phone directory and hit talk. After a few seconds, Cole heard a voice on the other end. "Lorena? Cole Sage. Is C.W. in? That's nice, that's nice, but this is an emergency. Thank you." Cole turned and began pacing again.

"Hello?" Langhorne came on the phone. "We're fine, Kelly is fine, yes sir. A friend of mine has been arrested. We need to see what we can do about getting him out of jail."

There was a pause on the line and Cole said, "Murder. Thing is, he couldn't have done it, he was at work. He works construction. For some reason, the sheriff deputies aren't buying his alibi. Yes, sir. Thank you C.W. I will, thank you."

Cole hung up the phone and turned to Kelly. "He said he would call a friend here in Orvin, and said for me to go meet him at the jail. If necessary, Langhorne will drive down here tomorrow."

"I know I can't stop you, but I still say this is something you shouldn't be getting involved in." Kelly's demeanor changed to one of quiet resolve.

"If he's innocent and I do nothing, what kind of a deal is that? You know as well as I do they shoot Indians and ask questions later around here. Old prejudices die hard. I'll be back as quick as I can."

"No, you can eat something first."

Cole sat down on the steps stretching his legs out. He set the cell phone down on the porch next to him. There was a surreal feeling to this situation. It felt strangely disconnected from Warren Poore's death. He thought back to an incident several months before. He stared across the yard as images of the past filled his mind.

Cole recalled approaching the door of the Children's Center. He heard the shouting of two men coming from the office.

"You only pretend to help. You only help people who don't know they are being used. You just want to be the great white father helping the little red brother. Nothing has changed in four hundred years!"

"That's not true." Warren Poore sounded defeated and unsure in his response.

"Little kids and women, coloring books and games are easy, but when there's a real problem, a man's problem, I can see you don't care."

"I think you're being very unfair. I have no idea how to help you."

"Yeah? And you're not willing to go out of your way to figure it out either!"

Suddenly a tall, dark headed man with sharp features and the build of an athlete burst from the office door. Cole looked at the man and realized his expression showed more disappointment and frustration than anger.

"You don't sound very happy, what's going on? Do you need some help?" Cole smiled as the man approached him.

"Well, this certainly isn't the place to get it."

"Then, maybe I could be of some assistance. What's the problem?"

"And who are you?" The man tensed and coiled like an angry rattler.

"I'm Cole Sage. I spent a lot of years as a journalist helping people with serious problems. Why don't we go over there and sit down and you tell me yours?"

"How about we go outside?"

"That works too." Cole moved to the door. Out on the sidewalk, Cole extended his hand to the man.

"I'm Michael Blackbear. I have a huge problem. And nobody will do anything to help me. I just returned home from two tours in Iraq. While I was there I met and married an Iraqi woman. We have a child, a son. While I was in country I did everything I knew to get them a visa so I could bring them home. There was no one I spoke to who was willing or interested in helping me. I was met with indifference, prejudice, and in a couple of cases, open hostility, about me marrying an Iraqi woman.

"I'm not sure I can do anything, but I do know a few folks at the State Department. I know some folks in Washington who deal with immigration issues. I did a story a few years ago about a case similar to yours. I can reach out to the same people again to see if they can offer some suggestions."

"Why would you do that?"

"Let's just say I appreciate your service. That, and I don't like it when people get the runaround."

"That's certainly better than that guy in there. He's supposed to be all about love for Indians. He wasn't even willing to hear my story the first time I came in. I have written letters, he doesn't answer. This is my third time in there. He said he would look into it but he didn't."

"You're persistent. I'll give you that. I can't speak for him, but you have my word I'll do what I can, if anything. I'll try to get you more information and possibly some help."

"I'm very grateful."

Blackbear put his number into Cole's phone. His words were kind in the end but rang hollow with disbelief. Cole had seen it a thousand times. Veterans who fought their way to the gates of hell and back, seen unspeakable horrors, given up careers, education, wives and sweethearts, and the normality of home, only to return to the country they fought for to be treated as the lowest of the low. From VA hospitals, disability claims, education benefits that somehow mysteriously turned to student loans, all tearing at the sinews of men and women who would have laid down their lives for the ungrateful, slow-moving, soul-crushing mechanism that is the Federal Government.

It was a national disgrace. All the "Thank you for your service" comments in airports, restaurants, and bus stations didn't move the needle a tick. It enraged Cole and he fought with thankless energy and faced hostility and disdain from the very people whose job it was to help Veterans. He would not give up and he picked up the gauntlet to do battle again.

Cole watched as Michael Blackbear walked away. He noticed an old man sitting and smoking on a bench not far from where they talked.

"Never changes."

"How's that?" Cole turned to face the voice.

"Ko-ree-uh. I was there three years. Purple Heart, Silver Star, bunch of other bangles they pinned on me. But you better damn well not bring home any slit-eyed women. No sir. Kill who they tell you to. Take all the whores you want. But fall in love with a nice girl and they all tell you you're a traitor to your race, just a homesick kid, it'll pass, go home and find yourself a nice American girl. These slopes, they're not like us." The old man was gritting his teeth. "Damn their souls. I loved her. Still do."

"Were you ever able to bring her home?"

"Never. I never made enough money to go back after the war. I got a letter in '82 saying she died of a female cancer. She never married. We kept our promise to each other. That ol' boy ain't never gonna see that girl, or his boy, again. It isn't in the national interest."

"That's not always how it works." Cole immediately wished he said something else.

"You're right. Once in a hundred, somebody does the right thing, or there's a C.O. that signs the right papers. Back then, nobody gave two hoots about the rights of anybody. Not like today, when the damnable chickens in the too-small cages got more rights than veterans. Makes my blood boil. And that Indian?

He ain't got no rights at all, lessin' some mobster wants to build a casino." The old man spat a brown gooey blob of tobacco between his feet.

"You've learned a lot. How'd you put all that wisdom to work?"

The old man looked up at Cole. His expression was one of half amusement and half disgust.

"You mean work?"

"Yeah, I figure you're retired. What did you do after the war?"

"Gave up for quite a while." The old man spat again.

Cole decided maybe he needed to cut the conversation short. He clearly was rubbing the old guy the wrong way.

"Automotive part procurement."

"Not sure I know what that is." Cole thought for a moment before pressing on. "Like a pick-and-pull junkyard?"

"No, more like stripping stolen cars in a chop shop." The old guy grinned at Cole as if to challenge a comment.

"Are you sure you should be announcing that to a stranger on the street?"

"You a cop?"

"No."

"Fibbie?"

"No."

"Then who cares? The statute of limitations ran out a long time ago. I got car parts scattered to hell and back. Probably all in the junkyard by now. Stopped choppin' about 20 years ago."

"I'm Cole, by the way. I'm supposed to meet my wife inside for lunch."

"You know the fella that runs this place?" The old man gestured toward the Center with his thumb.

"Not well. My wife volunteers a few hours a week."

"I wouldn't stand too close to him in the street."

"How's that?"

"He's not real popular in some circles. You might take an arrow meant for him."

Cole stepped a little closer to the bench and took a seat next to the old man. "What's the beef with him?"

"Kind of like that young fella who you were talking to. Ol' Poore talks a good game but does nothing for anyone beyond the kids. Been a few husbands come in looking for his scalp. Same old thing, White Man education replacing Indian tradition. Mary around here eats the sheep; it doesn't follow her to school. There ain't no hill and Jack and Jill have to haul water by the truckload. And Jesus ain't welcome at the Ghost Dance or Peyote rituals. These folks have been bamboozled by convert-or-die Spanish priests, phony do-gooders from the Government, and hell-fire missionaries for hundreds of years."

"Makes ya mad, doesn't it?"

"Me? Hell no, I hate Indians. Lazy, thievin', drunks. I'm what you might call an observer of human nature. White's are just as bad. They're either ingrates, dopers, drunks, or worse. Or they are a bunch of namby-pamby, do-gooder Baptists that would steal the pennies offin' a dead man's eyes, then lie to their mama about it, all the time hidin' their girlfriend from their wife."

Cole couldn't help himself and laughed. "Seems you don't hold anyone in very high regard."

"Ain't that. Listen, I'm just tellin' ya. If anything ever happens to the good reverend in there, check to see if he's got his scalp. Five'll get you ten an Indian killed him."

"It has been most enlightening chatting with you. My wife probably thinks I stood her up. I better go see what she has planned for lunch."

"If you ever want more education, I'm here Tuesdays and Thursdays most of the day. Otherwise, I reside at the third stool from the door at O'Malley's. I'll buy you a cup of coffee."

"How'd you know I don't drink?" Cole was genuinely curious.

"I didn't. But, I can't. Rotted my guts out years ago. Coffee with lots of cream keeps my seat reserved. Talk's cheap, the company is tolerable."

"I may just take you up on that."

"No you won't, but it is nice of you to pretend. You really gonna help that Indian kid?"

"The best I can." Cole smiled at the old guy and stood up. "Don't bet your last dollar on me not showing up. You'll need it to buy my coffee."

"I won't hold my breath."

Lunch with Kelly was a meatloaf sandwich she made the night before and a soda from the machine. The food didn't matter. He loved spending time with her and hearing in great detail what she was doing at the Center. It was trivial, mundane, and anyone else in the world would have found it boring, but he loved the twinkle in her eye when she talked and the chance he got to reach out and touch her hand.

Driving home after lunch Cole decided to go straight away and keep his promise to Michael Blackbear. Kelly wouldn't be home for a couple more hours. He dug out a couple of old notebooks from his file cabinet. To the rest of humanity, his filing system was nothing more than folders, papers, and small bundles of notebook pages bound with rubber bands.

To Cole, every file drawer was a specific time, article, incident, and the background information that corroborated his memory. He always slipped into a stream of consciousness self-talk that worked as a road map to just the right sheet or sheets of paper he was looking for.

There you are. Cole looked down at a piece of paper with a business card; Keith Strauss, U.S. Dept. of State. Cole carried the card to the kitchen and punched the number into the phone. He leaned against the counter and gazed out the window as he was transferred from one department to another.

Finally, the voice on the line said, "Mr. Strauss' office".

"Cole Sage, calling for Mr. Strauss."

"May I tell him what this is regarding?"

"It's a personal call."

"Please hold."

"There's a name I haven't heard in a hundred years. How are you doing, Sage?"

"I'm great, how's the world of high fashion diplomacy?"

"Not very high fashioned in this department. Once they figure out you're about to retire you inherit a pointless desk in a pointless department with pointless tasks."

"How soon till you retire?"

"Six months. It feels like an eternity. What can I do for you?"

Cole tried to bring Keith Strauss up to date on his location, marital status, and retirement, then dove into the matter at hand. "I met a local young man who did two tours in Iraq. He married an Iraqi woman in a civil ceremony. They have a child and he wants to bring them to the States. Seems he's had every door slammed in his face. Can you direct me to somebody who could possibly care?"

"Oh boy, I've been out of the loop for quite a while. Let me think a second."

"How about Angelo Firenze?"

"I hate to tell you this, Cole, but our old buddy Angelo had the bad taste to die on us."

"When was that?" Cole felt as if he'd received a punch in the gut.

"Almost two years ago, pancreatic cancer. By the time they figured out what it was, it was too late."

Cole stared out the window for a long moment. "I don't know what to say. Sorry."

"Yeah, we worked together for over twenty years. I probably spent more time with him than both my wives." Strauss gave a soul-deep sigh. "Let's get back to business. Let me make a couple of calls for you and I'll get back to you. What's this fellow's name?"

"Michael Blackbear."

"Branch of the service?"

"Army."

"Okay. Let me see what I can do."

"Thanks. I really appreciate the help. And, I'm really sorry to hear about Angelo."

"Yeah."

The line went dead and something in the grass moved just beyond the fence. It was a jackrabbit. Cole watched as it hopped, grazed a bit, and hopped some more. He wondered if the rabbit felt anything when a farmer shot one of his friends.

Cole spent the next two hours checking news sites on the internet and reminiscing about working with Strauss and Firenze. The time they spent together was actually very short in days, but they bonded and kept in touch until Cole moved to San Francisco.

The sound of Kelly's car door slamming was a relief to the tedium of killing time on the internet. He went out to meet her on the porch.

"Welcome home!"

Kelly gave Cole a big smile and held up two shopping bags. "Something special for dinner."

"Oh yeah? What?"

"It's a surprise."

"It won't be too much of a surprise because I intend to sit at the kitchen table while you cook.

Kelly laughed. "Lonesome?"

"Something like that." Cole went down the steps and took the two bags from Kelly and gave her a peck on the cheek. "Tell me something. Do you know a guy named Michael Blackbear?"

"Oh heavens, how do you know him?"

"I didn't mention it at lunch, but I ran into him when I came to see you at the Center."

"There's something wrong with that guy." Kelly shook her head. "He's been in the center a couple of times and always ends up yelling at Warren. I was ready to call the police once."

"He's a very frustrated guy. He married a woman when he was in Iraq. They have a kid and he wants to bring them home. He can't get any help."

"So, of course, you're getting involved." Kelly gave Cole a concerned frown.

"Well, kind of. I told him I would see if I could find somebody to help him."

"I think he's kind of scary. I hope you don't get tangled up in some kind of a crazy mess."

"No, I just made a call. We'll see what happens."

You haven't touched your lunch!" Kelly scolded coming back out onto the porch.

Cole looked up, still lost in his thoughts. "Uh-huh."

Funny, Cole thought. I can't remember what the surprise dinner was. He wondered if the old man's prophecy was fulfilled. A thought came and went so fast that Cole barely could process it. Michael Blackbear's face came back to him. Cole tried to dismiss the thought that Michael Blackbear could somehow be involved but knew if he was a cop he definitely would want to have a talk with him.

"I'll take it with me." Cole picked up the plate and stood. He took the plate to the kitchen and picked up his sandwich, grabbed his keys and sunglasses, and was out the door.

Chapter Eleven

Sometimes the trip to town seemed a blink of an eye. But today it seemed a hundred miles away. As Cole drove, he finished off his sandwich and kept replaying his first-time meeting with Michael Blackbear. He remembered the angry young man yelling in Warren's office. Looking back it was a volatile first meeting. The words of Michael Blackbear played in his mind with a whole new meaning.

"I've been here three times!" Blackbear had shouted. Why would he do that? If you weren't getting help, why press it? Why go to an Indian Children's Center, run by a semi-retired preacher that houses a daycare, parenting classes, and an afterschool program? What made Blackbear think Warren could be any help in an immigration case? Cole did not like where his thoughts were taking him.

He pulled into the only available parking space, about six cars from the police station. As he made his way to the door, Cole realized that Kelly was right. He only knew Michael Blackbear from their meeting and a couple of phone conversations. Their chats were strictly business, fact-checking, and information gathering sessions to fill in the blanks. Blackbear seemed like a good guy, but he'd met a lot of 'good guys' that turned out to be criminals, and worse.

Cole approached the desk inside the police department, identified himself and told the desk sergeant he wanted to see Michael Blackbear.

"Have a seat, I'll find someone who can help you." The sergeant mumbled something into the phone that Cole couldn't make out, and pointed him to a chair. For nearly an hour Cole sat as various people came and went. He read yesterday's paper, or what was left of it, a couple of tattered copies of *Sports Illustrated*, which bored him to death, and a year old copy of *Field and Stream*.

He was about to get up and have a word with the desk sergeant when the door opened and a man in a tan suit came in. He made knowing, friendly eye contact with Cole. "Mr. Sage?"

Cole stood and approached the man. "Yes."

"I'm Dick Selvin. I understand we have a mutual friend in C.W. Langhorne."

"Yes, we do."

"So, my friend, tell me what's going on here, exactly?" Selvin shifted his briefcase to his other hand.

"Well, exactly, I've been sitting here for an hour being completely ignored." Cole jerked his head toward the front desk. "Here's the thing, an acquaintance of mine, Michael Blackbear, has been arrested for the murder of Warren and Judy Poore. They were fine people. I've been acquainted with them for several years. Mr. Blackbear was at work at the time of the murder. Seems to me an easy alibi to prove, one way or the other. So, what I want to know is, why'd they bring him in?"

"That's why I'm here. It's an old, old story. Lock up an Indian, then time permitting, you go look for another option. Let's see what the real circumstances are. If it is as you say, we'll have him out of here in a jiffy. Let me take it from here." Selvin slapped his briefcase against his leg as he briskly approached the desk. "Sergeant, is it true that my client has been sitting here an hour?"

"Sounds right."

"And why is that?"

"I don't know. It seems that everyone is pretty busy."

"Let me talk to the Chief."

"The Chief is a very busy man." The sergeant was the gatekeeper, and as such he was doing a good job, but he also managed to irritate Selvin.

"Well, I'm willing to bet a crisp $100 bill he's not too busy to see me."

The sergeant huffed and picked up the phone. "What was your name again?"

"Selvin, Dick Selvin."

The sergeant pushed a couple of buttons on the phone. After a bit of a pause he said, "Chief, I've got a Dick Selvin out here that says you'd be willing to talk to him." The sergeant's eyes shot up at Selvin. "Yes sir, I see, yes sir, I understand, yes sir." He hung up the phone. "Please, come with me."

Selvin turned and motioned for Cole to follow. After a short walk down a well-lit hall, the sergeant opened the door into the office of Chief of Police Tuckman.

The man behind the large, mahogany desk got up and moved toward the door. "Dick, how are you?"

"I'm great, but my client here has been sitting out in your lobby for the better part of an hour waiting for someone to talk to him."

"You know about this, Sergeant?"

"Uh, yes sir."

"And why is that, Sergeant?"

"Uh, not quite sure, sir."

"Get Lieutenant Bishop in here right now."

The sergeant wasted no time leaving the room. Selvin and the chief exchanged pleasantries and a bit of small talk before there was a quick rap on the outside of the door.

"Lieutenant, come right in. Seems this gentleman has been waiting out in the lobby to talk to someone involved with, what was the guy's name again?"

"Blackbear." Cole turned toward the detective.

"That's right."

"What do you know about a Blackbear we're holding?"

The detective looked at the two men sitting in front of the desk.

"This is a good friend of mine, Dick Selvin, he's Mr. Blackbear's attorney. This is Mr. Sage, Cole Sage, a friend of Blackbear's."

"Ahh, I think I met your wife the other day at the Indian Children's Center."

"I believe you did." Cole couldn't get a read on the detective.

"Ok, here's what we've got. We have two dead people, and we have a guy who wrote two very threatening letters to one of the victims."

"So you made the jump from angry letter to murder? Is that right, Lieutenant?" asked Selvin.

"It's not much of a jump sir, you get an Indian riled up and they're likely to do anything."

"Are you aware, Lieutenant, that Michael Blackbear is a decorated veteran?" Cole injected.

"No sir, I was not." Bishop's sheepish response made it clear he didn't like being embarrassed in front of his boss.

Selvin looked over at Cole and gave him a look that indicated he preferred to do the talking. "Are you also aware that my client was working the day of the murder?"

"That's what he said."

"Well have you bothered to check?" Selvin was like a shark that smelled blood.

"I was planning to send a man out, yes."

"The question was, have you bothered to check?" The chief could see where this was going and was getting uncomfortable in front of Selvin, his friend.

"No sir, as of yet, we have not checked his alibi."

"I suggest my client be released since it will be quite easy to verify his employment, and his presence on the job, the morning of the murder."

The chief stood. "Can you gentlemen excuse us for a moment? I'd like to have a word with my detective."

"Not a problem." Cole stood first and made his way to the door. Selvin nodded in the direction of his friend, the chief.

Back out in the lobby Cole and the attorney were the recipients of vicious glares from the desk sergeant. "I have a feeling that our friend, the Lieutenant, is going to get one Grade A, first class, ass chewing." Selvin looked toward the desk sergeant and returned the glares with a big smile.

"I think you're right. That was some pretty shoddy police work." Cole neither smiled nor looked in the direction of the desk.

"No, that was some pretty blatant, racist police work."

The door opened and Lieutenant Bishop came from the chief's office and approached the desk. "Have Blackbear brought up here."

"Yes, sir." The desk sergeant made a call, grumbled something about the prisoner and glared up at Cole and Selvin.

Bishop turned and approached the two men. "There seems to have been a bit of confusion in our priorities regarding this case. I'm sorry you gentlemen had to come down here. This matter should have been settled earlier in the day."

"We are no longer at war with the Cheyenne people, Detective. Your misguided, racist antagonism toward them is not only antiquated but, quite frankly, disgusting and unprofessional."

"You think not? What do you call that out there?" Bishop shot his index finger at the front door, and turned and went back down the hall.

Outside a group was gathering in front of the police station. Selvin looked from the door to Cole.

"This doesn't look good."

"What is it?"

"Three of my clients have been brought in along with your friend. I will see to them next, the same kind of 'round up the usual suspects' mentality that your friend got caught up in. These fellas raised a ruckus at the Children's Center, and at Warren Poore in particular. Along with their salty language, I understand, threats against his person were made."

"Could any of them be connected to the murder?"

"My gut says no. But, there's one thing I've learned in this business, black is not always black as it looks, and white can be mighty dark underneath. I won't know until I see which one is most anxious for me to represent them."

It only took about five minutes for Michael Blackbear to be released through the front lobby. "Mr. Sage! Thank you so much."

"Don't thank me, thank Mr. Selvin here."

"I'm sorry, I don't understand."

"Good friend of mine called me and said you needed some help. I'm an attorney here in Orvin, here's my card. If this matter should cause you any more problems, don't hesitate to give me a call."

"I'm sorry sir, I appreciate your time and trouble, but I really don't have the money for an attorney right now."

"That's quite alright, Mr. Blackbear. We'll just consider this my pro bono case for the month. Selvin extended his hand to Blackbear. "I hope the next time we meet will be under more pleasant circumstances." Selvin returned to the desk for round two with the desk sergeant.

"I'd like my client to use the back door for his egress."

"His what?"

"Exit, escape, way out, departure."

"It's not available to the public. Anyway, what the hell does he need the back door for? He's an Indian, they're not gonna bother him."

Blackbear looked at Cole. "Let's get out of here if you don't mind. He's right, we should be OK."

Cole paused with his hand on the bar across the front door. The scene outside was not welcoming. There were ten to fifteen men on the sidewalk in front of the police station. Some wore their hair braided; others wore it long and straight. In the time Cole lived in Orvin there were no gatherings of Indians in town, at least not that he knew of. These men were angry and poised for confrontation.

"What are you waiting for?" Blackbear moved in close behind Cole for a better look.

The door opened to yells of "Free Tommy Running Dog! Let Samson Knight Go!" Several of the men carried makeshift protest signs. Upon closer inspection, Cole saw that the handles of the signs were not sticks, but two-by-fours and baseball bats."

When Cole pushed open the front door of the station it flew back at him, nearly breaking his wrist. He let out a howl of pain and shook his hand repeatedly.

"What is going on?" Blackbear leaned forward and looked out the window. "I see. I think we have a problem. Maybe I should go out first. These guys look pretty riled up."

Behind them, the desk sergeant laughed.

Cole tried again to open the door, this time with success. The chants and yelling grew louder as Blackbear and Sage left the building. One man stepped up and shoved Cole hard against Blackbear.

"Come on pig, why don't you arrest me?" A fierce man about Cole's height shoved him again, trying to get a reaction. Cole suppressed his urge to engage the angry man.

"He's not police." Michael Blackbear stepped between Cole and the angry Indian. "He just got me out of jail. Maybe you should try thinking before attacking someone."

"Maybe you shouldn't be so friendly with the whites." A man was in Blackbear's face.

"What's your problem?" Blackbear found himself facing four men. "What's going on here anyway?"

"They've arrested Tommy Running Dog, Richard Armendez, and Samson Knight."

"For what?"

"For the murder of that preacher. They didn't have anything to do with it. Somebody gets killed and they start rounding up Indians. We've had enough."

Cole tried to speak but was cut off by one of the men. "We don't need to hear from you. This is an Indian matter. You have no right to speak. We will handle this ourselves."

Suddenly a projectile flew past Cole's head and smashed hard against the door of the police station. As he turned, Cole saw a big splash of red paint running down the glass. From both sides of the crowd, police officers approached the group. "Y'all need to go home. You're not helping anyone's case. If you don't disperse you'll find yourselves cellmates with 'em."

There were shouts, taunts, and curses, in response to the police demand that they leave.

Michael turned to Cole with a worried look. "We need to get out of here, this is gonna get ugly."

Cole took two steps toward his car and was hit hard with the handle of a protest sign. Blackbear threw a crushing right-hand blow to the man's head, knocking him to the pavement. Cole staggered and was leaning against the wall.

"Move, hurry." Cole hesitated and Blackbear grabbed his arm and half pushed, half dragged him running down the sidewalk. Neither man looked back until they were nearly to the car.

Cole leaned against the front of a car, trying to catch his breath.

"You OK? That looks pretty bad."

Cole reached up and touched the knot rising on the side of his head.

Blackbear was looking back at the disturbance. The police waded into the crowd with nightsticks and began zip tying the protester's hands behind their backs. The intent of the bats and two-by-fours of the protest signs became apparent as the Indians swung hard fighting back the police. Several men hit the ground after stumbling over another man on the sidewalk.

"Will they never learn? Broken heads, broken bones, locked up for days. Probably jail time. They lose their job if they have one. For what? Those three in there don't care about them. They're thugs, trouble makers. They'll get out, probably before the fools that are getting beat."

Cole looked at Michael for a long moment before he spoke. "I've seen this before, a lot, other places, other races. It's a form of venting. You think rioters and looters care about anything other than themselves? Pent up anger, rage, frustration, hopelessness, are just looking for a way out. You remember that. We may have a long road ahead trying to get your family out of Iraq."

"You're right. I've seen it all my life. These guys won't listen to the tribal elders at all. They blame it all on the white man. They came here looking for a fight." Michael turned from the violence down the street, both physically and emotionally. "Look, I'm really sorry I had to call you, but I didn't know of anybody else that could possibly help."

"No problem, but here's an important lesson to learn. Rest assured, anything you put in writing that you shouldn't, will come back to bite you."

"Understood." Blackbear nodded.

"Good." Cole reached out and slapped Blackbear on the shoulder. "No problem, I'm beginning to see how things work around here. By the way, I got a call from the State Department from my contact there. I missed the call, but the message sounded promising.

It was too late to call back, so I'll return the call in the morning."

"Why must everything take so long? Maybe there's another way."

Cole disregarded the remark. There is no other way he knew of, and if this didn't work, he knew of no other solution. "Sometimes when things feel like they're taking too long, that's when suddenly things start to happen."

"I've never heard that one before." Michael looked at Cole and thought to himself, 'I do have another way'.

"We both learned a lesson today. What did you learn?"

"That it doesn't pay to be an Indian in Orvin."

Detective Bishop was still stinging from the dressing down he received from the Police Chief and the words of Dick Selvin rang in his ears. Now he would face Selvin again.

The door of interview room #3 creaked a bit as Bishop pulled it closed. Sitting at the table with their backs to the door were Samson Knight and his attorney Dick Selvin.

"Detective, this is a complete and utter waste of my client's time." Selvin was out of the gate with a hostile tone and a volume unnecessary for the size of the small room.

"Afternoon, Samson." Bishop completely ignored Selvin.

The detective took a seat at the table and pressed the red button on the digital recorder, starting both an audio and video record of the proceeding.

"Interviewing Samson Knight. Present: Lieutenant Martin Bishop, the accused, and his counsel Mr. Dick Selvin. For the record, please state your legal name."

"Richard Cowell Selvin."

"Mr. Knight, please state your date of birth."

"Méanéeše'he, sóohtoha, na'no'ena'nóhtoha." Samson answered in his native Cheyenne tongue and gave Bishop a defiant grin.

"Look, we can stay here for the full seventy-two hours or you can cut the crap and tell me your birth date." Bishop didn't look up from his note pad.

Selvin leaned over and whispered in Knight's ear.

"July 9, 1980."

"Lieutenant, we can all save ourselves a lot of time, and you another embarrassing blunder for the day, if you will simply check the booking log for the day before the unfortunate deaths of Mr. and Mrs. Poore, as well as the release record for the day after. You will find my client was incarcerated during that time, making his participation in their murder impossible."

The metal chair grated across the tile floor as Bishop scooted back. He stood clenching his teeth for a few seconds while he glared at Selvin, then left the room. He did indeed check the logs, and to his dismay, Selvin once again had him. Not being able to bear Selvin's *I told you so* smirk or another of Samson

Knight's moon-faced grins, he sent the nearest patrolman in to inform him he was free to go.

The revolving door of Indians arrested and released for public drunkenness, disturbing the peace, as well as more serious infractions of the law, left few of the tribe's troublemakers unknown to Bishop. Richard Armendez held the distinction of the only arrest Bishop ever made where a suspect drew blood from him. Bishop hated him and the feeling was more than mutual.

Making sure that Samson was out of the building, Bishop spent several minutes making and sipping a cup of coffee in the break room. There were bad days and then there were days like today when he wished he had become a shop teacher at the high school. He loved working with wood, fixing cars, and even Ag shop and welding broken pieces of farm equipment, and it would be better than what he faced today.

"This will be your third strike for the day, Bishop." Selvin popped off before the door clicked shut.

"Mr. Armendez." Bishop nearly choked having to address 'Snake Armendez' formally. "I suppose you have an explanation for your whereabouts on the morning of the Poore's deaths?" Bishop decided to forgo the formalities rather than face more humiliation at the hands of Dick Selvin.

"I was working."

"Working? That's a first. And where might you have been gainfully employed?"

"Sooner Moving. I helped move some people to Tulsa."

"I suppose you have proof of this?"

"Whatchu mean?"

"A pay stub, a contract, some kind of verification of this employment?"

"I got cash." Armendez thought he was boasting.

"That is illegal without a pay stub of some sort." Bishop pursed his lips and looked at Selvin for the first time. "Counselor, can you provide this documentation?"

"I'm sure we can." Selvin leaned over and whispered to Armendez."

"Hell, I don't know. We met in a bar. He said you want to make some money? I said sure. He paid me, I came home." Armendez didn't bother to whisper.

"So, you can't prove it."

"We will provide verification." Selvin was a bit less self-assured.

"Will. Meaning at some undisclosed time in the future."

"Soon as possible."

"Richard Armendez, until your attorney can provide a concrete alibi for your whereabouts the morning of the murders, I will be holding you on suspicion of murder." Bishop stood. "This interview will be resumed at the convenience of this department."

"I didn't do shit!" Armendez screamed at Bishop's back as he opened the door. "You said you would get me out!" Bishop turned at the sound of a deep groan from Selvin. Armendez had slammed his elbow into Selvin's face and knocked him from the chair. He stood over the attorney kicking him repeatedly.

Bishop, in what some might call a rather subdued manner, called down the hall, "Need some help in here!"

Three uniformed officers ran to his aid and into interview room three. Bishop walked to the desk. "Tommy Running Dog's attorney will be indisposed for a while. We will reschedule his interview at Mr. Selvin's earliest convenience." Bishop took a couple of steps from the desk. "Oh, and charge Richard Armendez with aggravated assault, with intent to do great bodily harm."

Chapter Twelve

Becca stood with her hands flat against the shower wall with the hot water beating down on the top of her head, over her shoulders, and cascading down her back. Her eyes were tightly shut and the cares of the previous days seemed to melt in the heat of the steamy shower.

The key slipped into the familiar lock. The click heard a thousand times before said welcome home. Matt Walker came into the house and looked around. He could sense that there was no one home. "Anybody home?" He called out. There was no answer. He carried his bag and backpack into his old bedroom and tossed them on the bed. As he glanced around he realized something was wrong. There were a bra and pair of panties lying on the bed, draped over the chair at his old desk was a pair of jeans, way too small for him. Against the wall next to the closet was a large, green duffle bag. He felt an uneasiness seeing the foreign objects in the room he knew so well.

Becca sensed the water cooling off. As much as she hated to, she shoved in the knob turning off the water. She stood for a long moment breathing in the steam. She wrung out her hair, pushed back the shower curtain, grabbed the towel off the rack and wrapped it around her head forming a turban. She took the big, plush, white terrycloth towel from the counter and dried herself. The mirrors were completely fogged up. She hated to leave the steamy warmth but felt foolish just standing in the middle of the bathroom with a towel wrapped around her.

She opened the door and made her way down the hall to her room. She entered the room and let out a blood-curdling scream.

Poor Matt was standing looking at his trophies on the shelf above the dresser and nearly jumped out of his skin at the sound of Becca's scream. He whirled around and yelled, "Who are you!"

"Who are you? What are you doing in the house?" Rebecca clutched her bath towel tight.

"I live here!" Matt shouted back. His fight or flight adrenalin kicked in and he was wide-eyed and not the least bit pleased.

"Oh, my goodness, Matt. Hi, umm, uhh-"

"I don't care who you are! You scared the crap out of me. It looks like you've taken over my room." Matt motioned towards the bra and panties on the bed.

"Yeah, just for a while." Becca's knuckles were white from her grip on the towel.

"Let me get out of here so you can dress. We need to have a talk." Matt went out the door, closing it a little harder than necessary. He went back into the kitchen just as he heard the front door open and the familiar sound of his mother's voice.

"Matt? Matt, honey? Are you here?"

"Hey, mom!" Matt called back from the kitchen.

Sharon came around the corner and into the kitchen and threw her arms around her son. "What a wonderful surprise. When did you get back?"

"About five minutes ago. Who the heck is that in my room?"

Sharon laughed. "That's Becca Poore." She turned and set her purse on the counter.

"Uh-oh." Matt felt his face flushing.

"What?" Sharon replied.

"I just yelled at her." He began to laugh. "She's not going to be happy with me. I didn't even recognize her."

"Becca and Cassie are staying with us for a little while."

"I was really sorry to hear about her folks. What on earth happened?"

"Nobody really knows at this point. The first thing we heard was that Warren shot Judy, then himself."

"No way, that could never happen," Matt interrupted, shaking his head.

"We all knew that. We knew that couldn't be. The next day the police determined that it was murder."

"Who would kill them?" Matt couldn't imagine anyone even disliking the couple.

"That is the question that has kept your father and I awake for a week. There's no clues, no motive, nothing was stolen. It's a senseless, barbaric--" Sharon burst into tears.

Matt reached out and pulled his mom close. "I'm so sorry. I know how much they meant to you." He felt himself choke up. "Where's dad?"

"He went to Warren and Judy's place to see if he could help with the cleaning. Some people from the church have gathered. It has to be done sooner or later and I couldn't face it, and I certainly wouldn't want the girls having to do it."

"Hello." Becca stood smiling shyly near the edge of the kitchen door. "Am I interrupting?" Becca's hair was dry, she was dressed and her voice was so sweet. Matt found himself smiling back at the lovely, young woman.

Sharon wiped her eyes, and responded, "No, no."

"Becca, I am so sorry. I didn't recognize you. I've never seen you without clothes before."

"Naked!" Sharon looked from Matt and then to Rebecca for an explanation.

"I wasn't naked! I had a towel around me."

"Okay, that was more flesh than I was expecting. You totally took me by surprise."

Rebecca smiled and could feel her cheeks redden.

"I'm really sorry about your folks. They were wonderful people and they really meant a lot to all of us. I'm so sorry."

"Thank you, Matt."

Sharon spoke and interrupted the moment between them. "I was so excited to see you, it didn't dawn on me to ask, what are you doing here, Matt? I wasn't expecting you for another month."

"There were some big doings at school and they canceled class for three days. I thought I'm getting the heck out of here."

"Well, I couldn't think of a better surprise. I am so glad to see you. Are you hungry?"

"Am I ever *not* hungry? What have you got?"

"Well if you don't mind leftovers, we have a ton of stuff from the funeral. How about a ham sandwich and potato salad?"

"Perfect."

"How about you, Becca? Are you hungry?"

"Yeah, now that you mention it, I am kind of hungry. I'll have the same."

"You kids have a seat at the table and I'll get it ready."

"Let me help you." Becca did not want to sit at the table face to face with Matt quite yet.

The kitchen fell into a soft comfortable silence. Becca pulled the bowl of potato salad from the refrigerator and handed it to Sharon. She took a tray of cold cuts and moved like a shadow behind her.

Sharon set the salad on the long side of the counter. "I'll get the bread. You get the mayo, no mustard for Matt. There should be some cheese wrapped up on the second shelf."

A few minutes later there were two plates, two sandwiches, and two scoops of potato salad sitting before Matt and Rebecca. Sharon made a pretty obvious exit from the room, and they sat for several minutes in very awkward silence.

"So." They both seemed to say at the same moment.

"You first." Matt took a big bite of his potato salad.

"So, what are you studying in school?" Becca tried a clumsy attempt at getting the conversation started. "I mean, not to be rude, but haven't we been out of high school about six years now?"

Matt chuckled. "Yes, we have, but I'm in my second year of veterinary school. And no, I didn't flunk out two or three times."

Becca hoped she hadn't offended him. "I wasn't suggesting you were a bad student, I just couldn't figure out why you were still in school. I'm sorry, that was rude."

"Not any worse than what my dad says. He's getting kind of sick of paying for college."

"I only went one year, to the community college. Then I worked to raise my support."

"Yeah, aren't you in, like, Honduras or something?"

"Guatemala." Becca corrected the common mistake.

"Yeah, yeah, a missionary, right?"

"That's right."

Another awkward silence fell over the room. Matt sat watching Becca mess with her potato salad. He was surprised at her shyness. He somehow remembered her being the lively one of the two sisters. Cassie was the brat; Becca was the fun one, though he would have never told her that's how he remembered her. He took a sip of his lemonade and thought how strange for them to be sitting at this table as adults.

He stood up and went to put his plate in the sink. He stood for a long moment with his lemonade, as he gazed out the front window. Nothing has changed. It is kind of a comfort. He smiled at his thoughts.

Becca looked up and watched him go to the sink. He's so tall, she thought, she remembered him being so much shorter.

He turned and opened a cupboard. "I bet mom's got some cookies in here." He rummaged through packages.

Becca looked at his profile. Gone was the ponytail he wore in high school. His hair was cropped in a stylish cut. His beard was very thick and he wore it closely trimmed. He turned back and faced her.

"So, dad's gone, and your sister's not here. What have you got planned for this afternoon?"

"Nothing, actually," Becca replied hesitantly.

"I need to drive out to the Mattson place. You remember John from high school?"

Becca remembered him, didn't like him but didn't know how to react so she just made a humming sound.

"Anyway, he's managing his dad's ranch now and I told him I would come out and take a look at a horse that got injured. Would you like to ride along? It would give you something to do."

Becca felt her face redden even deeper as she replied, "That would be nice."

"Okay, let me break the news to my mom and we'll be off if you're ready."

Five minutes later they were out at the curb and Becca stared at the passenger door of Matt's truck. She wondered how in the world she would be able to gracefully get into the vehicle. As she stood there pondering the situation, the passenger window rolled down and Matt's face appeared.

"Having trouble there, Shorty?"

"I was, how do I, umm-"

"Here, maybe this will help." Matt fired up the engine. A long, wide running board descended from under the truck. Becca sighed in relief and opened the door. She stepped up and hoisted herself into the truck with no further problems.

"This is a nice truck." She admired all the nice touches of the interior.

"I've been working part-time at a veterinary clinic. The old clunker Toyota that mom and dad gave me when I went away to college had breathed its last." Matt pulled from the curb and they were on their way.

"Mind if I play some music?" Matt reached for the knob.

The thought of riding out to the country listening to country music blasting made Becca regret her decision to come along. To her shock, the sounds of soft jazz came from the stereo. As they rode along there was something very familiar about the tune playing. To her surprise, she recognized a worship song they sang at church.

"What are we listening to?" Rebecca asked.

"It's a CD of a Christian Jazz group I saw at school. They're really good."

"Huh." Rebecca was taken by surprise. "I was kind of expecting cowboy music to come blasting through your stereo."

"And beer cans flying out the window and a Confederate flag flapping in the wind?" Matt grinned, knowing exactly what she meant.

"Something like that." Becca tasted her words. "You know, you're really not what I remembered. You were kind of a hellion in high school."

"Probably worse than you even knew, but when I got to college I realized that the Aggies tend to be a pretty wild crowd. You really can't party and keep your grades up. My sophomore year I realized a lot of them had fallen by the wayside. A buddy of mine, from one of my animal husbandry classes, invited me to Varsity Fellowship. It really turned me around and got me grounded."

As she looked at the side of Matt's face, Becca thought back to the boy she grew up with. They went to church and Sunday School together their whole lives, but you would have never known it from his attitude and behavior at school. This newfound maturity and his re-embrace of faith was a pleasant surprise.

"Tell me about this Guatemala thing." Matt wasn't sure how to broach the subject. "What do you do down there, exactly? Are you a nurse?"

"No, I wish. Actually, I work a lot with agriculture and improving the water supply to the towns and villages in my area. Town, now that's an exaggeration. The biggest town around is maybe 2,000 people. It's a market town called Santos Verde. Most of the villages are no more than ten or twelve families living in an area, defined by a river or the forest."

"So what do you do? I mean, to help clean up their water?"

"One of my main jobs is explaining to the people that they can't have their drinking well and their outhouse next to each other." She laughed at what that must have sounded like. "They always have them in far too close proximity to each other. It is such a rainy, wet climate that the sewage leaks into their water supply. So that keeps me pretty busy. Of course, there's the ministry side, where I work primarily with Junior High aged kids, and our team that does street evangelism."

"And how long have you been down there?"

"Nearly three years in Guatemala. Before that, I was in El Salvador for a year, but we left because it was just too dangerous."

"That's pretty cool." Matt admired her but had little understanding of why she would put herself in that position. "I always knew you'd do something important."

"Really?" Becca was amazed. "I didn't think you even knew I was alive when we hit about thirteen."

"Oh, you'd be surprised who's watching you and whose parents are talking about whom at the kitchen table."

The song on the stereo seemed to abruptly change to an upbeat number and they rode along listening to the music. About twenty minutes out of town Matt turned the car into a wide space with a heavy, wrought iron and brick gate. He reached over and took the cell phone from its holder on the dash and punched in a number.

A moment later he spoke. "John, it's Matt, I'm at the gate."

"Hold on." Becca could hear through his phone. As she looked forward, the gate began to roll back.

"Alright, halfway there."

"You're kidding."

"Well, that might be a slight exaggeration, but this is just the outer boundary of the ranch."

Becca found herself holding tight to the armrest and the door handle as the truck hit ruts and potholes on the gravel road. Several times Matt said 'Whoa', in a loud voice after hitting a particularly deep hole.

"You'd think with all their money they'd have a better road. How are you making it over there?"

"It's a good thing I don't get carsick." They both laughed and Matt swerved to miss a deep rut in the road. Becca found herself falling over the center armrest.

"There's the house," Matt announced, slowing the truck down a bit. "Look at that thing!"

"My goodness, it's a mansion!"

The house was a sprawling, two-story, white affair with pillars across a large, front porch area. "How many square feet do you think that monster is?" Matt crossed his arms and leaned on the top of the steering wheel.

"I don't know, it looks more like a hotel than a house." They both laughed.

"It's got to be the biggest place around here." Becca felt like a kid seeing a big city for the first time, except this was still Orvin, and this gigantic place was in the middle of nowhere.

Matt turned onto a road to the right. "We're not going to the house though; we're going to the barn, although it's plenty nice enough to live in. In fact, it has a three-bedroom apartment as part of the building." Ahead was a beautiful red barn trimmed in white and looking like something off a calendar. Standing in front was John Mattson, wearing a big, tan-colored cowboy hat and a belt buckle the size of a coffee saucer.

"Wait till you get a load of this guy." Matt pulled the truck across ways in front of the opening of the barn and turned off the engine. "This shouldn't take too long."

"No problem. I love horses."

"Well, the one we're going to look at cost ten times as much as my truck."

Matt opened his door and Becca did the same.

"Hey Johnny, how's our patient?" Matt led the way to the barn.

"I don't know, she's not very happy. I got all the stuff you asked for. It's inside."

"You remember Becca Poore, don't you?"

"Not this model. I guess we've all kind of grown up. You must be Rebecca 2.0. Nice to see ya."

"Hi, John. Good to see you, too."

The three went into the barn and there was a large table with a white cloth sitting in the middle of the stable, and a variety of bandages and bottles set out. Over the next half hour, Becca watched as Matt comforted the beautiful animal. He spoke to it in a kind and reassuring voice as he changed dressings on a large wound across its chest.

"She wasn't watching where she was going," John explained the situation to Becca. "She ran right through the barbed wire fence, hit it so hard the post pulled out and impaled her. We thought we were going to lose her. Matt got us a referral for one of his professors and we flew him in to take care of her."

Matt ran his hand along the horse's side and gently patted its rump. "It looks good. It's healing nicely."

"I really appreciate you doing this, Matt. To fly that vet back out would have cost another fortune."

"Not a problem, John. Glad to check her."

"So, what do I owe you, Doc?" John reached for his wallet.

"Shut up." Matt would not expect or accept, payment.

John fished out a hundred dollar bill and shoved it into Matt's shirt pocket. Matt tried to swat him away.

"I'm not taking your money." Matt protested.

"It's not for you. It's so you can take Becca out to dinner."

"We're not, I mean, I ..."

"Don't act innocent, Walker." At that moment John's cell phone rang and he took the call. "It's my dad; somebody has driven a truck through our fence. I hate to do this to you, but I gotta go."

"No problem. Later!"

On the way back to town Becca commented on the rekindled friend. "John seems to have turned out to be a pretty nice guy."

"Yeah," Matt shrugged. "It only took two stints in rehab."

"Oh, goodness. I guess we are getting older."

"Yeah, grandma." Matt impersonated the voice of a shaky old man.

"Thanks a lot!"

"You're older than me!" Matt laughed.

"Yeah, by what, three months? How do you remember that?"

"What?" Matt was feeling mischievous. "After all your birthday parties my mom dragged me to?"

"I didn't go to any of yours," Becca said.

"You weren't invited."

"See? You *were* a snot. I told you." They both laughed.

For the next twenty minutes, they chatted as if they had been friends their whole life. They *had* known each other their whole lives, but they really had never gotten acquainted.

They pulled up in front of the Walker house. "Dad's home. Hey, before we go in, I hope John didn't embarrass you too much with that dinner comment."

"No," Becca answered with a disappointed tone to her voice.

"So, where *are* we going for dinner?" Matt asked brightly. "This Benjamin is burning a hole in my pocket."

"You don't have to take me to dinner just because John suggested it."

"I was going to ask you out anyway. He just made it easier and more affordable." Matt smiled widely. "And you'll probably get to go to a nicer place. It will be a nice way to get away from things and clear your head a little bit."

"This afternoon has worked wonders, Matt. I actually feel human again. Thank you for asking me to go with you."

"Shall we go in?"

Chapter Thirteen

"Cole? I need you." Kelly's voice said more than her words. She was frightened and there was something very wrong.

"Are you okay? Where are you?" Cole prayed she hadn't been in an accident. She only left the house a little while before.

"I'm locked in the Center. Please, can you come? I'm scared."

By the time Cole said, "On my way" he was already running to the car. Never a great driver, and with a tendency to be cautious, he drove to town with a total disregard for speed limits or stop signs. He took the corner at Long Street faster than he should and fishtailed, nearly losing control. Just ahead he could see three police cars blocking the street in front of the Center. Cole pulled over and parked, hoping his screeching and sliding went unnoticed.

In front of the Center was a large group of people yelling and screaming and chanting. The police presence calmed some of his fears, but Kelly must be frantic. The closer he got to the crowd, the clearer their chants became.

"Free, free the Orvin three! Free, free the Orvin three!"

The six policemen stood in a horseshoe around the group. It seemed odd to Cole that they hadn't dispersed the crowd. Cole made his way closer and stood at the rear of the patrol car closest to the door of the center. By his estimation, there were close to fifty people in the crowd. The makeup of the crowd was almost entirely Indian. The group Cole encountered the day before at the police station was primarily men, but the crowd in front of him was half women.

Across the front of the windows in red, runny paint someone sprayed *Make America Native Again!*

Cole glanced to his left. One of the policemen was approaching him. "Hey, I wouldn't be here if I were you. These people are getting pretty wound up. And I don't think some white guy gawking at them is going to go down well."

"My wife is inside the Center. I need to get her out of there."

"Well, you sure as hell aren't going through the front door without losing your scalp." The cop laughed at his own joke.

"Then what do you suggest I do?"

"I suggest you either let this run its course and they'll all leave in a little while, or you can go around and get her out the backdoor, that is if she can hear you."

"Why are you letting this go on this way?" Cole's words wiped the smile off the policeman's face.

"Because there are six of us and fifty of them. No sense throwing fire on gasoline. We'll let them tire out and then get them to leave."

"And if they decide to break out the windows or burn the place to the ground, then what?"

"Then I guess we wait for the cavalry to arrive." The policeman chuckled again. "They'll tire out in a bit."

"I hope you're right." Cole pulled his cell phone from his pocket and began walking back to the car. "Kelly, I'm out front. I'm going to go around back and take you out that way. I'll be there in a second." Cole got into his car and did a u-turn in the middle of the street and pulled into the parking lot of Johnson's Insurance, cutting through to the alley behind. He turned left and hastily moved down the alley to the back door of the Center. He got out of the car and pounded hard on the back door. He could hear the yelling and screaming echoing off the buildings. Within moments, Kelly opened the door.

"This is insane! What is wrong with these people?"

"I don't know but let's get out of here." At that moment the sound of breaking glass echoed through the building. Cole pulled Kelly out the door and slammed it.

"Wait, I have to lock it!"

"That's pretty pointless if the windows are broken out in front. Get in the car."

Kelly started to get in the car. "Wait, what about my car?"

"Where is it?"

"It's in front."

"We'll get it later." Cole got in and continued down the alley.

"Can you explain to me what this is all about?"

"The police have arrested three Indians on suspicion of murdering the Poores. Just like Michael Blackbear, they've all three had run-ins with Mr. Poore. Two of them had the police called on them at the Center. The crowd is saying that they all three have alibis."

"Then why don't they let them go?" Kelly turned in her seat to look at Cole.

"Because, my darling, they're Indians."

"Don't be silly. This is the twenty-first century."

"Oh yeah? Explain that to Michael Blackbear, Tommy Running Dog, Richard Armendez, and Samson Knight. We're not in San Francisco anymore. Somebody along the line forgot to explain to these people due process and civil rights."

"I knew there was an element in the Cheyenne community that doesn't like the Center, but I had no idea that the white people were just as bad, or worse, toward the Indians. I guess you never really know a place till you've lived there a few years. I think we're just now starting to see below the surface of our little town."

"What are you doing down here, anyway? I thought you were going shopping." Cole approached a stop sign on the corner.

"I was, but I remembered we were going to take an inventory of supplies and I thought I would do it while it was nice and quiet."

"Well, you certainly missed the call on that one. When did the crowd show up?"

"About ten minutes after I got here I started hearing a commotion out front. Then there was pounding on the doors and windows, people were screaming and swearing. That's when I called you."

When they got to Long Street, Kelly looked back and saw the graffiti and the broken window. They had hung a banner from the awning that said *Indian Culture! Not White Fairytales!* They rounded the corner and headed for home.

Kelly began to cry. "It makes everything we've tried so hard to do seem so pointless."

"It does indeed." Cole accelerated.

"When we come back later to get my car, we'll see about securing the building and replacing the window."

"*We* won't be coming back. I'll have Ernie run me back to get your car. You can call somebody else to take care of the rest." Kelly turned and looked out the window and barely spoke the rest of the way home.

On the kitchen table, Michael divided, counted, and re-stacked his take so far. $20,000, two robberies, and now only halfway there. It was almost a week since he robbed Marco's. The fear of learning what the police knew, or what was reported, kept Michael from watching or reading the news. "One more should do it. They're not ripping me off again." Michael's words seemed to echo in the small kitchen.

He placed the money back in a small box and walked it out to Mary Wilson's shed. He felt a sense of pride outsmarting the police by hiding his gun and money. If he left the bag of jewels and gun in the house when they made their surprise visit, he would still be behind bars, but, rather than a murder, they would have him for the hold ups. The first of the week will be the perfect time to hit his next store. Not only would he be able to get the jewels, but if he were able to surprise the merchant when they arrived, he could not only get jewels but the weekend's receipts as well.

An old, tattered phone book was on the kitchen table. He didn't understand why he still had it, but it would come in handy in deciding where he would go next. Flipping to the J's in the yellow pages he scanned the list of jewelers. The biggest jewelry store in the county based on the size of their ad was M&J Jewelry Mart. He circled the number with a pencil and reached for the phone. He quickly punched in the number and waited for someone to answer.

"What time do you open on Monday? Thanks." He placed the phone back on the base on the counter. If they open at ten, I will be there at a quarter to nine. Michael closed the phone book.

The weekend went by as normally as Michael's nerves would allow. He attended a tribal gathering in honor of the oldest member of the tribe who was turning 100 years old. He spoke with old friends and enjoyed the barbecue provided by the tribal council. Sunday he slept late and spent the afternoon watching old black and white movies on TMC. The need to get out and do something eventually made it impossible to concentrate on the movies.

Somehow his car found its way to Shelly Matera's house. She was no longer there. While he was in the army she married a mechanic from Tulsa who was the cousin of his friend, Merle.

'I will wait for you as long as there is dust in this old town.' Her promise rang in his ears as he stopped his car in the middle of the street. His mind went back to a dusty afternoon in Iraq when he received a letter from Merle telling all about going to Shelly's wedding, not realizing no one bothered to tell Michael.

He sighed deeply. "You shouldn't have come by here." Halfway between the car and the house, the image of Shelly smiling and waving goodbye the day he left for the Army played like a hologram. If he were not such a coward he would have asked her to marry him then and there. In the back of his mind, he thought of being killed in a war far away. It made him realize he would have to wait. The blast of a horn jarred him from his thoughts. He hit the accelerator and left the area. He bought two burritos from a roadside taco stand, ate one and put one in the refrigerator before going to bed.

A ray of bright sun pierced through the window and across Michael's face. His first thought was that he overslept, but checking the time it was just a little past 7:00. He shaved, showered and retrieved his gun from Mary's shed. He started to eat the burrito he saved from the night before, but his nerves would not allow him to take more than a couple of bites. He paced nervously until there were only twenty minutes left before his determined time of reaching M&J Jewelry Mart at 8:45.

The large employee parking area behind Jewelry Mart was also used by employees of Kerry's Supermarket to the left of the jewelry store, and Western Wear store to the right. Michael parked the car out of the direct line of M&J's back door. From his vantage point, he would have plenty of time to determine who would arrive at their back door first.

At five minutes to nine a neatly dressed man, gray at the temples, in a pale gray suit, his tie yet to be knotted, left a silver Mercedes Benz and took the first steps toward the back door of the jewelry store.

Michael stepped from his car, the blue burka in one hand and his gun in the other. He didn't slam the car door. As quietly as he could, he slipped in behind the man from the Mercedes. The man was four yards from the back door when Michael slipped the burka over his head.

"Don't turn around and don't do anything foolish."

"What do you want?"

"You and I are going in the store, you are going to fill a bag for me and I am going to leave. No one will get hurt if you do what I say."

"This is a very bad idea. My other clerks will be here soon."

"Hopefully I'll be gone by then, just do as I say, open the door, turn off the alarm and let's get this over with."

"As you say." The man slipped the key into the door.

"Slowly. Alright, alright, slowly."

The man opened the door and stepped inside. To the left of the door was a keypad for the alarm. It began to beep as he pushed in a series of five numbers for the code. Michael pulled the door until he heard it click behind him.

"Everything you want is in our safe."

"Then open it."

"I just didn't want you getting excited when you saw the showcases empty." The man crossed the room to the safe. It was nearly as tall as he was with a large brass combination lock in the front. Michael noticed the man's hand tremble as he began turning the combination. As the last number was entered the man turned the large handle and opened the safe.

"Here." Michael thrust out the Wal-Mart bag. "Fill it." Without hesitation, the store manager began taking trays and slipping them into the bag. "Shake 'em. Shake 'em."

The man did as instructed and then tossed the trays aside. He repeated this action nine times.

"Now, where are the raw stones?" Michael stepped a little closer to the man.

"They're in this box."

"Ok, dump it." The man reached in the safe with both hands.

Michael heard tapping on the glass coming from the front of the store. In that moment of distraction, the man spun about and pulled the trigger of a gun that was mounted inside the box. Michael felt a burning in his side and saw the rage in the manager's eyes.

Without thinking, he shot the manager once in the chest and once in the face. Michael quickly grabbed the bag, ran out the back of the store, slamming the door hard behind him. The pain in his side was growing worse by the second as he got into his car and shut the door. He left the keys in the ignition and was out of the parking lot in just a matter of seconds. He made his way back to the highway and home.

After two tours in Iraq with never so much as a scratch, Michael Blackbear was shot by a middle-aged jewelry store owner. The pain combined with the adrenaline of the shootings put him in a heightened state of awareness. In the army, he was trained to kill. In his job, he did nothing but help the people of Iraq. As he drove, the images of his wounded comrades being loaded into helicopters and rushed to hospitals in and around Bagdad made the wound in his side even more surreal.

Somehow, I must get in the house without anyone seeing me. His garage door opener remote was misplaced ages ago. On occasion, he pulled his car up onto the dirty weed patch of a front lawn and washed the car. He decided he would pull the car up there again, this time with the car door facing the front door. The closer he got to home, the worse the pain became. He felt the urge to pee but thought that maybe the two sensations were blending together. He relaxed and felt the warm urine run into his pants and mix with the blood. He sat for a long moment staring at his front door, wondering if he could make it the few feet to the door. Later, he would hose out his car, but for now, he must somehow get into the house.

There was a thunderous pounding in Michael's head. He opened his eyes wide and was unable for a moment to determine where he was. There was a tremendous pain in his knee and as he turned his head he saw he was lying on the floor just inside the front door. He had passed out and collapsed. His right leg was bent at the knee, and it was under his other leg.

The house was in the shadows of dusk. He had no concept of how long he was out. Michael struggled to straighten his leg and a pain shot through his side and the ceiling exploded in white sparkling stars. I must feel my side, he thought, but the gooey half coagulated blood held his hand and arm to the floor like thick molasses. He rolled to his left with a deep, guttural groan, freeing himself. He felt his side and the gooey blood.

Breathing heavily he made it to his hands and knees. Half crawling, half dragging his aching leg, he moved down the hall to the bathroom. Moving as close as he could to the bathtub Michael reached in and turned on the water. He realized he must have blacked out again because when he opened his eyes the water was reaching his elbow. With great effort and incredible pain, he pushed himself to his knees and rolled into the tub. The water was warm. He tore open the front of his shirt popping off each button as he went.

He gently began running his right hand over his abdomen, gently washing away the gooey blood as he went. He reached the wound and gently ran his fingers around the hole left by the bullet. The pain was lessened by the water and he was able to reach onto his side, feeling the gooey blood and rubbing it until he could feel the skin beneath. He knew from his medic training in the Army that this kind of wound is cause for a great loss of blood. He placed his hand full over the wound and tried to remember what lay beneath. Did the bullet strike any vital organs? The bleeding seemed to have stopped.

The water in the tub was growing increasingly cool and he knew he must get out before he got a chill. He rolled to his side, felt for the plug at the drain and pulled it out. As the water subsided, he managed to get to his knees and grabbed the vanity next to the tub with both hands. With great effort and even greater pain, he threw his knee over the side of the tub and felt his foot land flat on the floor. Using his leg and his arms, Michael pulled his other leg up from the tub and stood before the mirror above the vanity. He removed his shirt and let it drop to the floor. The wound was closer to his side than he first thought. He turned ever so slightly in an attempt to see if there was an exit wound. A larger hole showed where the bullet passed through. It was an ugly, but clean wound. The bullet struck mostly flesh and a bit of muscle in his side.

In the drawer of the vanity, there was a bottle of aspirin. The second drawer down he found a half bottle of old alcohol. He kicked off his shoes, unhooked his belt, unzipped his jeans and let them drop to the floor. Stepping on the cuff of his jeans Michael pulled his leg from the soaked denim. He stood in his shorts and socks and stared into the mirror. "You can do this." His voice was shaky but in his eyes there was determination.

As he turned to leave the bathroom he remembered an ace bandage that he bought for a sprained ankle. Retrieving the bandage from the drawer he took the alcohol and aspirin and made his way to the kitchen. Halfway down the hall, he began to feel lightheaded and nauseous; he needed to use the wall to lean against to make it the rest of the way.

He set the bandage, alcohol, and aspirin on the kitchen table and went to the cupboard. From the first shelf next to the stove He removed a box of salt. He dumped the bottle of aspirin on the table and poured a small bit of the alcohol over it and began crushing the aspirin with the bottle.

Satisfied the paste was nearly smooth he poured salt on top, adding a bit more alcohol onto the mix. Again, he remembered his army training. A skinny Medic who looked about sixteen gave a lesson on emergency medical attention of wounds when none was available. His theory was, a chemical burn in the field works as well as a flame to cauterize a wound. Seal it; kill any possible infection as soon as possible. Michael hoped the Medic was right and continued to mix the strange compound.

A clean dishtowel would have to act as a bandage. There was only one in the cabinet. He groaned and thought how his buddies in Iraq would laugh at his ridiculous attempt at doctoring himself as he tore the dishtowel into four long strips. Michael scooped up some of the salt and aspirin mixture, gritted his teeth, and pushed it into the bullet hole on his side.

He gasped, clenched his teeth, and rocked back and forth, nearly passing out from the burning pain of disturbing the wound. Scooping up the remainder of the mix, he shoved it into the hole in his back. Panting heavily, he began to wrap the dishtowel strips and then the ace bandage around his abdomen. The task done, he stood, intending to go lay down on his bed. The room grew dark and he passed out hitting the kitchen floor with a heavy thud.

Chapter Fourteen

"I have to run into town for a little while. Would you like to come along?"

"Are you going to go to the movies? Getting an ice cream cone? Or, going to the used book store?"

"No, I have to meet Rebecca Poore at the Center."

"I'll pass," said Cole. "We are going to have to take your car in and do something about the damage," Cole added.

"I still don't understand someone doing that to our car. How did they know it was even mine? I was several spaces down from the Center in front of the empty building.

"Well, I'll bet you $500 it was done by someone who knew you from the Center. There were lots of women in that mob. They just stuck their finger through a wad of keys and clawed the full length of our car."

"Why would they do that?" Kelly asked bewildered.

"Because you work at the Center."

"Do you really think it's that simple?"

"They are simple people, my dear. Look what happened to our car at church. Real nice bunch of

Christian people you've got there. Who carries a knife that big to church? And do you really believe nobody saw somebody punching four big holes in our tires?"

"I stuck up for an Indian, brought in a lawyer, and basically made the cops look stupid. There's a lot of police and Sheriff's Department people at the church."

"You can't blame the church, and you certainly can't blame God for some jerk slashing our tires. They may have just seen your car in the church lot. That's a pretty nasty assumption you're making."

"I'm not blaming the church, just some of the racist jerks who go there. Better?"

"What is the matter with you? You sound as bad as the Indians. Hate is hate. This is not like you. I'm disappointed."

"I'm sorry. I got a bit carried away. You're right. Maybe I did. The church has nothing to do with it. All the same, it's pretty scary to have your car vandalized in the church parking lot. People are acting really crazy about this whole Blackbear thing."

"Maybe I do want you to come with me." Kelly sighed and shook her head. "What happened to our little town?"

"I'm sorry, sweetie. I am just disheartened and frustrated as you are with what's happening. I shouldn't have thought twice about going with you."

"I still can't believe that the people of this town could turn on us like that."

"Not us dear, me. You were just in the wrong place at the wrong time."

"What about the car?"

"Could have been anybody's." For Kelly's sake, Cole backpedaled his feelings. He still believed it was someone in the crowd that knew it was her car.

When they arrived at the Children's Center, Lt. Bishop was already there. They parked next to him and he gave a wave of recognition.

"Good morning, folks," Bishop said. "What happened to your car?"

"Are you being funny?" Cole asked. "It got this treatment while we were sitting in church."

"You're not serious." Bishop frowned and turned toward the windows.

"Whole church full of cops, too."

"Cole." Kelly was not pleased with Cole still implying cops were involved.

"When did this happen?" Bishop jutted his chin toward the damage at the front of the Center. The front windows were now covered in plywood. The banner was gone, but the spray paint was still visible.

"That is the section that said *Native Again*." Cole pointed out. "Two days ago I spoke with one of your men in blue watching the whole thing. He seemed to really be enjoying it. Didn't lift a finger to stop it or break up the crowd. He joked about calling in the Cavalry if it got out of hand. Looks out of hand to me."

"What about that bunch of Indians attacking the station?" Bishop showed deep resentment in his voice. Bishop was unwilling to give an inch. Thinking better of the idea, he didn't continue, just looked at Kelly motioning toward the door. "Shall we go in?"

Kelly moved toward the doors, keys in hand. She turned and whispered to Cole. "Not another word."

"Kelly, here's Rebecca." Cole motioned at the door. He didn't look in Bishop's direction. He knew all he needed to about the detective.

"Oh good, we're all here." Becca gave everyone a welcoming smile.

Bishop moved to the door, briefcase in hand.

"Good morning, Rebecca." Cole smiled. Being the last one through the door he locked it behind him.

"Good morning, Mr. Sage. I didn't expect to see you here."

"Please, call me Cole. It seems my wife needs a bodyguard. I'll stay out here."

Cole's comment wiped the smile from her face. She frowned and followed the other two into the office.

Neither Becca nor Kelly wanted to take the seat at Warren Poore's desk. Detective Bishop placed the briefcase on the desk and popped the latches. "Here are your files back." He took the short stack from the briefcase and placed them on the desk. "You have some serious problems here, ladies."

"Meaning?" Kelly asked.

"Well this is a nonprofit organization, and by Oklahoma State Law there's an annual accountability report due, along with the minutes of all meetings signed by the chairman and the secretary, number one. Unless they're somewhere else, there are no minutes from any meetings in this material. Didn't you tell me, Mrs. Sage, that these were all the files?"

"Yes sir, I did."

"Aren't you the secretary of this organization?"

"No, that would be Maryann Kopek."

"Would she know where those would be?" Bishop asked.

"I doubt it." Kelly shrugged. "Her title is more like an honorary thing for being a volunteer. But, I'll see if she knows where anything is."

Bishop took a deep breath, then looked from Kelly to Rebecca. "Well, quite frankly, that's the least of your worries."

Kelly glanced at Rebecca. She was trying to think of anything that could be worse. What was to come next didn't enter her mind. "What do you mean?"

"According to our officer from Financial Crimes at the station, there are some serious discrepancies in payouts and balance sheets. To put it bluntly, it looks as if somebody has been skimming money from the organization and doing a lousy job of covering it up. I suggest before we get any more involved, you folks do a real thorough search for more records, receipts, or canceled checks. You need to get this straightened out, like yesterday. You understand what I'm saying? Is there an accountant you use?"

"I don't know." Becca's head was spinning and she wanted to throw up.

"Neither do I. I'm just a volunteer, yet I find myself getting deeper and deeper involved simply because no one steps up to do things," Kelly explained.

Becca steeled herself and asked the one question she really didn't want the answer to. "How much money is missing?"

"It's no small amount. It's in the thousands, forty at least, and that's just a quick police audit. When the State auditors get a hold of this, and if you can't balance it, somebody's going to be in big trouble. That is unless the one doing it was one of your parents."

"That could never be." Rebecca jumped to her feet. "Why would they steal money from what is basically themselves?"

"I don't know, but people do it all the time." Bishop was hardened enough from his years on the force to know that was the case nine times out of ten. "How many people have access to this material?"

"Just Warren, I thought." Kelly was trying hard not to think the worst.

"Do you keep this door locked?"

"No."

"Then anybody has access to it." Bishop pursed his lips, then sighed. "Look, the door's not locked. People come and go all day long, including some of the poorest people in the county. You have a bunch of volunteers, and an organization, it seems, that doesn't report to anyone who would hold them accountable. You have a real mess here, ladies. It is the determination of our financial affairs officer that there is substantial embezzlement of this state-chartered, non-profit. That is a felony, and we take felonies real serious around here. Do you hear what I'm saying?"

"If we can find the discrepancies nobody will get in trouble, right?" Rebecca's question sounded more like pleading.

"My dear, that's a very generous thought, but frankly, you're not going to find anything, anywhere, and somebody is going to go to jail. We made copies of all these books, and our people are digging deeper. I would appreciate it greatly if you would do the same and give us anything you find out."

"We'll do our best, but I really don't think either one of us is qualified to do the kind of audit you're suggesting."

"You two are all I have, so do your best, but I suggest you get a good accountant or attorney to work on this. We'll meet up again in a few days to see where it's all going. Like I said, we have copies of everything. I will let you know what our people figure out."

Kelly looked at Becca, who was still standing in the corner of the room. Her thoughts ran to the incredible weight that the poor girl suddenly found thrust upon her. I didn't sign up for this, she thought. At the same time, I can't abandon Rebecca either. Her head spun with thoughts and fears. Did Warren steal the money? Ridiculous, Kelly dismissed the thought. He borrowed it! He borrowed money. But, for what? Her mind raced until Bishop broke in.

"Any questions before I go?" Bishop picked up his briefcase and moved toward the door. "I'm not the bad guy here, and I'm sorry to add to your stress at this time of grief, but, you have to get to the bottom of this. I will give you a couple of weeks. Then I have to act."

"Thank you, Detective." Rebecca stepped forward and shook his hand.

Kelly looked at Bishop with an expression that said 'I don't want to be involved'.

Bishop left the building and the two women sat in silence. Neither spoke for several minutes. The sound of brakes and a honking horn out front broke the spell.

"I don't know about you, but I could really use a cup of tea." Kelly stood and moved to the door.

Rebecca looked at Kelly and shook her head. "I am so over my head here. Where do we even begin to find what he's asking for?"

"When I was a kid my mom kept a budget. On the last day of the month, she would sit down with a sheet of paper and draw a line down the middle. At the top of one side, she put a plus and on the other side she put a minus. Then she would list all the monies that came in during the month. On the other side, she wrote down everything she spent. She would add it all up, subtract one from the other and give it to my father. He would look at it and either say, 'We've got money left, or, what on earth have you done?' Then they would laugh."

Rebecca looked at her and said, "And?"

"I don't know, I was just a kid. But, maybe that's a good way for us to start."

"Do you think they could be wrong?" Rebecca asked.

"Everybody makes mistakes. Maybe they didn't understand the system being used. You only have to be off a column or two. But let's have a cup of tea before we get started. You put on the kettle. I'm going to go out and talk to my husband."

Kelly went outside where Cole was sitting on the hood of the car.

"Do you really think somebody is going to attack your car again?"

"If you'd have asked me that last week, I would have said don't be silly. This week the response is the same. Funny thing with words, how a simple phrase can have two completely different meanings, yet be the same. So, what did the cop say?"

"He said somebody has been embezzling money from the Center." Kelly threw her hands up as if to say, 'What next?'

"I knew he was in there too long to just be returning a bunch of paperwork. So, now what?"

"So now Becca and I are going to go over everything with a fine tooth comb. Would you like to go home and come back for me later? This is probably going to take a while."

"What do you two know about finding an embezzler? Shouldn't you call in a CPA?"

"Yes, but I have an awful feeling I know who it is and I would just as soon Becca find it for herself."

Cole moved to the driver side of the car.

"Aren't you going to ask who it is?"

"I don't want to know." Cole opened the car door. "I think this is a case of, better leave it to the professionals. Of which, I remind you, you are not one. I love you, Kelly, your heart's in the right place. Now, let's work on your head." Cole gave her a broad smile and winked.

Kelly returned to the office and Becca stood holding two steaming mugs of tea. "I got us chamomile. I figured the calming effect might do us both good."

"Good thinking." Kelly took the cup. "So, where do we start?"

"I was thinking while you were outside, Cassie wants to go to college to become an accountant. She's always been a whiz with numbers. Maybe she can take a look. After all, she's as big a part of this as I am."

"Yeah, she helped your dad with the books. Maybe she can spot it."

"Let me ask you something, Kelly, you're kind of new to town and you don't have all these lifelong connections that the people here have. What do you think is going on?"

Kelly thought for a long moment. Deep inside she was starting to get a feeling she didn't like. The idea of what was going on was beginning to formulate, but without more evidence, she wasn't about to say anything.

"You're right, Becca, I am new around here. All the people here at the Center were strangers to me a couple of years ago."

"How did you get to be the Chairman of the Board?"

"Oh heaven's Becca; I'm not the chairman of anything. Your dad asked me to be on the board and I declined. He said it was just kind of an honorary position and that if I were going to carry the keys and be able to let people in and out I should probably have some sort of a title."

"But, you seem to be the one in charge. I mean, after my dad, everybody seems to look to you for direction."

"Maybe that's because I have the biggest mouth." Kelly chuckled and gave a shrug. "Don't worry. We'll get this all straightened out."

"Yeah, hopefully, Cassie can spot the problem. I really have a funny feeling that it's just a big mistake."

Bishop said outside help. I hope another person close to the organization isn't a mistake, Kelly thought.

Becca took her cell phone from her pocket and punched in a series of numbers. After a few seconds, she said, "What ya doin'? ... We could sure use your help here... You're the numbers person in the family and it seems we have a problem... Well, the police think there's something funny with the accounting. You said you wanted to be an accountant. So this is your big chance... Could you come now?... That would be great. See you in a few."

After her call, Kelly and Becca sat quietly sipping their tea, lost in their thoughts. About fifteen minutes later Cassie arrived.

"So what's this about the cops thinking something's wrong?"

"They seem to think somebody was embezzling money from the Center's accounts. Their Financial Crimes guy seemed to think there were double entries and irregularities in deposits." As Kelly explained, she watched Cassie close for a reaction.

"We were hoping that since you helped dad with the books you could either find the mistake or find out what's going on. You know how bad I am with numbers," continued Becca.

"I would call what I did, help. I totaled and double checked long columns of numbers. I didn't really even know what they were. Just a fresh pair of eyes." Cassie looked back at Kelly. "I thought you were in second command around here. Can't you do it?" She turned back to Becca. "Can I talk to you alone?"

Becca looked at Kelly as if to say 'what do I do?'

"No problem, I'll finish my tea in the main room. This is a family thing, anyway." Kelly left the room and closed the door behind her.

"I don't trust that woman, Becca. Who is she anyway? She's a total stranger. We don't really know her; she's only been here a couple of years. She could be the one stealing the money."

"I don't think that could be. Daddy had full confidence in her."

"He saw good in everybody. He was too gullible for his own good. He was always getting taken advantage of. I say we send her packing."

"I don't think that's fair, Cassie. Whatever happened to 'innocent until proven guilty'? If you go over the books and find something wrong, we'll decide what to do then. But, she doesn't write checks, she doesn't make deposits, she's just a volunteer."

"Oh, so now I'm a suspect."

"I didn't say that!" Becca was surprised at her sister's reaction.

"Well, I'm the only one besides dad who made deposits and wrote checks."

"Well, you certainly wouldn't steal from the Center." Becca tried to reassure her sister and calm her ruffled feathers.

"So what do you want me to do exactly?" Cassie huffed and plopped down in her father's desk chair.

"Just go over this stuff, you know, checks and balances, and see what the police could be talking about. And then, explain it to us."

"So you're gonna keep that woman around?"

"Well, she does seem to have the confidence of everybody that works here. They all seem to look to her for guidance. I like her and I trust her."

"Whatever. But if you're wrong, it's on you."

"If I'm wrong, sure, I'll take responsibility."

Becca moved to the door. "Kelly?"

"I'll be right there."

As Kelly entered the room, Becca smiled reassuringly. "We've come up with a plan. We just need to have some family understanding."

"I think that's a wonderful idea. How long do you suppose something like this will take, Cassie?"

"I don't know, a couple days." Cassie didn't look up from the papers she shuffled on the desk.

"That's great. So we'll be able to start the new week with a plan of action."

"I'm not doing it over the weekend." Cassie sneered. "I have plans."

Becca, always the peacemaker, said, "That's fine, just the sooner you can get it done, the sooner we can put this black cloud over the Center behind us."

"So I guess we're done here." Kelly pulled her phone from her purse. "I'll have my husband come and get me."

As the girls gathered their things to leave, Becca's phone rang. "Oh, hi Matt."

"I have to run out to Mattson Ranch again. I was wondering if you'd like to ride along and we can have lunch on the way back."

"Where are you now?"

"I'm at my friend Aaron's house. Are you home?"

"I'm at the Center. I was just getting ready to leave."

"I'm five minutes away. I'll be right there."

"Well, aren't you two the lovey-dovey pair." Cassie's words were coy and teasing but her tone was sarcastic.

"It's nice to get reacquainted. He's nothing like I remembered. We seem to have a lot in common, and it's fun to talk to him."

"Doesn't hurt that he's a tall hunk either, does it?"

"It certainly doesn't hurt." Becca giggled and glanced over at Kelly. Kelly winked at her and gave her an approving smile.

"I think I'll wait outside. Matt said he'd be here shortly. See you guys later." Becca left the office and the building.

"It's nice your sister has found somebody. It must be hard coming back to town when everyone you know is getting older, married, and connected."

"Yeah sure, leave it to her. She always wins the prize, finds the Easter egg with five dollars in it, and does all the right things."

"What's eating at you, Cassie? Becca is trying really hard to get through this and you go around looking like you've been sucking on lemons. Have you two always been at each other? You know, it makes people around you very uncomfortable to be in the middle of it."

"Then maybe you shouldn't be in the middle," Cassie snapped. She snatched her purse off the desk and left Kelly standing alone in the office.

Kelly blew out an exasperated breath. "Well, you certainly handled that well." She moved toward the door and turned out the lights. Leaving the Center, Kelly wished she didn't have to go back. Cole was right, it's not her responsibility. Out on the sidewalk, there was no sign of Cassie, but Becca was sitting on the bench nearby.

"Well, lucky you." Kelly moved closer to her.

"I know, right? I certainly wasn't expecting Matt to be so sweet and friendly."

"He's a great catch, Becca."

"Oh, no, it's nothing like that, we're just friends."

"Oh, is that right?" Kelly smiled. "Let's see how long that lasts. All the same, I think you're a pretty lucky girl."

"I think so too, but I'm not going to read anything into it. I'm a little too fragile at the moment for any more big disappointments."

"This doesn't look like a disappointment to me." Kelly pointed up the street at Matt's approaching truck. As Matt parked in front of the bench, Becca gave a coy wave.

"I hope you have a wonderful time. I'll be in touch."

"Thank you." Becca stood clutching her purse in front of her.

The door opened and Matt jumped out of the truck. "Hey, ready to go?"

Matt looked over at Kelly. "Kelly, right? I've heard nice things about you."

"You, too."

Matt looked at Becca and shyly looked down at the curb.

"This should be fun." Becca moved toward the truck.

"If driving back out to the ranch excites you, you've got a strange sense of fun." Matt gave Becca a big grin. "I can guarantee you are going to love lunch though."

"Is that so?"

"I've got a table all reserved."

"You're kidding, where?"

"Big Pete's Barbecue, of course, best place in town."

"Very funny," Becca laughed.

Matt opened her door. "Your chariot awaits."

Becca turned and smiled at Kelly as she hopped into the truck.

"Drive careful Matt, you have precious cargo," Kelly said as Matt closed the door and hurried to the other side.

"Don't I know it." He gave Kelly a thumbs up.

Chapter Fifteen

"What are you so busy doing?" Kelly stood in the archway into the den. Cole always referred to the room off the front door as his office, but Kelly loved the couch, fireplace, and the bookcase that gave her a place to relax, read and reflect.

"New book." Cole looked up and smiled with a cat-that-ate-the-canary grin.

"Really?" That's exciting. What's it about? Is it a biography kind of thing, or something you wrote about, or…?

"Nope." Cole interrupted. "It's a historical mystery."

"Really?"

"Don't sound so shocked."

"No, it's not that, it's just, I didn't, I mean…" Kelly tried to find a way out of her poor choice of words. "When did you come up with this idea?"

"In the shower."

"Really?"

"That's three, Kelly. I can write fiction." Cole's sudden defensiveness took Kelly off guard.

"I'm just surprised. You've talked about all kinds of books, their stories, and stuff like that. This is a totally new idea? I was just kind of surprised, that's all." She crossed the room, put a big toss pillow behind her, and lay back on the couch.

"What are you doing?" Cole looked at her in wonder.

"I want to hear the story. I want to be comfy. So, let 'er rip. You have my undivided attention."

"It's just a seed. A bunch of random thoughts still wet from the shower." Cole chuckled in half embarrassment and half amusement at Kelly's interest.

"Yeah, so?"

"So? So, nothing. It's rough and some of the plot might be kind of disjointed."

"Ok, I get it. Not perfect. Not a book. Not ready for public exposure." Kelly shrugged. "No excuses. You've been typing for the better part of an hour. So read to me already!"

Cole laughed merrily and began to read. "OK, the working title is *The Tears of an Angel*."

"Like it."

"I can hear the boots crushing the gravel up to the steps of my parent's house. Like the heartbeat of demons steadily coming closer. All through June and July 1942, people, Jews, have been taken away in trucks. Now it was our turn. Someone turned us in for harboring Jews, sharing our food, our home.

"This part is still a work in progress. In the truck, a mother gives her girl *The Tears of an Angel* diamond. She tells her that it will help her. She does not explain or offer how, but she tells the girl it is very valuable. She tells her that children are not usually searched." Cole paused to think. "I'll have to figure out how the mom knows this. She tells the girl if it appears they will do a search, to stick the diamond up inside her."

"I'm not sure about that part." Kelly interrupted.

"History, not Sage."

"OK, go on."

"They're all taken to a concentration camp. Mother and daughter never see father and two brothers again. Later, weeks, months maybe, whatever, Mother and daughter are loaded on a train and moved to a Concentration camp in Poland.

"They are able to stay together, but the second year, mother and daughter are separated. The girl goes to a children's home. The kids are used as child labor in a factory, what kind, I don't know yet. The mother is gone forever.

"Because she is so small, she's like ten or twelve and small for her age, the girl spends the war in a factory going under machines cleaning up. She befriends an older woman that sneaks her food every day from her plate and gives her a pair of socks she steals from somewhere.

"All the time she keeps the diamond, through community showers, de-lousing, all kinds of stuff. Only once does she have to, you know." Cole used two fingers to motion her inserting the diamond.

"Near the end of the war the factories are one by one shut down, she is moved from camp to camp, factory to factory. Finally, she is moved to Auschwitz main camp and endures hunger and the terror of death. She watches skeletal people sent to the gas chambers, at one point she is forced to sort their clothes. She gets sick, malnutrition-ed..."

"Malnutrition-ed? That's not a word." Kelly teased.

"I know, but these are notes. I needed a word, and I grabbed that one. Anyway, she survives and the camp is liberated. Not wanting to be the captives of the Americans or Brits, she sneaks off the transport truck and hides in a truck carrying crates of some kind. The truck goes to France. There she heads for Paris, on the road, trains, trucks, walking. She steals from farmers, nearly gets raped by German deserters.

"Then she gets caught by a farmer's wife, a widow, trying to get milk from one of their cows. It's snowing and she's starving. The woman takes pity on her and gives her a job milking cows on the farm through the winter. She finally reaches Paris, finds school friend."

"Where is she from?" Kelly was finding the whole thing a bit farfetched but was trying to stay engaged.

"I don't know. Can't be Holland, too Anne Frank-ish."

"Got it. How's she find a friend in Paris? I don't get it."

"I don't know, at the Louvre, Eiffel tower." Cole was showing signs of frustration.

"No. She's a refugee, not a tourist. Where would she get money for a ticket?"

"If I might continue," Cole sighed showing his rising frustration, "She sells the diamond and leaves for America with the aunt of the school friend. The woman is wealthy and needs a companion."

"Then why would she sell the diamond to go? Wouldn't the aunt buy her a ticket?" Kelly's excitement about helping tell the story was growing, as Cole's feeling of enthusiasm was sinking.

After a pause that was a bit too long, Cole continued. "The woman introduces her to a family from their country that lost a son in the war, and they adopt her, send her to school. Goes to Sarah Lawrence. She meets the grandfather, a professor at the college. He hooks her up with the son of his eldest daughter. The girl marries the guy, who's rich, yada yada.

"Husband finds a diamond, buys it back. They live happily ever after. Our girl, now a Grandmother, gives it to her granddaughter who is getting married. She is the one that our girl/grandmother is telling the story to. The end."

Cole leaned back from his laptop and closed the lid. Kelly didn't speak for a long time. She watched as Cole pretended to plug in the mouse.

"It's a nice story," Kelly finally said.

"You hate it."

"What's going on, Cole?"

"What do you mean?"

"Why are you writing this book? Or any other for that matter?" Kelly sat up and faced the desk.

"I'm a writer. It's what I do."

"Did. You *were* a newspaperman, a journalist. You wrote non-fiction, the news, your opinion, and insights. You didn't write novels."

"So?"

"How long has it been since you quit the Chronicle?"

"I don't-"

"Four years. Let me rephrase the question. Why are you doing this?"

"The money."

"We don't need the money. Fame? Limelight? A return to your former glory days?"

"I don't need that." Cole was lying, and he prayed Kelly wasn't seeing through his desire to write again.

"I'm worried about you. Do you realize you just read me a Harlequin romance fairy story with World War Two thrown in?" Kelly was beginning to see Cole's veneer cracking. She hit the nail on the head. He found himself living at a snail's pace when he was used to running, going, doing, chasing a story, a lead, doing interviews and being at the very heart of the news of the day.

"I don't know what to do with myself."

There it was, Kelly thought. She gazed at Cole sitting in the chair at the desk and realized he was defeated. He looked old, sad, and lost. Her heart was breaking.

Kelly leaned forward. "What do you mean, sweetie?"

"I don't know what to do with myself!" Cole's eyes flared as he looked up at Kelly. "You do all your volunteer stuff, ladies Bible studies, whatever else you do, I got nothin'."

"You could volunteer. There are men's Bible studies, there are places to help."

"That's you, Kelly. Not me. I go to church. The people there are not like me. We have nothing in common. What am I going to volunteer to do, plant daisies downtown, hand out candy at the Christmas parade? I'd kill myself." Cole tried to sound sarcastic with a twist of humor, but the pathos of his voice could not bury the truth just beneath the surface."

"What you're saying is you hate it here."

"What I'm saying is I have no one but you to talk to. As much as I love you, I need people. People with interests other than Friday Night Football at the high school, and drinking beer at the Legion Hall." Cole was getting wound up. "I don't give a royal rip about corn prices, the weather, or the Dallas Cowboys, or whoever it is they cheer around here. And, my gosh, other than the ribs at Big Pete's and a sandwich at Ernie's I haven't had a decent meal since we moved here.

"Well thank you very much!" Kelly said indignantly.

"Not your cooking. You know what I mean. Don't you miss real Italian Mia Sophia's ravioli? Kowloon's Dim Sum in China town? Korean BBQ, Rosenberg's Deli? I'd kill about now for a Chicago style hot dog. I miss buildings more than two stories high. I miss Mick Brennan, I miss Chris Ramos and Chuck Waddell, I miss Olajean, I miss Hanna." Cole's voice cracked, he looked down. "I miss the kids, and I miss my Jenny." Cole put his hands over his face.

Kelly fell silent. She didn't know what to do. She didn't know what to say. She crossed the room and stood behind Cole. She put her hands on his shoulders.

"Don't."

"I had no idea you were hurting so." Kelly spun the chair around and hugged Cole.

"I feel like a fool. I don't know what has come over me. I have you, what else could I want?"

"All the things you mentioned. I'm so sorry. Let's go. Let's go on a trip. Anywhere you want. You know I'd love some Chicago deep dish Pizza, some Memphis barbecue, or maybe we should just get on a plane for Paris."

"We have to do something." Cole squeezed Kelly tightly.

Michael Blackbear gently pulled off the bandage from his wound. There was a yellowish tinge to the blood in the salt and aspirin packing. I hope that's not infection, he thought, as he examined the bandage closer. Not being able to make a clear determination, he applied a new bandage and repeated the process on the exit wound. He wrapped the Ace Bandage around his middle tightly. The burning pain seemed to recede the tighter he wrapped it.

The idea of getting the last monies he needed quickened his pulse. The Coyote would get his, and the process could begin. Most importantly, he would be done with the guys at the Chew'n'Chat.

He retrieved a navy blue t-shirt from the dresser drawer in his room and slipped it over his head. Carefully minding his right arm he slipped it through first, then the left. The bathroom was a bloody mess. He began to run water in the tub. He gathered up the bandages and strips of towel he tore two days before. Grabbing another towel, he began to wipe down the sides and rim of the tub. A bloody path ran over the edge, down the side, and onto the floor. He rinsed the towel and continued cleaning. Satisfied that the tub was clean he moved to the sink and repeated the cleaning process.

Picking up the wastebasket full of bandages, wrappers and shredded towel, he carried it to the kitchen and dropped it next to the large bloody oval on the floor. Using his foot, he pushed the towel around trying to clean the gooey mess. He fished under the sink and found half a bottle of ammonia. He poured ammonia directly on the spot. Under the running water, the bulk of blood rinsed from his towel. Painfully lowering himself to the floor, he used his right hand to scrub. Finally, the spot and the thick, sticky mess were clean. The stinging smell of ammonia filled the air.

Glancing around the kitchen for any sign of his injury and finding none, he took the trash can to the backyard and the 55-gallon drum. He dumped the trash inside and set it on fire. As flames danced above the barrel he moved over to the shed belonging to the neighbor and retrieved the Wal-Mart bag and its contents of jewels and watches.

As he glanced towards the road he saw his car was still parked close to the front door. Another mess to take care of.

"What's that?"

He hadn't noticed that Mary Wilson was standing on her back porch.

"Nothing, I was just talking to myself."

"You okay? You're walkin' funny."

"Yeah, I'm okay, I pulled something in my side." Michael continued walking into the house. Mary continued to talk to him but he ignored her. He put the bag on the table. Under the sink was a small pail he filled with water, added some ammonia, grabbed his towel, and went out to the car.

The cushion of the seat and the back were covered with blood. Hard as he scrubbed, the gray, cloth fabric of the seat wouldn't give up the cordovan stain. Maybe I should just hose it out, Michael thought in exasperation, but it would stay wet too long, he decided. He would pick up some upholstery cleaner at the auto supply store on his way home. In the meantime, he would cover it with a blanket. He put the bucket and towel in the house, got the bag, and departed for the Chew'n'Chat.

When he arrived at the café, the usual group was assembled near the back. This time, however, there was a black man sitting at the table. As Michael approached the booth the boss looked up and said, "In a minute. Get lost." Michael stood for a long moment staring at the small white purse with gold clasp and strap rings that was sitting on the table.

"You deaf? I said later."

Michael turned and walked back to the far end of the counter near the door. He sat down and the waitress came through the swinging door from the kitchen.

"What can I get you?"

Michael glanced around at the placards thumbtacked on the wall announcing various specials and food prices. "I guess I'll have some of that pie." He pointed at the glass case behind the counter. "And a glass of milk."

"What kind of pie? We have four kinds."

"I don't care, just pie."

"No need to get snooty with me, I'm no mind reader."

"Sorry. Cherry. Give me cherry pie."

"We don't have cherry."

"Then whatever you've got. You said you have four kinds. Just bring me a piece of pie."

The waitress opened the glass door on the case, slid out a pie tin and slapped a piece of pie onto a small plate and tapped the pie server hard on the plate. She whirled around, set the plate in front of Michael, took a fork from under the counter and dropped it next to the plate. Without speaking, she turned, filled a glass of milk from the jug in the small refrigerator, brought it back, and set it down next to the pie.

"There." She turned and went back through the door into the kitchen.

Michael took his time eating the pie. It didn't help that it was some sort of unidentifiable, coconut/banana/custard, cream, yellowish stuff that he really didn't like. He drank the milk to get the taste out of his mouth and waited.

It was nearly fifteen minutes before the black man walked through the café past him. He looked neither right nor left. He left without a change of expression or making eye contact. Michael wasn't sure if he should approach the table again or wait until they called him. After a couple of minutes, he stood. He glanced back at the table and the boss motioned him with two fingers to come.

Michael slid into the booth, setting his bag on the table. "This is it. This is the last of it." His tone was the same one he used when dealing with hostile villagers in Iraq.

The man sitting next to the boss raised his sunglasses and perched them on top of his head. He looked at Michael with a hostile glare. "You're not very grateful."

"Grateful? You give me pennies on the dollar and I'm supposed to be grateful?" Michael stared into the eyes of the man across the table. For a long moment, it was a battle of wills who would blink first.

The boss broke the spell as he reached across the table and took the bag. "Enough." He opened the bag and looked inside; reaching in, he stirred the contents about.

"Twenty thousand." Michael's suggestion was uninvited.

"What are you, a comedian?" The boss snapped the bag shut and set it between himself and the man who stared at Michael.

"That's how much I want. I don't want to negotiate. This stuff is worth ten times that. Give me the money and that will be the end of it, and you'll never see me again."

Michael felt something shove hard against his side, sending a fiery bolt of pain through his wound. It only took a moment to realize the man sitting next to him shoved a gun into his ribs. A familiar metallic sound came from beneath the table. The man next to the boss pulled back the hammer on his gun.

"I give you nothing. This is my commission for putting up with you. You're right. I'll never see you again. If I do, *nobody* will ever see you again. Now get the hell out of here."

Between the shock of the boss' words and the incredible pain in his side, Michael was unable to breathe. Michael raged inside. He was helpless to react. Unarmed and crippled with pain, there was no choice but to comply.

"What are you, stupid too? Get lost." The man sitting next to him jabbed him again even harder in the side. Michael gasped in pain. He saw stars and a wave of nausea swept over him.

It took forced concentration for Michael to slip out of the booth. He was lightheaded and needed to grab the backs of the stools along the counter as he made his way to the door. It took all his strength to keep from staggering.

As he reached the register the waitress yelled, "Hey, you didn't pay for the pie. Hey, you owe me five bucks."

Michael pushed open the door with his right hand. He raised his left hand and middle finger as he went through the door, the waitress still yelling at his back. As he opened the car door, he winced and grabbed his side. It was wet. He looked at his hand and it was covered with blood.

"I gotta get out of here." Michael gasped for air as he fumbled for his keys fighting to start the car. The engine turned over and he put the car in reverse. As he backed up he heard the scrape of something metal. He realized he hadn't closed his door and it was scraping the car next to him. He didn't stop, he just pulled it shut.

On the road and heading for home he felt like he was looking in the wrong end of a telescope. He recognized the feeling, and he knew he was passing out. The gravel crunched beneath his tires. He shook his head violently, the ratcheting sound of the rumble strips signaled he was driving off the road onto the shoulder.

He pulled back hard and swerved wildly, crossing into the oncoming lane. A small, silver car honked repeatedly and Michael pulled back into his lane, narrowly avoiding a head-on collision. After driving less than a half mile, he pulled into the parking lot of a Dairy Queen. He rounded the building and parked near the dumpster and out of sight from the road. He rolled to his right, pulling the blanket on the back of the seat with him as he slipped into unconsciousness.

When Michael opened his eyes it was dark. For a moment, he was unable to understand where he was, or how he got there. He used the steering wheel to pull himself upright. A parking lot light flickered above him. There were two cars in the drive-thru. It was then the whole scene at Chew'n'Chat came back to him. He retched hard and threw up onto the floor of the passenger side of the car.

The angry face of the man that he killed in the jewelry store came to him up from the darkened floorboards. He had killed a man, and the fruits of that violent act were now gone. Stolen. Unattainable. He would never be able to bring Miriam and his son to America. He cursed himself as he felt for the keys and started the car. At that moment, he didn't care if he lived or died.

Chapter Sixteen

When Cole pulled up in front of Ernie's Deli, he could see Georgia and Ernie through the window chatting behind the counter. Of all the people in Orvin, they meant the most to him. He thought back for a moment of meeting Ernie, and his help clearing the mountain of tumbleweeds on his little inherited farm. He remembered the times Ernie would come over with a sandwich wrapped in waxed paper, and say, "Try this, see what you think." Cole never dreamed at the time that he would be sitting in front of a place like Ernie's Deli.

Georgia turned and spotted Cole. She smiled brightly and waved. Cole waved back. He chuckled at the memory of his first meeting with Georgia in Kansas and how nasty she was to him. Now he felt she was more his sister than a cousin.

Cole got out of the car and went inside. "Hey cuz! How ya doin' today?"

Three people turned and looked at Cole when Georgia answered, "I'm great. Good to see you."

It was enough of an oddity in Orvin that the attractive black woman in the Deli was married to Ernie the Greek, but the idea that she was the cousin of a white guy left their mouths agape.

Cole went to the counter and fist bumped Ernie, who said, "What's with the bump on your head?"

"I bumped into a sign downtown."

"It looks painful." Ernie grimaced at Cole as he walked back toward the kitchen door. "Don't have to order, I know what you want."

"Maybe not. I was kind of in the mood for a turkey sandwich."

"The hell you say. I won't fix one. You're gonna have a Reuben, just like always."

"Ernie, for heaven's sake, let the man have what he wants." Georgia stood, hands on her hips, looking at Ernie like he had lost his mind.

"That just ain't right. He's never changed his order before."

"You're right. Fix me a Reuben." Cole knew a change of his order could knock the earth off its axis in Ernie's world.

Georgia laughed mightily. "You two are like a couple of kids." Her attention shifted to the three people at the table rising to leave.

"Thank you, see you next time. Was everything okay?" Georgia gave them a friendly smile.

"Best in town," one of the men answered.

"Thank you, Georgia." The woman in the rhinestone-pocketed jeans waved. "See you next time."

"Another satisfied customer." Cole was pleased to see the deli growing. He felt a vested interest, having watched it go from Ernie's dream to a thriving business, with Cole's cousin as wife and partner.

"Looks like you've got the whole place to yourself." Ernie stuck his head out the pass-through from the kitchen.

"I always try to time my arrival after the lunch rush." Cole watched Georgia clear the newly vacated table. "I thought maybe we could have a chat."

"Something wrong?" Georgia frowned.

"Does something have to be wrong for me to come and see my favorite cousin?"

"I'm your only cousin. Have a seat, I'll bring you a diet coke and join you." A few moments later Georgia came with his Coke Zero and an iced tea for herself. "Wowee. Feels good to get off my feet."

"Business good?" Cole took a sip of his soda.

"11:30 to 2:00 it's crazy. After that, we might as well go home."

"Order's up."

The sound of the plate on the metal shelf turned Georgia's head. "Well, bring it out. Your legs ain't broken."

A moment later Ernie came through the kitchen door holding the plate and shaking his head. As he passed the rack on the counter he grabbed a bag of Fritos and headed for the table.

"I haven't seen you since the day the preacher fella got shot. How you been doing?"

"I'm fine. I guess."

"That's a pretty weak alright." Georgia took a sip of her tea. She set it on the table and looked at Cole. "Kelly says you've been in kind of a funk lately. What's up with that?"

"Oh, I don't know."

"Yes, you do. Spit it out."

"I was thinking that I was going to settle in, write a book, then another, and it's just not going to happen."

"The hell you say! I thought you were a famous writer." Ernie looked at Cole like he just said he was going to have a sex change operation.

"Whatever fame I might have had was as a journalist, a newspaperman, a reporter of facts. I didn't realize how difficult it would be to move from telling the truth to making up a bunch of stories. I've started and stopped half a dozen different book projects. I've got a folder full of titles, snippets, partial outlines, and it's all crap."

"I kind of see how that's a totally different style of writing, but you're a clever guy. Seems like, with all the places you've been and things you've seen, writing books would be a snap." Georgia's response was one of thoughtfulness and concern.

"Well, that's what I thought. The problem is, every time I go to write a story it comes off like reading a newspaper article. I spent my whole life *not* writing flowery descriptions, embellishing the action, or adding to the facts. That's a mighty hard habit to break."

"You should have Ernie help you. He can't stick to the facts to save his life! He makes up stories all day long."

"Hold on now, I do not."

"Yes, you do." Cole and Georgia spoke at the same moment. All three broke into laughter.

"I tell you what. How 'bout you come down here and work the counter and I take some time off?" Georgia smiled. "Just imagine you two, Abbott and Costello, working in a sandwich shop. I don't know if it would draw customers or drive them all off."

Cole took a bite of his sandwich.

"Well, if you can't write books, what are you gonna do?" Ernie leaned forward. His face showed real concern for his friend. He knew the undoing of Cole's dream was a serious matter and not to be taken lightly. "If you don't write these books…"

"Sometimes wantin' ain't gettin'." Georgia set her glass down. "I dreamed once upon a time I was going to go to the Olympics. I had it all figured out. I could just see myself standing on the podium getting my medal. When it didn't happen I thought it was the end of the world, but it wasn't. Who says you have to work at writing books anyway?" Georgia looked at Cole for a long time before he spoke.

Cole wiped his mouth with his napkin. "I don't have a plan B. What am I gonna do, sit on the front porch?"

"I would." Ernie grinned.

"Yeah, for about two hours. Then you'd be off doing something else, fishing, mowing the grass, working in the yard, driving your tractor around or inventing a new sandwich. I can't do any of those things; moreover, I don't want to."

The bell rang when the door opened. A group of six women came in chattering, yakking, and laughing as they made their way to the counter.

Georgia quickly went to her side of the counter. "My goodness, where'd ya'all come from?"

"We had a meeting of the Oklahoma Settlers Association and we're starving."

"You don't look that old." Georgia teased. "Well, I'm glad you're here. What can we get you?"

As Georgia took their orders, Ernie stayed behind at the table, still deep in thought. "I know what's wrong with you."

"What, pray-tell, might that be?"

"You need a dog. Dogs are good for telling your troubles to. I tell mine stuff I'd never tell Georgia. He listens, looks up with his big brown eyes, never interrupts, never gives me advice, and when I'm done I feel a whole lot better."

"The hell you say." Cole teased.

"Don't make fun. I'm being serious. You can take it for walks, watch it chase rabbits. Dogs are a lot of fun."

"I've never had a dog. I wouldn't know the first thing about having a dog."

"That's the great things about living in the sticks. All you have to do is feed 'em, make sure they've got water, and have a place for them on the back porch in the winter time. They're good for keeping the varmints off your land too."

"I can see that you have thought this through. I appreciate the idea, but I don't think Kelly would go for me having a dog. I think her last pet was a cat. I hate cats. Unfortunately, I unknowingly mentioned that in an all too unpleasant way when we were dating.

So, the whole idea of having pets has been off the table ever since."

Ernie stood. "Think about it. I'm telling you, you can't have the blues when you got a dog."

"Thanks, buddy, I'll take it into consideration."

The women at the counter began to file over where two tables were shoved together and continued their clucking and chuckling without interruption. Georgia handed Ernie the orders at the pass-through window, explaining some of her notes. She came back over to the booth where Cole was finishing his sandwich.

"I want you to know I understand what you're going through. You've spent your life in the fast lane, and now you've come to a place that pretty much runs backwards. That's got to be a real shock to your system. You know, this pace of life isn't for everybody, and you might just be one of those people. When you were here before you had San Francisco to go back to. Being here was kind of like a vacation, even though it was a lot of hard work. Now, take this with the love it's given, Kelly could make friends with that soda machine and talk to it all day long. You, on the other hand, don't cozy up to people like that."

"Well, I don't know about that." Cole protested but knew in his heart that Georgia was right. She always was.

"Oh, you can charm the cover of a baseball, but then you're on your way. You're used to extracting information and not worrying about ever seeing the person again. It's a whole other ballgame letting people into your world and making real friends. I bet you a hundred dollar bill that Ernie is the only friend you've got in this town."

Cole reached out to Georgia with his palm up. "Pay up."

"Oh yeah? Who's your other friend?"

"I got you, babe," Cole sang.

Georgia laughed, "Don't flatter yourself. We're not friends, we're family. You're stuck with me."

Cole reached over and took her hand. "I don't know what I'd do without you."

"Well, it feels like we're fixin' to find out."

"What's that supposed to mean?" Cole frowned and let go of Georgia's hand.

"That means, my dear cousin, I see the taillights of your car headin' out of here."

Cole did not respond. He sat looking down at the tabletop and the last two bites of his sandwich. He did not want to accept what Georgia was saying. But, she hit the nail right on the head.

"Order up."

Georgia stood up and patted Cole on the cheek. "Don't worry sweetie, God's got a plan. It will all be alright. You just don't know what it is yet." Georgia moved to serve the table of women. "Here we come, ladies," she called across the room.

Cole took a long drink of his soda and watched as Georgia gracefully served the women at the table happily exchanging in heartfelt banter. He envied her transition. She was not the woman he first met in Wichita four years ago. As he popped the last two Fritos in his mouth, the image of Georgia's mother, his Aunt Lottie, came to his mind. Although he didn't know her all that long she held a very special place in his heart. He never realized until this moment how much he missed her. She was so wise and so charming. What I wouldn't give, he thought, to sit down and have a piece of her sweet potato pie and have a nice, long talk.

In a way, Georgia was just like her mother. She had a way of seeing through a problem and right to the heart of the matter. Cole knew without a doubt he just moved to the top of her prayer list. Her faith and her love for him would not let him stray far from her thoughts. He thought himself a very lucky man to have found these two strong, wonderful women. To have gone for so many years with no relatives and to be blessed with them was one of the greatest gifts of his life.

Cole stood, blew Georgia a kiss and waved at Ernie. "See you two later. Best Reuben ever! I'll think about the dog."

Brooke spotted Cole next door through the side window of Randy's Computer Repair shop and waved happily. Cole couldn't help but smile back at the lovely girl with the beautiful smile. He opened the door and stepped into the shop. "You look very chipper today."

"Why shouldn't I? It's a beautiful day, business is good, and you're here."

"Flatterer." Cole winked and crossed the room. "Where's my favorite hacker?"

"Shhh! Don't say that in here." Brooke looked through the pass-through where Randy sat.

"Why? Is the place bugged?" Cole gave the room an exaggerated visual once-over.

"Very funny." Randy appeared through the archway into the workshop and approached the counter. "Come on back."

"Why would I want to do that when the pretty girl is out here?"

Brooke rolled her eyes and blushed, and gave Cole a dismissive wave.

"What are you doing out and about? I thought you were writing the next great American novel." Randy took his chair at the workbench. "Grab a seat."

"It's hardly that. Kelly hates it." Cole pulled over a tall stool.

"She said that?" Randy's eyes went wide.

"Not exactly, but I could tell."

"What's it about?"

Cole took a deep breath. "Which one?"

"How many are there?" Randy gave Cole a confused look.

"I've started, and gave up on, three so far."

"I'm telling you, you need to write about your life and the weird, crazy stuff you have got caught up in. Just the stuff since I met you could fill ten books. Serious, write what you know. You are the one person in the world who doesn't need to make stuff up."

"You ever thought of being a motivational speaker?"

"Isn't he wonderful? He always has the right answer!" Brooke stuck her head over the counter into the back room. "Sorry, I wasn't eavesdropping, but you guys talk so loud they can hear you next door."

"Hey, I didn't come here to talk about my problems. All that book stuff isn't important." Cole looked into Randy's eyes. He could tell he knew he was lying. "I just had lunch next door and thought I'd drop in and say hello."

"Well, I'm glad you did. There's a lull right now, we can have a chat. What's this I hear about you getting attacked by Indians?"

Cole reached up and felt the lump on the side of his head. "Never a dull moment in Orvin town. It's kind of a long story, but the long and the short of it is, I went to help get a friend of mine released at the police station and a riot broke out."

"Is that how you got the knot on your head? I wasn't going to say anything but, geez Cole, what happened?"

Cole winced. "That bad, huh? I was hoping it had gone down."

"Looks like you've been in a bar fight." Randy leaned in for a better look.

"Yeah, I got hit with a protest sign."

"Where did you find a protest around here?"

"There were a bunch of Indians raising Cain in front of the police station."

"What was that all about?"

"The police rounded up four guys for the murder of Warren Poore and, believe it or not, they were all Indians." Cole shook his head.

"And you know *who* that needs bailing out of jail?"

"That's the long part of the story, a guy named Michael Blackbear. He's a veteran trying to get his wife home from Iraq. He went to the Center asking for help. Warren said he couldn't, wouldn't, didn't know how, or something. Anyway, it seems Michael wrote a couple of nasty letters to Warren. The cops found them in the files during the investigation and figured that was enough reason to bring him in as a suspect."

"Did he do it? Wait, dumb question, otherwise, you wouldn't have bailed him out."

"You haven't heard the best part yet. Kelly got trapped the next day inside the Center when about fifty angry Indians decided to protest that, too. We went out the back door just as they broke the front windows out. This place is getting nuts."

"You're not kidding." Randy slipped a disc into the tray on the computer and pushed it in. "It's really changing around here. I mean, remember the first year or two we were here? There was no crime to speak of at all? Have you seen the news about the guy holding up all the jewelry stores?"

"No, I've been kind of busy. This whole thing with the murder of the Poore's, Kelly and the drama at the Children's Center, then throw into the mix my assistance on Michael Blackbear's immigration problem, I haven't had a moment to read or watch the news these days." Cole gave Randy a jerk of his head as if to say, 'go on'.

"Well get this, a guy has been holding up jewelry stores. He even killed the owner of one. Here's the goofy part. He wears one of those head cover thingies like Muslim women wear."

"You mean a burka?"

"Yeah, yeah, the headdress with the mesh screen across the eyes. The news has been calling him the Burka Bandit."

"Oh, clever." Cole rolled his eyes.

"Anyway, he's robbed three jewelry stores so far. So, even though they've got him on two security cameras, there's no way to tell who he is." The computer on the workbench beeped and Randy typed something on the keyboard. "Where in the world does somebody around here get a burka?"

Cole was suddenly transported from the room. Time and space swirled around his head. There was a rolling, cramping ache in his chest. Bits and pieces of conversations, fragments of images, and phrases from his note pad, all played back like a grainy, distorted video. He grasped frantically at thoughts and ideas knowing the familiarity of all those things pointed only one way.

"Iraq."

The word tasted dirty in his mouth as he realized that a returning soldier from the war would be the obvious person to have one. He knew, at that moment, the Burka Bandit was Michael Blackbear. A wave of nausea came over him.

"Funny. I'm serious, where around here would somebody get a burka?"

Cole ran his fingers through his hair and interlaced them on the back of his head. He closed his eyes as thoughts rushed through his mind. Michael had tried everything he knew, he was just grasping at straws when he tried to get Warren to help him. He said there was another way. No, he said there was a *different* way. Oh, what *did* he say? His thoughts screamed inside his head. Cole slowly turned his head and looked at Randy.

"You alright? You look like you just saw a ghost." Randy was clearly perplexed.

"They wouldn't. They would have brought one back with them from the Middle East. *I* know who it is!"

"What?" Randy stared at Cole waiting for a response.

"It's the guy I got out of jail!"

"You kidding me? How do you know that?"

"I just put two and two together. Think about it. You've got a guy desperate to bring his Muslim wife to the United States. In his mind, he's exhausted every avenue to get it done. Even though I'm trying to help him, it's not moving fast enough, he said to me, "maybe there's another way". Well, the only other way would obviously cost a lot of money. Money that he doesn't have. Who else is gonna have a burka, but a guy who served two terms in Iraq and has a Muslim wife?"

"That's crazy, but it's just crazy enough to be right."

Cole pulled his cell phone from his pocket. He flipped through his contacts and hit the number for Detective Bishop. Cole glanced up at Randy and raised his eyebrows.

"Bishop, Cole Sage here. I know who the Burka Bandit is."

"Oh, yeah?"

"Yes, it's Michael Blackbear."

For a long moment, Bishop did not respond. "Michael Blackbear? The guy you helped spring from jail? The guy that you said was some kind of decorated war hero? Now you think he's robbing jewelry stores and shooting people?"

"Think about it, it makes sense. He's a veteran. Who else is going to have a Burka?"

"Look, Sage. Do you have any idea how many veterans there are in this county? Tell you what, you write books or do whatever it is you do and leave the detective work to me."

The line went dead. Cole was stunned. He looked at Randy, bewildered and exasperated. "He hung up! He didn't even want to hear what I had to say. He hung up!" Cole flipped the phone repeatedly in his hands.

"Sure makes you miss Detective Chin, doesn't it?" Randy recalled what a great team they were back in the day.

"More than you know, buddy. More than you know."

Chapter Seventeen

Michael Blackbear woke and looked at his watch. It was 1:35. He had been asleep for nearly twenty hours. He rolled and felt a dull ache in his side. For a long moment, he didn't recall even getting home. He made it into the house but passed out on the sofa. The vile acrid taste of vomit was still in his mouth as he tried to stand and go to the kitchen. A ray of light was streaming through the front windows. He bent over the sink, splashed his face and rinsed out his mouth.

Miriam, I have failed you. How could I have let them steal the jewels? I must think how to do this. Michael splashed his face again, cupped his hands and took another mouthful of water, rinsing hard and spitting. He thought of the Coyote and the $40,000 he needed to bring his wife and son across the border. What if they didn't have to cross the border? He suddenly stood as straight as the wound in his side would let him. What if I just went to Mexico? What if they just came that far? We could live there, or go farther south to Central America or South America. His words and thoughts brought a wide smile to Michael's face.

I can do this. All I have to do is meet them there. He went quickly to the bedroom and got the card with the Coyote's number just in case, but surely it would cost less than half to get them as far as Mexico, anything beyond that, we could live on. Dollars go a long way south of the border. He looked at the number and chuckled. That's it, that's what I'll do.

He pulled off his bloody T-shirt and tossed it into the basket in the corner. He looked in the bathroom mirror at his bandage. It was completely blood soaked. Peeling it off he turned to see the one on his back. It looked fine. He kicked off his shoes and peeled off his jeans. He turned the water on in the shower, removed his socks and underwear and stepped inside. He couldn't remember when he last took a shower. Brown, dried blood ran down his leg and swirled down the drain. He rubbed his hands through his hair and the warm water seemed to clear his head. Except for the dull pain in his side, he felt renewed. He peeled the bloody bandage away and let the warm water hit his chest, shoulder and run down his side. He ever so gently cleaned the blood from his body. He washed, shaved, and shampooed his hair. Rinsing and turning off the water, he stepped from the shower a new man.

He dressed in clean clothes and returned to the kitchen. He opened a can of ravioli from the cupboard, got a beer from the refrigerator, and took a seat at the table. "I will need road money", he said out loud as he took his first bite. Then he remembered the dead jeweler. He knew that adding murder to the robberies would intensify the search for him. I need to do this quickly, and then I need to leave.

His thoughts were racing with this new plan. Where can I get money and lots of it? Banks are no good, most have a guard. Grocery stores? Pawn shops? Department stores? And then it hit him, a check cashing place. What day is it? He wondered. He looked at his watch, it was Thursday afternoon. Friday would be their big day, Thursday they would have to be prepared. He checked his watch again; it was nearly 2:00.

He glanced around the bottom of the sofa for his phone and realized it must be in the car. Outside, he found his car parked at a weird angle in the yard. The window was down. He opened the driver's door and spotted his phone in the passenger seat. Not wanting to reopen his wound that was beginning to heal, he rounded the car and opened the passenger door and retrieved the phone. Walking back into the house he spoke a voice command, "Okay, Google. Check cashing". On the screen, he saw *USA Payroll Advances and Check Cashing*. The directions said it was ten minutes away.

Michael went into the house and pulled his large military issue duffle bag from the closet. He began stuffing his clothes, and anything small of value, along with pictures and a small, framed display of his medals from the wall. He took the bag and put it in the trunk of the car. Then he retrieved his gun and money from Mary Wilson's shed. He entered the house one last time. He removed the small satchel of mementos from his bottom dresser drawer. As he closed the front door, he realized it would be for the last time. He kissed the tips of his fingers and touched the front door. You've been a good house. He got in the car and headed for town.

Orvin seemed quiet for a Thursday afternoon. It was the lull between school being out and folks getting off work. USA Check Cashing was situated in the parking lot of a building once occupied by a car rental company. Orvin just didn't have enough business to keep them operating. There were two cars parked on the side that Michael figured belonged to employees. There were no cars in front. He reached in the glove box and slipped out his powder blue burka. He carefully determined his exit route. He parked far enough away from the building that it would be difficult to read his license plates, and his car was common enough that he could easily disappear among the other makes and models of the same color. He dropped the clip from his gun. There were only three bullets, more than enough he thought. I won't be shooting it anyway.

He wadded up the burka tightly and moved toward the side of the building where the blinds were drawn. The large red and blue neon sign in the window shone brightly. As he stepped onto the sidewalk in front of the building, a car pulled up. A woman in her mid-forties got out of the car, crushing her cigarette on the pavement as she blew a plume of smoke into the air. She looked at Michael but didn't smile. For a moment he thought of going back to his car, but then realized she might work into the plan quite well.

He followed her into the building to see a young man of no more than twenty sitting behind the glass counter. He looked up from the magazine he was reading. The woman stepped to the window and slid her check into the transaction tray.

"Good afternoon, Jennifer." The young man recognized the return customer. He turned to open a drawer and took out a stack of bills. At that moment Michael slipped the burka over his head. He knew the clerk hadn't looked in his direction. As the clerk began to count cash on the counter in front of him, Michael stepped forward and shoved the gun into the woman's neck.

"Hey!" Michael shouted straight into the slotted speak-through unit in the bullet resistant glass. "I want you to put all that, and every cent you have in this place, in a bag. Do it fast or I will blow her head off. I know you don't want that, so give me the money now."

The young man looked up, first into Jennifer's face and then at the large looming blue burka over her shoulder. "Don't hurt her please, I'll do it, I'll do it." In less than a heartbeat, there was a large, metallic, grinding sound, and the slam of a large security grate hit the floor behind him. Michael spun around to see he was trapped like a rat in a cage.

He shoved the woman hard to the left and fired the gun at the clerk through the pass-through tray. The bullet ricocheted off the metal and smashed into the wall, missing the terrified clerk completely. Within seconds the clerk was on the far side of the room and on the phone. Then he crouched down out of sight.

For the first time, Jennifer spoke to Michael. "Please don't hurt me; I just came in to cash my husband's check. It's my son's birthday. Please, please don't do anything foolish."

"Shut up!" Michael screamed. "Or I'll shut you up." He pointed the gun in her direction. He frantically paced about the room. He went to the grate and grabbed it, trying with all his might to lift it but it was locked and wouldn't budge. For several minutes he paced trying to think of how to escape, but there was none.

In the distance he could hear police cars approaching, sirens screaming. Out the window, he saw two cars, with blue lights flashing, approaching from his right. Michael frantically pounded against the grate. Two cars pulled up in front of the building. Without getting out of the car a voice came from the police car.

"You cannot escape. Lay your weapon down. It's over."

Michael turned and looked at Jennifer. She was crying and huddling in the corner. He walked to the corner where she sat, grabbed her by the forearm and yanked her to her feet. He pushed her hard towards the grate, grabbed her by the neck and shoved her face into it, and put the gun to her head.

The voice from the police car was instantaneous. "Hurting her will make no difference. Don't do anything stupid. You can't escape, lay your weapon down, it's over." The officer was well trained and didn't deviate from the script.

Behind him, Michael heard a phone ringing. He turned to see the young clerk approaching the window. He'd put a cordless phone into the tray and pushed it forward and he quickly disappeared again.

The patrolman in the second car opened the door and stepped out. A cell phone was to his ear. He nodded at the other officer and the amplifier voiced a command. "Please pick up the phone."

Michael looked from the patrolman to the other car, and back. Jennifer whimpered and trembled. Not releasing her neck, he spun her about and pushed her hard towards the counter. "Sit down, right there." He pointed with the gun to the floor in front of the window. Taking the phone from the tray, he spoke in a flat, deep, emotionless, tone. "Let me out of here or I'll kill her."

The voice on the other end was calm. "My name is Peter, what's yours?"

"Don't play any negotiator games with me. Let me out of here, or I kill the woman. I'm in this deep. It doesn't matter anymore. I don't have any options. What I do have is a hostage and a demand for you to let me go."

"You know I can't let that happen. So, how are we going to end this peacefully?"

"We're not. I want to talk to somebody and I want to talk to them now."

"Alright, who would you like to talk to?" The patrolman was almost conversational, but the slight quiver in his voice betrayed his nerves.

"I want to talk to Cole Sage. Get him down here."

"Who is Cole Sage?"

"He's the only person in this town I trust."

"I'll see what I can do. In the meantime, I want you to just relax and think about ending this peacefully."

Michael backed up and slid down the wall under the counter until he was seated on the floor. He spread his legs wide, grabbed Jennifer by the arm, and pulled her hard towards him and over his leg where they were seated together, she in front of him, shielding his body from the outside.

Buried in the flushing sound of the toilet Cole could hear his phone ringing. He quickly ran to the kitchen and picked up the phone from the table. "Hello?"

"Is this Cole Sage?"

"Yes, it is." Cole didn't recognize the voice on the other end of the line.

"This is Chief Tuckman, Orvin PD."

"Good afternoon Chief, what can I do for you?"

"It seems we have a situation."

Cole did not respond and waited for the Chief to speak.

"We have a man who has taken a hostage during the process of robbing the USA Check Cashing place on McKinley."

"Okay. Why are you calling me?"

"Because he is asking to speak to you. There is a woman he's taken hostage. He refused to speak to my men and demanded to speak to you. It seems you are the only person he trusts. I have a strange feeling its Michael Blackbear, the fellow you helped get out of my jail."

Cole's heart sank. He was right. While he thought over his hunch that Blackbear was the Burka Bandit, he struck again. Cole felt the fire of rage go up his spine.

"Maybe you should have another chat with Bishop first."

"Why's that?" The snap of the Chief's response showed his displeasure at Cole.

"Because I called him and told him I believed Blackbear was the one robbing the jewelry stores. He blew me off. It seems to me this could have been prevented."

"We can discuss the shortcomings of my department later. I need you to get down there as quickly as you can. Do you want me to send a car to get you?"

"No, it would be faster if I just drove myself."

"Then I'll meet you there."

"Don't let Bishop near me. Understood?"

As Cole drove to town a hundred scenarios ran through his head. If only Bishop listened. Why wasn't Michael patient? What could I possibly say to him now? Hi Michael, what is it you want from me? Hi Michael, please put the gun down. With every scenario, Cole saw a dead woman on the floor. Please don't do this, he thought. The image of Michael firing at the police flashed across his mind. He envisioned Blackbear's body whipping and jerking as dozens of rounds from the police were fired into him. Cole slammed the steering wheel with his wrist. I have no words!

As he approached the check cashing business he saw four police cars and a SWAT team truck in front. Two policemen blocked the entrance as he pulled up.

"I'm Cole Sage, Chief Tuckman called me."

"Park over there." The patrolman pointed at a space behind the SWAT truck. "The Chief is in that Suburban."

Cole did as instructed and made his way to the white Suburban with the police shield on the door. Spotting Cole, the Chief stepped out of the vehicle.

"Thank you for getting here so quickly."

"I may be here, but I don't have the slightest idea what I can do."

"Just talk to him. We have a phone connection with him. He's been waiting. Let him see you. We'll see what he has to say." The Chief pointed at the patrolman holding up his cell phone.

Cole walked over and took the phone and waved toward the window. "Hello? Michael, are you there?"

"Mr. Sage, you gotta get me outta here."

"That's not going to happen. You know they're not going to let you out."

"Then I'll kill the woman."

"No, you won't. You're an honorable man. You've just got yourself into a situation you don't know how to get out of. Put the gun down and come out."

"I have nothing to lose." Michael paused for several seconds before he continued. "I'm not getting

Miriam and my son here, and I'm not going to prison."

"We don't know that. You need to give yourself up. We need to get you someone to talk to, a professional, a counselor. This is not you speaking. Please, end this and let me see what kind of help we can get you." Cole looked at the policeman standing with him. Cole took another shot at it. "Michael, let me talk to the lady."

"Why?"

"Because she's probably scared to death. I want to tell her you're not a bad guy. You're just in a bad place."

Michael put the phone to Jennifer's ear. "Hello?"

"Hi, my name is Cole Sage. I just wanted to let you know that the man holding you hostage isn't really a bad guy. He's in a very dark place, and I'm going to do everything I can to get him to release you. I need you to stay calm. Can you do that for me?"

"Yes, please, please get me out of here."

"I'll do the best I –"

Michael jerked the phone away from Jennifer and put it to his ear. "If she dies, it's on you, Sage. Go tell whoever's in charge. I'm serious, and I don't want to die in here but I will if I have to."

"Nothing is on me, Michael. This is all about you." Cole was not going to let Blackbear guilt him into doing or saying anything. He was growing angry at the behavior of someone who depended on him for help. "I'll go talk to the Chief. I'll see what I can do. Just stay calm."

Cole waved, handed the phone back to the patrolman and moved over to the Chief who now stood near the SWAT truck.

"What did he say?"

Cole shrugged. "Nothing any different. He's demanding to be set free or he'll kill the woman. I don't know what I'm doing here. I don't know what to say. He said he didn't want to die in there, but would if he had to. He backed into a corner. I don't know what to say to convince him otherwise."

"What does that mean? You giving up?" The Chief barked. "Look, there's a back door to that place. The manager is driving in from Enid. My SWAT guys are ready."

"So, you're just going to go in, guns blazing?"

"You suddenly have a lot to say for a guy who doesn't know what to say. It is my decision as to what we're going to do. This has to end sooner rather than later. The longer he's in there, statistically, the worse the potential outcome."

"How much more time do I have?" Cole was at a loss of what to say next, but the image he saw of Michael being shot to pieces by the SWAT team came back to him.

"I figure the manager will be here in the next ten minutes. She was called by the alarm company when that grate went down."

Cole turned and walked back to the patrol car and took the phone. "Michael? Are you there?"

"Go ahead."

"They're going to kill you. Plain and simple. You don't have to die. I don't want to see you die.

And, I know you don't want your son growing up knowing his father was killed by the police, or that you hurt an innocent woman". Cole stepped around the car and walked towards the windows.

"What the hell are you doing?" The Chief screamed at Cole's back.

He continued to move toward the window. He stood against the window and put his left hand up and placed his forehead on the glass. "I can see you. Can you see me?"

"Yes."

"I just want to look you in the eye and have you tell me this is how you want your life to end."

There was a long pause as Michael stood. He grabbed Jennifer by the arm and lifted her to her feet. They both moved towards the window.

Michael was now standing at the window with only Jennifer between him and Cole. "I want you to promise me something."

"What is it?" Cole felt a positive outcome slipping away.

"I want you to tell my son I did this all for him."

Cole found himself bristling at Michael's words. "You really think that will make it alright?"

Tears began to roll down Michael's cheeks. "Nothing will make this alright."

"Then let's end it now. Let the woman go and give yourself up."

Michael raised his hand and wiped his eyes. "Lift the grate, I'll come out."

"Thank you." Cole turned and blew out the breath he had been holding. He walked back to the Chief. "He's coming out. He's not going to hurt the woman. Promise me you won't do anything rash. Otherwise, this has all been for nothing. I want your word of honor that you, or your men, won't do anything stupid."

The Chief stared at Cole. "You really think he's going to let her go?"

"Yes, he's going to let her go and surrender. Let me take the gun from him. Please, let me do that. Please, let me do it."

"You really think that crazy Indian is going to hand you his gun?"

"No, I believe that a decorated United States Army Veteran will keep his word."

The Chief stared at Cole for a long moment. "It's your funeral."

Cole saw a car coming into the parking lot. A woman stepped from the car and approached the Chief and Cole.

"I'm Rebecca Beeler, I'm the manager."

"How do we get that grate up?" The Chief motioned toward the door.

"It's on a double remote system. I have a key here, and a remote here." Beeler held up a group of keys on a black, spiral key holder.

"Do you have to be inside the building to raise it?"

"No, sir. It's on the left side of the windows."

"Tompkins!" the Chief yelled to the SWAT Commander. "Escort this lady where she needs to go."

Cole jogged back to the sidewalk. "Michael, they're raising the grate. I told them you would surrender the gun to me. I told them I trusted you and that you were an honorable Veteran of the U.S. Army and would keep your word. I hope that means something to you."

"It used to. But you have my word anyway."

Cole glanced to his left and saw the manager inserting the key into a chrome plate on the wall. There was a whizzing noise and a slight clunk and the grate began to roll. As the grate rose above the door, Cole moved closer to the front of the door. He intentionally stood between the police and where Michael would come out the door, using himself as a shield to make sure the Police Chief kept his word.

Michael moved Jennifer to his side as they approached the door. They stood motionless at the door for a long moment before Cole reached out and pulled it open. The mechanism locked it in place. "Let her go, Michael."

Michael leaned forward and said softly into Jennifer's ear, "I'm sorry. Forgive me." He gave her a slight nudge on her shoulder. She ran from the building not looking back.

"You used to be a newspaperman."

"Yes, I did."

"So, you know the news people will interview you when this is over."

Cole chuckled. "You know, they probably will."

Michael smiled and said, "You've been a good friend. I wish things were different."

"Me, too."

"I want you to tell the news people something for me."

"Alright."

"Tell them that the war in Iraq had one more casualty." Michael raised the gun to his temple and fired.

Chapter Eighteen

The vibration of Becca's phone distracted her from the note she was writing. She put her yellow notepad and pen down and saw Matt's photo appear on Face Time. "Hi, Matt."

"Hey, there! How's it going?"

"I was hoping I would get a call from the Horse Whisperer tonight."

"I was getting kind of concerned. I hadn't heard from you in a couple of days. Is everything okay?"

Becca took a deep breath and bit her bottom lip. I will not allow myself to cry, she thought. "No, I don't think it could get any worse." As much as she tried to avoid it, Becca began to choke up.

"Hey, hey now. What's all this? Talk to me, what's happened?"

"The police brought back the books from the Center. They had taken them as part of the investigation. The police auditor found that someone was skimming money from the Center's accounts."

"Do they suspect someone?"

"Thankfully, any suspicion of wrongdoing by my dad was removed. So, the whole idea of him being depressed about the financial state of the Center disappears like a puff of smoke. You see, money has been removed twice from Center accounts *since* my parent's death. That means that there's really only one person who could be taking the money. Cassie."

"That's a pretty heavy accusation to make, Becca."

"I'm not the one making it, Matt. The police found that someone withdrew large amounts of money four times from the Center account."

"Are they going to arrest her? I mean embezzlement is a pretty serious crime."

"They don't have any other suspect. At least not that they have told us. Detective Bishop said for us to sort out the mess. Then it would be the decision of the Board, or me, how to proceed. Kelly Sage said that the Board needn't be involved because it was just an honorary position. That puts the whole responsibility back on me. I don't want it. What am I supposed to say? What am I supposed to do?" Becca covered her mouth with her hand and sobbed.

"Hey, it will be okay. Let's think this through together. I'm sure we can come up with a way to resolve it without involving the police. I mean, what would she be doing with large amounts of money? She must still have it. Just have her give it back."

"It sure explains a lot." Becca sniffed. "That's why she's been so nasty to me, its guilt."

"You'll need to do it in a kind and gentle way; otherwise it could get really ugly."

"Are you serious? I can see it now. She'll start calling me Miss Goody-Goody or Better Than Thou or one of the other horrible things she's been calling me lately. Oh, Matt, I am so angry. I think I've skipped being hurt, disappointed, and in disbelief and went straight to just wanting to choke her."

For a long moment, neither one spoke. Becca found herself sitting with her fists clenched.

Matt was the first one to speak. "Listen, I get it. I'm not sure how I would react, but yeah, I'd be really mad. How about I drive up and we do it together? Would that help?"

"You're sweet, but I don't think that would work. It would be two against one, and she's resentful enough as it is. But that is so kind of you to offer."

"It's not really kind. I just think that it could be a very volatile situation and I could be there in case it got out of hand. I don't want anything happening to you. Have you told my folks about this?"

"No, you're the only one. But, Kelly's not stupid. I bet she's figured it out. She was there when the police returned the books."

"I don't want to throw gasoline on this fire, but do you think she's done anything else?"

"What do you mean?"

"I don't know really, it just seems that if you're willing to steal from a charity and your father-- is there anything of value that could have been taken from the house, jewelry, anything like that?"

"I can't bear the thought of that. Let's not think about that right now." A deep sigh came through the phone. Becca looked down at her yellow pad and underlined Cassie's name several times. On Matt's end, he wore a sad and concerned expression.

"I'm so sorry, Matt. I didn't mean to dump all this on you. It's just that I've been laying here on the bed thinking and crying and worrying, and trying to figure out what to do."

"You can dump your problems on me anytime you want, or need, to. I want you to know I'm here for you and want to help you any way I can. You really matter a lot to me."

Rebecca was surprised by Matt's declaration. She couldn't find words to respond the way she wanted. She changed the subject. "I think I should talk to her sooner rather than later. So, I guess I'll do it in the morning."

"You'll be in my thoughts and prayers. Let me know how it goes."

"Thank you, Matt. I care about you, too. I better get some sleep now. Good night."

"Good night, Becca."

"Good morning, sleepyhead." Sharon greeted Becca as she entered the kitchen.

"It smells wonderful in here." Becca walked toward the stove.

"I'm making your favorite cranberry popovers, and that bacon, potato, and egg dish you like so much."

"You are the best, Sharon." She kissed Sharon on the cheek and gave her a squeeze of her shoulders. "Is Cassie up yet?"

"Oh yeah, she's been up for about an hour. She just left a couple of minutes ago to take the dog for a walk. It's so nice having you guys here. If for no other reason, I don't have to walk the dog." Sharon laughed and stirred the potatoes.

"How long till the popovers are done?"

"Oh gee, at least 20 minutes. I thought I'd wait till you got up so they would be hot and right out of the oven."

"I think I'll go join Cassie, she probably went to the park. There's something I need to talk to her about. It shouldn't take long."

"Okay, I'll wait to put them in the oven until you get back."

"Where's Russ, by the way?"

"Oh, he left too. He's meeting his buddies down at the donut shop. He says it's the only thing I can't cook."

Becca grabbed her lightweight jacket from the rack in the hall and headed down the street. As she approached the park with its slightly rolling hills, she saw Cassie and the dog standing by the little lake. She dreaded another confrontation with her sister. But, maybe the serenity of the surroundings would make things easier.

Cassie looked up and as she spotted Becca approaching. She let go of the dog's leash. The dog immediately ran to meet her.

"Hey, boy! You out for a walk?" The dog kept hopping up and hitting Becca with his front paws. "Okay, Okay, down, get down." Becca patted the top of the dog's head and then scratched it behind the ears. "Let's go back and talk to Cassie." As if knowing exactly what she meant, the dog turned and, leaping and jumping, it ran back to where Cassie stood watching her sister.

"What are you doing down here?" Cassie was not pleased to see her sister.

"I've come to talk to you."

"You couldn't wait till I got back to the house?"

"Cassie, I understand why you're so angry."

"What's that supposed to mean?"

"Kelly and I went over the accounts in preparation for the reopening of the Center. Why didn't you tell me you'd taken money from the accounts?"

"I did no such thing." Cassie snapped.

"There's no sense in denying it. We've checked the bank. We've checked the accounts and we've discovered your feeble attempt at copying daddy's signature. All you had to do was tell me that you borrowed the money."

"You think you're so smart. Miss perfect, always has the answers, always knows the way, and loves getting the goods on me."

Becca took a deep breath and bent down and patted the dog's back. "I wasn't the only one who knew." There was a long silence. Then Becca asked, "What did you do with all that money?"

"I don't have any money," Cassie snarled.

"Stop it!" Becca stood and faced her sister. "I'm sick of your lies, I'm sick of your attitude, and I'm sick of this whole stupid charade. You don't like the Center, you don't like its mission, and you want to leave Orvin. I get it. So you took the money and squirreled it away for your eventual departure. I get it. What you don't get is that you could have had the money. I'm sure mom and dad would have been happy to get you started wherever you wanted to go."

"There you go again! You always think you know everything. Well, they wouldn't give me the money. I asked for help, dad said no. I pleaded with mom, and in her usual, mealy mouth way she said, 'It's up to your father'. Do you know how much it costs to go to college these days? Do you have any idea what an apartment costs? You might be happy to live in a hut in the jungle, but I'm not. I didn't take a vow of poverty. They wouldn't give me any money so I figured out a way to take it. What are you gonna do about it?"

"Unfortunately, embezzlement is a crime."

"So, are you gonna have me arrested? Then arrest Maryann too! She signed the checks for me. She could copy dad's signature perfect." Cassie put her wrists together and shoved them out toward Becca.

"That's not true. Maryann is--"

"What, your surrogate mommy? She needed money to pay Molly's medical bills so she was eager to help. We all have a price, Becca. You have to make a decision. You want in?"

"I don't have to do anything. The police examined the books and they're the ones that found the discrepancies. Kelly and I couldn't believe there would be money missing, so we went through the books ourselves, trying to prove them wrong. Kelly also found a letter in daddy's drawer."

"There's no letter. I went through everything, all the files. Everything."

"Well, you missed it because it had fallen from the top drawer and was caught up on the drawer below."

"Liar! You're just trying to trap me."

"I don't have to trap you, it's all laid out in a letter that daddy wrote and hadn't given you. It said he forgave you and asked you to return the money, and that he would help you with your plans. So you see? You stole the money for nothing."

"You're just like him, condescending know-it-all, self-righteous, overbearing, obnoxious cow, I hate you! I hated him, and I hated your mealy-mouthed mother. I'm glad they're dead."

"What are you saying? How could you talk like that about our parents? Did they know you felt like that?"

"They do now. I went to the house to tell them."

"What do you mean?"

"I went to the house and I told them how much I hated them. And do you know what your father's response was? Do you know what he said to me? He said that 'mother and I will pray for you and we'll get you some help if you need it'. And then, mother said. 'Yes dear, listen to your father. He knows best.' I couldn't stand it anymore so I shot that mealy mouth bitch in the chest. And then I shot him. And I would do it again, over and over and over."

"Oh Cassie, Oh Cassie! Please, please. We need to go see someone. We need to get help."

"Stop it! Stop, shut up, you're just like them."

Cassie reached in her jacket pocket and pulled out a small pistol. "You're so excited to go to heaven. Let's send you there! She pointed the gun at her sister."

Rebecca stepped forward and said, "Go ahead if you think that will solve your problems." She took another step and stepped on the dog's foot. The dog howled in pain and jumped back, bumping into Cassie and giving Becca a window of opportunity to lunge forward and grab the gun.

Cassie swung her other hand and hit her sister with the side of her fist in her face. Temporarily blinded, Becca continued to struggle to get the gun away from Cassie. Cassie lunged out again, striking Becca just below her ear. Becca pushed hard against her sister and they both tumbled to the ground. Cassie reached out and grabbed a handful of Becca's hair, pulling her head back hard. She tried to maneuver the gun now pressed between them.

"I hate you, I hate you!" she screamed.

Becca struggled to try to free her head and twist enough to be able to open her airways. Cassie continued to twist and pull the gun until she felt it was pointing in Becca's direction. She squeezed the trigger and sent the bullet into her own chest and through her heart.

The two lay still on the grass as Cassie's hand dropped from Becca's hair. As she tried to rise from the top of her sister she looked through her tears into her sister's dead eyes and frozen angry face. Becca rolled onto her back, the dog licking her face.

A man in his forties in a pair of gym shorts and a blue t-shirt ran up to where the two girls lay. "What's going on? Oh my God!" He pointed at the circle of blood on the front of Cassie's powder blue shirt. "What have you done?"

"Call the police." Was all Becca could mutter.

As Becca lay on the grass panting, in the distance she could hear the wail of approaching police cars. The first vehicle to arrive on the scene was an ambulance. It looked so strange coming across the grass, adding to the surreal swirl of confusion. Moments later, two police cars sped across the park and stopped on either side of the girls.

The man who called in the report called out in a frantic rapid-fire report. "The dead one has the gun! The dead one has the gun!"

With guns drawn, two officers approached Becca. "Are you hurt, miss?"

"No, but my sister's hurt."

One officer reached down and offered Becca his hand. "Let's get you up."

The other officer knelt and put two fingers to Cassie's neck. Looking up, he shook his head. Two paramedics were standing at the ambulance waiting for instructions from the police officer. "This is going to be a while," the officer said to the paramedics. "You can stand down."

The younger officer who helped Becca up guided her fifteen to twenty feet from the scene. He keyed the radio attached to the epaulet on his shoulder. "We need homicide and forensics at the park ASAP."

Turning to Becca he said, "What's your name?"

"Rebecca Poore."

"Are you any relation to the couple that was murdered recently?"

"I'm their daughter."

"And who is the woman over there?"

"That's my sister. She killed them."

"How do you know that, miss?"

"She told me before she tried to shoot me."

"What's her name?"

"Cassandra Poore."

"Are you okay?"

"No, I'll never be okay again."

The officer pointed at the bench facing the small lake. "This will take some time; maybe you should have a seat over there."

Without saying a word, Becca walked to the small bench facing the lake and took a seat. Russ and Sharon's dog slowly walked up to her as if he knew there was something terribly wrong. Becca patted the bench. Ratchet jumped up and lay down with his head in her lap. She gently stroked his neck as she watched three ducks bobbing in the lake for food.

It took nearly fifteen minutes for Detective Bishop to arrive in his dark blue, unmarked car. He parked on the street and walked to where the two black and whites and the ambulance were parked. The forensics team got busy taking pictures and swabs from Cassie's hand. One technician was standing with Becca taking a sample from her hand as well.

Upon seeing the detective approaching, the head Medical Examiner turned and met him twenty to thirty yards from the others.

"What have we got?" Bishop nodded toward where Cassie lay.

"Apparently the deceased pulled a gun on her sister, a struggle of sorts ensued and the gun went off. The one with the gun took the bullet. The girl on the bench is going to need some medical attention. I've been holding off sending the paramedics till you got here and released them."

"What's the matter with her?"

"She took two or three pretty good blows to the face, her eye is swollen shut and she's badly bruised on the neck."

"Has anybody spoken to her?"

"Reynolds took her over and sat her down, got her name, but nothing since then."

"Alright, I'll go have a talk with her." Bishop moved towards where Becca sat.

"Hello, Rebecca." Bishop approached the bench and took a seat next to the sleeping dog. "You want to tell me what happened?"

"It wasn't her." Becca was still looking at the ducks. "I don't know who that person is. It's not the person I knew and loved as my sister. She's a stranger to me."

Bishop shifted his weight and turned slightly towards Becca. Waking the dog, Ol' Ratchet growled and got down from the bench. "You know, sometimes people do things so far removed from our experience and understanding, they truly do feel like strangers. What started this?"

"I confronted her about stealing money from the Center." Becca turned for the first time and looked Bishop squarely in the face. "When you returned the books, Kelly Sage and I tried to prove you wrong and went through them, but you were right. There were serious discrepancies in the bookkeeping. But, it wasn't until Kelly found a letter from my father that our suspicions became a reality."

"Where is that letter?"

"Kelly still has it."

"And what did it say?"

"It implied that my sister was embezzling money."

Becca looked back toward the ducks on the lake. "I used to come here when I was in high school to read. I never noticed the ducks before."

"Where did the gun come from, Rebecca?"

"Cassie had it in her jacket pocket."

"I meant, where did she get a gun?"

"It was my fathers. She did it, Detective."

"She did what?"

"She killed my parents."

"How do you know that, Rebecca?"

"She told me just before she pulled the gun on me. I don't think she really would have shot me, I really don't. But, I don't know what happened. All I remember is the dog yelping and jumping and the next thing I knew, Cassie and I were tumbling to the ground. I tried to grab the gun, and then it went off."

"I'm going to need for you to come downtown and make a statement."

"Whatever you need. Somebody needs to let Sharon know not to make the popovers."

"I'm sorry?" Bishop glanced around the park.

"Sharon and Russ Walker. We've been staying with them. We didn't want to go back to our house.

Sharon was making me popovers for breakfast. I told her I'd only be a few minutes."

Marty Bishop stood, and for a long moment looked across the little lake at the ducks swimming toward the shore. He thought of bringing his children to this park. He remembered when they were little bringing little bags of dried bread to feed the ducks. It seemed so unfair, he thought, that there was a dead body lying where children play.

Becca's words rang in his head, 'She did it.' What a horrible thing to say about your own flesh and blood. As many times as Bishop had been in similar situations, the idea of killing a member of your own family still made his temples pound.

He looked over at the body lying on the grass, "I'll get someone to take you the station. We'll let Mrs. Walker know."

"There is one more thing."

"What's that?"

"She didn't do it alone. Cassie told me Maryann Kopek forged the checks. She needed money. She helped." For the first time, Becca began to cry. Would there be anyone left in her life?

An older officer with a big belly drove Becca to the station.

"I knew your dad. A fine, fine man."

"Thank you." Becca rode along looking out the window.

"When I was new on the force, my partner and I were on a call. A young couple was fighting in the street, screaming and yelling to beat the devil. We rolled up and tried to get them to calm down. My partner, Marlin, said to me, "You take the guy and I'll see to the girl." For some reason only God above knows, he headed for the guy. He was directing this young fella to the back of the patrol car. Out of nowhere this kid pulls out a knife, whirls around and stabs Marlin. He stuck him four or five times in the side, then threw the knife onto the lawn of his house. Without a word he fell face down in the street, arms spread eagle."

Becca turned and looked at the policeman. He stared straight ahead as he spoke.

"Marlin bled to death. Right there. The ambulance guys said the knife hit his kidneys and liver. I went to a very dark place. Your dad saved my life. Somebody in his church, to this day I don't know who, said he should go talk to me.

"He prayed with me. That was the last thing I thought I wanted. He took a bottle of cheap bourbon from my hand and poured it down the drain in the kitchen. They went through the cupboards and poured all my liquor down the drain. That's been almost nineteen years ago now. I'd be dead, or worse if he hadn't challenged me to man up. Yes, sir, he was the finest man I ever met. You know, he did my old man's funeral too. God's giving him a big hug about now, I have no doubt." Emotion began to overtake the officer and he drove the rest of the way to the station in silence.

As Becca stepped from the patrol car, the policeman smiled at her. "Your daddy's watching you darlin'. It's all gonna work out in the end. If it doesn't, it ain't the end. Your dad told me that years ago."

"Thank you."

The patrolman walked her into the station and to a small room off the main hall.

"I'll leave the door open. When they finish with you, I'll carry you home."

Chapter Nineteen

In the three months since the murders of Warren and Judy Poore, Orvin drifted back into its same old, slow, uneventful self. The death of Michael Blackbear seemed an eternity ago. Still, as he lay in the dark at night, Cole was haunted by the image of the young veteran raising the gun to his head.

Cole dreaded going downtown today with Kelly. Since Rebecca Poore took over the Children's Center, Kelly reduced her days of volunteer work each week down to two. Three weeks ago she actually forgot it was the day she was supposed to go in. In gratitude for her generous help during the transition, Kelly was asked to be one of the four people to hold the banner at the dedication and re-christening of the Center.

The words on his monitor became just funny, black marks on a white background as Cole let his eyes fall out of focus, and he drifted deep into his own thoughts. This was the third book he had started in as many months. After reviewing *Tears of an Angel* he realized what a foolish, overworked and, frankly, silly idea the story of a girl and a diamond in WWII was. His second book was an attempt at a science fiction novel. That, too, was abandoned after he realized he couldn't come up with a satisfactory means of the hero actually getting to go back in time. His latest effort was the story of a journalist caught in a web of corrupt politicians, the mob, and his own conscience. He was nearly ten thousand words in, but it slowed to less than a drip of words on the page per day.

Cole stared at the folder on the monitor labeled *Books Ideas, Outlines*. He hit delete, and in two keystrokes it was gone, as were all his fruitless attempts at being a novelist.

He heard a noise in the kitchen and called to Kelly. "What time do we have to leave?"

"About half an hour, are you ready to go?"

"Ready as I'll ever be." Cole closed his laptop. He leaned back in his chair and tried to remember the name of the girl who was killed struggling with her sister. He started to ask Kelly but decided bringing up painful memories was probably not the best idea on what was meant to be a happy and exciting reopening.

"You're not ready to go." Kelly not only sounded annoyed but she was frowning as she moved toward the desk.

"What's that supposed to mean?" Cole stood, reached his arms out and turned around.

"You're really gonna wear a pair of jeans?"

"Why, yes, I am. What's the matter? Isn't my belt buckle big enough? You're the only one that's going to be seen. Nobody cares what I wear. Besides, I intend to sneak off the second that ribbon is cut and go to the post office."

"Alright, I'm going to run upstairs and finish getting dressed."

An hour later, Cole found himself standing in a group of around forty people listening to speech after speech; by the mayor, the head of the Chamber of Commerce, and the president of the Rotary Club. He felt quite proud of himself having made it through all the speeches so far. Now it was Rebecca Poore's turn at the podium.

The royal blue dress she wore was modern, age-appropriate, and quite flattering. Her hair was pulled back and tied with a matching ribbon. For the first time Cole saw her in make-up and, all-in-all, she looked quite lovely.

Rebecca stood for several seconds looking out over the crowd. "As you all know this has been a very dark season for my family. Many times over the last three months I have questioned the wisdom of continuing with this project. To be truthful, at times I questioned my sanity. The crowd stood silent. "Laugh, it was a joke." Rebecca gave a broad smile and the twinkle in her eye showed a woman in complete control of her surroundings and her determination to achieve her goals. "My father," She looked skyward for an almost undetectable second, "My father had a favorite Bible verse, Galatians 6:9. 'Let us not grow weary of doing good, for in due season we will reap, if we do not give up.' Since his death, it has comforted me not just by God's love, but it was like having him with me, and his arm around my shoulder, as I took on tasks that at times seemed more than I could bear.

"Today, as we gather here to honor my father's dream and dedicate the new Warren Poore Children's Center, I want you, the people of my hometown, to know that it is my dream too. My father had a good idea, but it didn't go far enough. I want this Center to be a tool for mending the hurts and long-held, wrongful beliefs that have kept the people of this community apart. No one is to blame, and everyone is to blame. White, Hispanic, Indian, African-American, every member of this community is welcome and will be represented here.

"It is my belief, and goal, that this Center will raise up a generation of children that will be free of prejudice, hate, and distrust of their neighbors here in Orvin. So, please join me in pledging a commitment to seeing that this dream becomes a reality."

Rebecca left the podium and, along with Kelly and the other speakers, moved to the front of the doors. A pretty redheaded woman from the Chamber of Commerce, with the help of her boss, unrolled a yellow ribbon with the words *Congratulations*. It sparkled with way too much glitter she obviously applied after its purchase. Rebecca Poore was given the three-foot ceremonial scissors.

"There's someone I want up here with me during this ribbon cutting ceremony, without whose help, support, and encouragement I could have never gotten the Center reopened. Even though it was mostly done on Face Time, I couldn't have done it without him. Matt Walker, could you please join me?"

From the side of the crowd, a handsome young man in Wrangler jeans and a crisp, blue, oxford cloth shirt approached Rebecca. She reached up with her free hand grasping the collar of his shirt and pulled him towards her. She gave him a kiss to the applause of the onlookers.

"That was just a nice way of saying Thank you," she giggled. "I guess this is where I say thank you to everyone, and I declare the Warren Poore Children's Center open for business." Rebecca whacked at the ribbon with the scissors. It didn't cut so she tried it again. Still not cutting, Matt reached into his pocket for a small pocket knife and slit the ribbon in two. Then she added, "I told you I couldn't do this without him." The crowd laughed and applauded.

Rebecca turned, opened the double doors and said, "Come take a look. We've got cookies and a big cake, lots of coffee, and some pretty good punch."

Cole made his way through the crowd to where Kelly stood to chat with the young redhead from the Chamber of Commerce. "I'm going to run over to the post office." Cole held up the blue envelope containing Jenny's birthday card.

"Don't you want some cake and coffee?"

"Yeah, maybe when I get back."

"Okay, I'll be here."

Cole turned and made his way from the crowd.

"Hey there, Mr. Sage."

Cole greeted the clerk at the window by waving the envelope in his hand. "Got one going to Paris. Got any kind of fun stamps?"

"Let me go look."

A couple of minutes later the clerk returned with three sheets of stamps and an envelope. "Say, you know somebody expecting something from the

State Department? This was undeliverable. But, look here, your name made it through."

There was a splash of something dark across the address leaving only fragments of Orvin, OK, the zip code, and Cole's name at the bottom left corner.

The clerk looked intently at the envelope. "One of the gals in the back recognized your name."

Cole looked at the return address. His stomach flipped over.

It wasn't just the State Department; it was the U.S. Citizenship and Immigration Services.

"You okay, Mr. Sage? You look a little peaked."

"I'm fine. The stamps?"

"Well, we've got *Flowers of the West*, *Lena Horne*; I got a couple of *John Lennon's* available."

"Never liked him. I'm a George guy, myself." Cole looked over the stamps spread out on the counter.

"I'm a George guy too, George Strait." The clerk grinned.

Cole gave a weak chuckle looking down again at the envelope.

"And here are some Mr. Rogers, and a whole sheet of these silly Scooby-Doo things."

"This is for my granddaughter's tenth birthday, those seem a little young. Got anything else?"

"Well, let's see." The clerk pulled out her drawer under the counter and lifted the tray. "I've got these left."

Cole looked down to see three stamps illustrated with colorful kites.

"Perfect, give me those." Cole put two dollars on the counter.

"I don't need the change. Just use all three of those stamps. I'm in kind of a hurry."

Out on the sidewalk, Cole approached a bench in front of the Post Office and began to tear open the envelope. As he sat down, he pulled the single sheet of trifold paper from the end of the ripped envelope and began to read.

> Mr. Blackbear,
> We are pleased to tell you that your application for your fiancée Miriam Al-Omari, and your son, is being processed. We have made attempts to reach you by phone with no success.
> We have forwarded the letter of approval to the American Embassy in Bagdad for her to pick up at her earliest convenience.
> It is also our pleasure to inform you that as family of a Veteran of the United States Army and of the conflict in Iraq, we are extending to Miriam and your son transportation on an Air Force transport plane with a destination of Vance Air Force Base, Enid Oklahoma. Details and arrangements to be worked out in country by US military personnel. The necessary documents will be included in the packet sent to our Embassy in Bagdad.
> Congratulations, we are pleased to be able to bring your family back together again.

Sincerely,
Susan Waltham
Secretary to Donald W. Syverson
Under Secretary of State

Cole folded the letter and returned it to the envelope. The sidewalk was busy for a Saturday morning. A young woman with long, dark hair pushed a stroller passed him and smiled. Cole nodded.

A Styrofoam cup caught by the wind bounced down the sidewalk. Hitting a seam in the concrete it bounced and caught by a gust, it blew into the gutter. It bounced twice and rolled into the street. A pick-up rolled by missing the cup, but the little, green Fiat that came next smashed it flat.

Kind of like life, Cole thought. I think I'll use that in a book. He made an 'oomph' sound. "Forget it."

Cole's mind shifted to Miriam and the little boy. How would they react to getting their Visa? He was sure no one notified them of Michael Blackbear's death. When she couldn't make contact with him, would she still make the 7,000-mile journey to a foreign country where she didn't know anyone, with no promise of meeting up with the father of her child? Would the Immigration Officials let her stay without an American husband or fiancé?

Cole sighed deeply and slapped his thigh with the envelope. He struggled within himself for an answer to the question that he wouldn't let formulate. What was his responsibility in all this?

"When did you take to sitting on benches?"

Cole looked up. Standing in front of him was the old guy he met on the bench in front of the Children's Center the same day he met Michael Blackbear.

"I figured you'd be down with all the swells at the ribbon cutting."

"How you doin'? Have a piece of my bench." Cole grinned and scooted over a bit.

"Whatcha got here?" The old guy reached for the letter.

Cole grinned. There was nothing shy about the old guy, no filters and no worry about social convention. Cole handed him the letter.

"Kind of the ending to a sad story."

He began to read the letter. "Blackbear, isn't that the fella that was holding up the jewelry stores?" What do you suppose his idea was?"

"Another way."

"How's that?"

"He gave up on the legal options and decided to buy their way here. The cops found the phone number of a known Coyote in his jeans pocket."

"And here's the help he needed." The old guy handed the letter back to Cole.

"Yep."

"So what now?"

"I have no idea."

"Way I see, it ain't your rodeo, ain't your horse, somebody else can clean up after it."

"I've been sitting here thinking what I might have said, or done, different. I think I have come to the same conclusion."

"You can't regret things. It will drive you crazy. Look at me."

"What do you mean?"

"I have regrets that put me on benches and barstools."

"What's your biggest regret?" Cole watched the old guy look at his hands, his thoughts forming.

"I guess it all comes down to this town."

"How so?"

"I wish I'd left this one-horse-mud-hole years ago. No, that ain't it. I wish I never came back after the war. I wish I'd seen the world. I regret that. I wish I could have seen the world." The old guy looked over at Cole. "You seen the world?"

"Yep. I have been all over the world. Six of the seven continents and I lost track of countries."

"Which one did you miss? There are seven, right?"

"Antarctica."

"Hell, that don't count. Nobody there. I would have loved to see people in other places doin' what they do, see how they dress and eat what they eat."

"Travel memories are the one thing nobody can ever take away from you. Those people you meet, the food, the history. You're right."

"So, tell me. What do you regret?"

"Not much, to tell the truth. But you know--" Cole stopped. He thought of Ellie. He thought of the years he spent thinking about her. That was his regret. Though he would never speak it. "Looking back, I think God guides our path. There are things I would have changed, sure. Thing is, I wouldn't have what I have now. So, I guess you can't dwell on the past. Like Dylan said, 'Don't look back'."

"Who's Dylan?"

"A fella I grew up with."

"I think he was onto something." The old guy slapped his knees. "Yes sir, I think he was onto something." He nodded and lifted his chin toward Cole. "So now what?"

"What do you mean?"

"You've got leavin' written all over your face. All I had to do was mention seein' the world and you were already gone. Your woman know you feel like that?"

Cole laughed. It felt fake, forced, and contrived. "I think she just might."

"If I was your age, no way would I use up my life sittin' around here. That's all I'm doin', sittin' around waitin' to die."

"You've got a long time before that happens. Maybe we should chop a few cars." Cole grinned at the old guy.

"You don't look like a chopper. What did you do before you got here?"

"I spent my whole life as a newspaperman."

"You a writer?"

"That's what they paid me for. War correspondent, political and community social issues, murder investigations, you name it, I wrote about it."

"I'll be damned. You should write a book!"

"I've been trying. I think the well's gone dry." Cole shrugged.

"What have you been writing about?" The old guy was genuinely interested.

"I started out writing a book about corrupt officials and the mob, then a time travel science fiction thing, the last one was about a girl with a diamond she carries through WWII and concentration camps."

"You know about all that stuff?"

"Apparently not enough."

"How's that?"

"When I read it back, it was all crap. It wouldn't hold anybody's interest, it just sounds silly. It certainly wouldn't sell. Funny thing. Just before I came down here for the ribbon cutting, I deleted it all."

"What's that mean, exactly? I'm not a computer guy. But it don't sound good."

"It is exactly what it sounds like. I had it all in a file and I hit the delete button, erasing it all from the computer. Good-bye and farewell."

"Isn't that kind of like building a house, then burning it to the ground?"

Cole looked at the old guy and smiled brightly. "That, my friend, is a brilliant analogy. That is exactly what it is like. The thing is, though, these houses were shacks." Cole laughed and smiled at the old guy with appreciation.

"You don't seem none to upset about it."

"Not a bit."

"So what are you gonna do now?"

"Well, since you won't chop cars with me, I'm not sure."

"I'm serious. Don't poke fun at me. I ain't pokin' fun at you." The old guy was clearly offended by Cole's repeated reference to his criminal past.

"Sorry, I meant no disrespect. I truly don't know."

"How many years you in the writing game?"

"Almost thirty."

"And you been all over the world?"

"A lot of it. Where'd you live?"

"Chicago and San Francisco, mostly."

The old guy considered Cole's answers before speaking. " 'To thine own self be true.' I heard that somewhere."

"Shakespeare."

"You makin' fun again? When would I have read Shakespeare? I believe it was in a Willie Nelson song. An old one. Anyways, you need to write about the stuff you saw. Make it like an adventure story. You can start with that crazy Indian friend of yours. Write a detective story about him. Hell, you got the wow finish right there." The old guy pointed at the envelope from the State Department.

Cole slapped the palm of his hand with the envelope. He looked at the guy for a long moment. "You're right. It has all the key elements of a great mystery."

"So where do you start?"

Cole squinted. "I'm going to start with meeting you out in front of the Children's Center."

"Why would you put me in a book?"

"Because you're like the chorus in a Greek tragedy."

"What in the Sam Hill does that mean?"

"In ancient times all the old Greek plays would have an oracle, or a group of people, who stood off to the side of the stage and, from time to time during the course of the play, they would explain what was going on. That's what you're going to do in the book."

"But we've only spoken two or three times."

"That, my friend, is why they call it fiction."

"That's the dangest thing I've ever heard of. Here I've spent my whole life trying to stay *out* of the newspaper and you come along, a newspaperman, and put me in a book!" The old guy laughed heartily. "Can I have some cool gadgets like MacGyver?"

Cole looked at him and grinned. "Let's not get carried away." Cole stared at the grill of the pickup parked in front of their bench. He thought about how he could change the facts of the location and the facts of the story enough to not draw direct parallels. Changing the names is easy. So is changing the town and the state. The Children's Center can be a battered women's home. This will be a piece of cake, Cole thought.

"Hey, where'd you go?"

Cole chuckled. "I was already laying out the book in my head."

"Just like that?"

"Just like that."

Cole stood and extended his hand to the old guy. "I can't thank you enough. I feel like I have a whole new lease on life. I can do this."

"Well just make sure I get a copy when you're done."

Cole took two steps away from the bench, turned and said, "I'll even autograph it."

Cole had only taken about ten steps when he turned back to the old guy on the bench. He was gone. *I don't even know his name,* Cole thought and chuckled. *I'm sure I'll run into him again.*

Cole strode towards the Children's Center with new confidence and purpose in his step. He could take what he knew and write what was true, all wrapped up into a mystery novel. *I finally have got something that I feel confident about writing.* Three more steps and Cole came to a complete stop. He pumped both fists in the air at shoulder height and said out loud, "I've got it!" He nearly made the couple that was approaching him jump off the sidewalk. *Michael Blackbear said it himself. He gave me the title. I've got the title,* The Last Casualty. *It's perfect. Wait till I tell Kelly.*

THE END

COLE CUTS

Exclusive sample from Book 10

ONE

"No entiendo." The dark man in the sweat-stained work clothes shook his head and shrugged signaling his lack of understanding.

"I need a worker. Trabajo." The driver spoke through the passenger side window of his small green Toyota pickup.

The Hispanic man laughed and smiled, nodding his head. "Si! Trabajo. Me."

"That's right." The driver got out of his pickup and around the back to where the man now stood. He took a small stack of folded bills from his pocket and held them up. There was a twenty showing and it hid the other ten one-dollar bills neatly.

"OK." The dark-skinned man smiled and nodded.

"Now?" The driver pointed his index finger to the ground and bobbed his hand up and down at the wrist. "Let's go. Vamanos." He jerked his outstretched thumb to show motion.

"Si. We go."

The driver of the pickup pointed at the small duffle bag the worker carried, then to the back of the truck. As the newly hired man moved to put his pack in the bed of the truck, the employer stepped aside letting a shiny chrome bar slip from his jacket sleeve into his hand. With a swift, powerful movement he swung the bar, striking the worker at the base of his skull killing him instantly. The force of the blow sent him falling face-first into the truck bed, leaving his legs to dangle over the side. In one quick movement, the driver of the truck grabbed the man by the ankles and rolled him into the back of the truck.

Moments later, the dark green truck was tossing gravel behind it as it sped away from the desolate stretch of road. The driver tapped rhythmically on the steering wheel while the music from the CD player filled the cab.

"Going 'round the world in a pickup truck. Ain't goin' down 'til the sun comes up." The driver couldn't contain his excitement and the rapid beat of the song matched his heart rate.

He looked over at the chrome bar laying in the passenger seat. A flash of light danced about the cab from its freshly wiped down mirror surface. Fifteen minutes later, he reached his destination. The well-worn path through the dry grass down to the river was rutted and filled with shallow potholes.

Near the end of the path, the little truck turned and headed along the crushed grass parallel to the river under the spreading branches of an old Black Walnut that towered above the water below. This area of the river was no good for fishing. The locals all went a half-mile downstream to a bend that formed a series of deep pools.

The driver got out of the truck and took a look around the area. This time of day it was too late to fish and too early for the high school kids to come out to party. This was his section of the river. Not by right or conquest, but because nobody else cared about it.

He tilted the seat forward and pulled a pair of blue latex gloves from a McDonald's bag. He removed them from the box preventing any possible visual in his truck. Half the pickups in Oklahoma had Mickey D's bags or beer cans floating around the floorboards or behind their seats.

He looked down in the back of the truck and smiled. "One down, eleven million to go."

The tailgate came down with a thump. He grabbed the dead man's feet and pulled them toward the end of the bed.

"Too many beans and tortillas make Juan a lard ass." A heavy groan accompanied a second yank of the body.

Rolling the dead man face down, he let his legs fall at the waist. The killer put his arms under the dead man's and lifted him upright. "My gawd, you stink."

To drag a dead body is no easy task. The killer was in excellent physical condition, yet he grew winded and found himself struggling to get his victim to the riverbank. Once his foot twisted in a gopher hole and he stumbled, nearly falling under the weight of his load.

As he reached the path down to the river, he gave the dead man a shove and let gravity and the slope of the bank take him to the water's edge. He moved quickly and methodically to remove the man's clothes. He tossed them carefully into a three-foot circle of rock he laid out before his first kill. There must be organization, proper methodology, and undistracted concentration. This would be a long and bloody battle if he was to win the war. And he would win.

As the man lay naked on the bank of the river, the killer thought for the briefest moment how very much he looked like a woman, smooth hairless skin the color of his morning latte, oddly curved for a man. He found himself ever so slightly aroused.

Giving his head a hard shake in an effort to focus, he took the dead man's wrists and pulled him the rest of the way to the water. A large flat rock sat half in the water and half lodged in the bank. He moved the body as close as he could to the rock without the possibility of it falling into the slow-moving water.

The man returned to the truck and took a small hatchet from the back. He felt the bit of the hatchet's head and admired the finely honed edge he put on it. He once again took a long moment to look around the area, up and down the row of trees and the narrow path that led to the popular end of the river. Deserted, neglected, and isolated, he was alone with his task.

Maneuvering his victim's dead weight was the part of this undertaking he struggled with the most. It must be done, so he soldiered on. He took the dead man's right hand and placed it as close to the center of the rock as he could. He picked up the hatchet and, in one forceful stroke, severed the hand from the body.

Removing a small black nylon bag from his pocket, he placed the right hand of the man in the bag.

"Thank you." The killer nodded down at the body.

Grabbing the other arm, he rolled the corpse over repeating the action, only this time the hand was palm up. He did not place this hand in the bag nor did he speak. He took the ankles again and turned the body placing both feet on the rock.

The bones and tendons of the leg made the removal of the feet more difficult, Sparks shot from the rock as the steel hatchet struck. It took two forceful blows to remove them.

He took the two feet and remaining hand to the water's edge. He submerged each and washed them. He thought of Jesus and washing the disciples' feet. He, too, claimed a symbolic spiritual cleansing. This alien to his land, this army of lawbreakers, must be redeemed. He laid the feet on the hard sand of the shore. Yet, as he washed the left hand of the dead man, he felt more of a kinship to Pontius Pilate.

"I am innocent of this man's blood." In his heart, he believed the words he quoted.

When his tasks were completed, he made his way up to a row of trees away from the site where he dismembered the dead man. About fifty yards down the bank, he threw the feet into the river. He moved another thirty feet or so more and threw the hand with all his might, trying to reach the other bank, but fell short and it landed in the water with a silent splash.

Returning to his pickup, he retrieved a red plastic gas container. Back at the fire pit where he tossed the dead man's clothing, he doused them completely with gas. He lit a wooden match from a box in his pocket, and set the pile of clothes alight, then tossed in the box of matches.

Tearing a small branch from the walnut tree he carefully brushed away any sign of his footprints in the soil. He picked up the hatchet and got back in the truck. Once seated in the truck, he swept away the last mark of his presence at the scene and closed the door.

Following the rutted path back to the main road, he stopped for a moment. He lowered the sun visor and took a CD from the holder. "Garth, you won't do for the ride back." He ejected the disc from the player and replaced it with the new selection.

The lilting strings of *Vivaldi's Four Seasons* filled the cab. He slipped the ejected CD into the holder, flipped up the visor, and pulled onto the road and headed back to Orvin.

****

"Cole, you have to do something about this dog!" Kelly showed her growing frustration with the new member of the family.

"He's just a puppy."

"Puppy! It's as big as a horse! It eats like one, too!" Kelly was getting madder and wasn't about to take Cole's platitudes any longer.

"What do you want me to do?"

"Tie it up, muzzle it, better yet, get rid of it." Kelly stood looking at her devastated flower beds. "Do you know how hard it was to get these flowers to take hold? Look at them! That animal's destroyed them all." Kelly burst into angry tears.

Cole stood at the top of the porch steps looking down at Kelly's flower beds. It was an impossible situation and he knew it. There would be no peace until the dog was dealt with.

"So, you want me to get rid of him? What am I going to do with him?"

"Give it back. What kind of a person dumps a dog on somebody anyway? We didn't ask for it. I certainly don't want it. Give it back." Kelly stood, her hands on her hips, surveying the damage.

"Ernie thought he was doing something nice. I don't want to hurt his feelings."

"Nice! Nice would have been, 'Hey Kelly, would you like a dog?' Nice would have been, 'I have a puppy that needs a home'. Nice, is not 'Here, I brought you a dog'! Why didn't you say no? I would have. Where'd he get it anyway?"

"A guy was asking around the deli. Ernie thought of us."

"Then he can give it back to the original owner. Really, come on, that's not a dog, it's a pony!"

She was right and Cole knew it. The dog had to go. As if on cue, the big golden blond dog came bounding around the corner of the house. The half German Shepherd, half Saint Bernard pup was almost the size of a full-grown Lab already, and it was headed straight for Kelly.

"Duke!" Cole shouted at the dog, but life always switches into slow motion before a disaster.

The dog hit Kelly at full speed, its huge paws landing on her shoulders knocking her onto her back. The dog stood above her licking her face as she swatted at it demanding it to stop.

Cole raced down the steps to Kelly's aid. "Duke! No! Bad dog!"

Kelly rolled to her side away from the slobbers of her unwanted pet and scrambled to her feet. "That's it!" Kelly raced up the steps and into the house.

The dog turned and jumped up on Cole. He patted the dog's side. "Now you've done it, you big dummy." Cole pushed the dog off him. "We better get out of here until things cool off. Let's go for a walk."

The fields of the countryside were a great place for a big dog like Duke to romp and run. The leash of a city dog would be pointless. Jackrabbit chasing and the manic sniffing of everything in sight was part of the fun for the dog. Expending some of his boundless energy was a bonus for Cole. The walk was good exercise for Cole and, truth be told, he loved the times outdoors with Duke.

The gate creaked and Duke shot through it like the holding stall at a horse race.

"Duke! Wait!"

The dog raced toward the road. To the right, a white F150 truck roared up the road. Cole broke into a jog and headed for what he knew would be the scene of a tragedy. As he ran he could envision the unwavering Ford plowing into the body of the oblivious dog.

"Stop, you stupid mutt! Please! Stop!" Cole desperately called as he panted and tried to speed up.

The pipes of the truck sounded like the roar of approaching thunder. Cole stopped and watched as the dog and the truck drew ever closer to a fatal collision. The throaty blare of the truck's air horn filled the air, but it didn't slow.

Cole covered his eyes unwilling to witness the devastation to come. The horn blared two long blasts and Cole sensed the sound moving to his left. He peeked through his fingers to see Duke running back to where he stood.

Cole's heart raced as the dog ran back to him barking happily. He didn't know whether to hug him or kick him in the butt. He settled for a slap on Duke's rump as he circled Cole with the joyous freedom of leaving the fenced yard.

The warm morning air was welcome after the cold harsh winds of winter, and the rains of spring. Cole stretched his arms wide as he strolled along. Duke ran from tree to tree and did circles in the freshly plowed ground across the road. The thought of getting rid of the big, golden beast saddened Cole. He really was growing attached to the overgrown pup. Kelly was right though, he was no dog trainer, and the "chew it" period was becoming costly. Cole's favorite desert boots and a pair of Kelly's expensive heels fell victim to Duke's need to chew.

If he would admit it, not only to Kelly but to himself as well, he put up little resistance to Ernie's gift and was actually pleased with the thought of a combination watchdog and pet. His heart sank as he watched Duke take off after a rabbit.

"It's not your fault." Cole sighed.

The sight of Duke in a full extension gallop was a thing of beauty. The grace and power of the youthful animal was a promise of things to come. Cole smiled at the thought of Duke catching up to the rabbit. He was sure the dog would have no clue what to do with it.

As they continued down the road. Cole whistled a mournful tune. For a moment he lost sight of Duke. Oh, great, he thought, scanning the horizon. To his right, he spotted Duke. The dog was running full out toward him. This was not normal. The end of the walk usually ended with Duke's tongue out and panting and then a leisurely stroll back to the house.

Fifty yards or so from Cole, Duke began to bark. There was a sense of urgency about the sound of his barking. It wasn't the happy bark of the day in the fields. The dog was trying to tell him something. That's silly, Cole thought. But as Duke drew nearer the pitch of the bark changed. Reaching Cole, Duke first stopped in front of him, then gave a sideward jump. He barked and ran, circling Cole, then in short, halting bursts back toward the field across the way.

Without thinking Cole began walking in the direction of the field. Duke ran ahead stopping every few yards and turned as if to see if Cole was still following. On a grassy knoll, he could just see over the drop to the river. On a clearing near an edge of the riverbank, Duke stopped and barked at something on the ground. The tall grass kept Cole from seeing what was disturbing the dog until he reached Duke and the edge of the field.

On the ground was the body of a man, spread eagle, face down, wearing nothing but a pair of worn boxers. His hair was black, long, and matted with blood. Cole stared as he realized the man's hands and feet were hacked off.

Sensing his job done, Duke returned to his master and sat waiting for approval.

The trip back to the house and the wait for the Sheriff's department to arrive took nearly twenty minutes. In the interim, Cole tried to explain to Kelly how Duke led him to the body.

"He acted like he knew what he was doing, Kell." He came and got me. He did everything but lead me by the hand. I've never seen anything like it. I thought that stuff only happened in movies."

"The body, the person, are you sure it was a man? You said the person had long hair."

"Not long, long. Just longer than most people wear these days. He was brown. I think maybe he was Mexican? He was the strangest color, Kelly. Like a grey-brown. The weird thing is there was no blood anywhere."

"You mean stranger than the absence of feet and hands?" Kelly's words were soft and in no way ironic. "Why cut off feet? Hands, I can understand. No fingerprints to ID the victim. But feet?" She gazed at Cole. "Are you OK?"

"Yeah, yeah fine. It's not like I haven't seen dead bodies before. In the Congo, they stacked them like firewood. I saw whole villages massacred in Cambodia. This wasn't like a murder, a stabbing, or a gang shooting like in Chicago. This was harsh, cruel. This poor guy was violated, humiliated, dumped.

"You never told me you'd seen--" Kelly's voice trailed off.

"I didn't mean to upset you. I'm sorry, I was kind of thinking out loud."

"I'm not upset. I'm hurting. For you and your memories."

"A long time ago." Cole moved to Kelly and took her in his arms. "A long time ago."

The sound of tires on gravel, along with Duke's barking, announced the arrival of the Sheriff's deputy. Cole moved out to the porch.

"Mr. Sage?"

"Yes. This is my wife, Kelly." Cole turned and smiled reassuringly at Kelly.

"So, you want to tell me what's going on?" He seemed far too relaxed for a murder investigation.

"I was walking my dog and he came upon a body." Cole pointed down the road. "He's at the back of the field, next to the river."

"He?"

"Yeah, a man, Hispanic I think." Cole frowned at the thought of the man's body.

"You good enough to show me?" The deputy asked.

"Yeah, I'm fine." Cole stepped down from the porch.

"Hop in." The deputy gave his head a jerk in the direction of the passenger side of his cruiser.

"We'll be back in a few minutes. You want to hang onto the dog?"

"Sure," Kelly said, watching Cole get in the car.

As they backed out of the drive, the deputy turned the squelch of the radio down a bit. "My forensic guys are on their way. You have any idea who the victim is?"

"No. No idea. I think he was dumped." Cole looked straight ahead.

"How would you know that?"

"I've seen a lot of bodies in my time. Newspaperman in Chicago and war correspondent." Cole thought he better explain his remark. "There's no blood. Anywhere."

"Huh. Chicago. Lot of bodies around there."

"It's a lot worse now. Still, there were plenty."

"So which field?"

"Down a ways, by that row of trees." Cole pointed.

Without hesitation, the deputy turned down the dirt path next to the trees. "Old Nelson's not gonna like this. I'm surprised he hasn't given you hell for being on his land."

"Never met him."

"You're the one who inherited that farm, right?"

"That would be me." Cole's head rocked and hit the side window as the car hit a big dip in the path.

"You folks have really done a nice job on it."

"A lot of the credit goes to Ernie Kappas, my neighbor."

"Oh, the fella that owns the sandwich shop. With the black wife."

"She's my cousin."

"No shit," The deputy exclaimed. "I'll have to hear that story sometime."

"There!" Cole pointed at the river. "The body's along there."

The deputy stopped the car and they went the rest of the way on foot.

"Man, they did a number on him." The deputy was taken aback by the sight of the half-naked man lying halfway between the dirt and the water. From the way the man's face lay in the sand Cole realized his face was bashed in. "So which of these prints you suppose are yours?"

Cole picked up his foot and rested it on his knee, showing the deputy the pattern on his cross-trainers.

"Got it." The deputy moved back to the car. A few moments later he returned with a roll of yellow tape and a handful of wooden stakes. "Better mark this off."

The radio squawked and a crackling voice filled the air. "Hey, Steve, where you at?"

The deputy returned to his car and turned on the red and blue roof lights.

"I see ya," the voice responded.

Within minutes, the forensics team took control of the scene. They set about taking pictures, examining the body, and taking a temperature reading to determine the time of death.

Cole leaned against the car watching. A few minutes later another deputy and plain-clothed detective in a dark blue Chrysler arrived on scene.

"Hey, how you doin'?" The man extended his hand to Cole.

"Detective Chrisman. Call me Todd."

"Cole Sage."

"I take it you found the body."

"I did."

"How's that for detective work?" Chrisman grinned.

Cole sighed and his sneer showed his discomfort at the detective's quip.

"Too soon?" Chrisman shrugged.

"A bit."

"I know you probably already told Steve there what happened, but if you wouldn't mind… "

"I was out with my dog. Not leashed. He was running around chasing rabbits and rolling in the grass. He disappeared for a minute or so, and the next thing I know he's racing back to me barking like crazy. So, I followed him back to the scene and that's when I saw the body. No, I didn't touch anything. I got no closer than about twelve feet. The deputy has already identified my shoe print. I returned home and called you guys."

"That it?"

"Pretty much."

"Hold tight. I'll go see what there is to see." Chrisman started towards the deputy. "Hey, Stevie!" Chrisman called out as he made his way to the deputy.

One of the men from the forensics van retrieved a gurney and a black body bag.

"We double as Coroner's deputies," The man said passing Cole.

Cole nodded.

The deputy returned to Cole after about ten minutes. "How 'bout I run you home? We could be a while. No sense you just hangin' around. I'm sure you have better things to do."

"Thanks, if you don't mind, I think I'll just walk home."

"No problem. I'm Steve Knight. We sure appreciate your help." The deputy extended his hand and Cole shook his hand.

"I don't know how much help I was."

"You got us here before he got ripe, that's a lot in my book." Knight smiled. "We'll need you to come down and give a formal statement."

"Gotcha. I expect I'll see you later." Cole glanced up at the arrival of yet another Sheriff's car. "Quite the turnout."

"No doubt. Chrisman will be point on the investigation. Nice meetin' ya."

"Yeah, you too." Cole turned toward home.

"Hey, thank that dog of yours!"

Cole waved, his back to the deputy.

****

"What is that dog doing now?" Kelly stepped through the kitchen door. "Cole! Please do something about your dog!" Kelly got no reply. "Where are you?"

The muffled answer came from upstairs, "Bathroom!"

The pawing and barking continued. Kelly made her way to the front door. Throwing open the door she saw Duke now sitting on his hind legs staring up at her.

"What is it? Did Timmy fall down the well?" Kelly asked sarcastically.

The dog barked and pawed the doormat, drawing Kelly's eyes downward. Sitting on the mat was a foot, ashen grey and drained of blood. The dog barked up at her.

"Cole!" Kelly let out a blood-curdling scream.

About the Author

Micheal Maxwell has traveled the globe on the lookout for strange sights, sounds, and people. His adventures have taken him from the Jungles of Ecuador and the Philippines to the top of the Eiffel Tower and the Golden Gate Bridge, and from the cave dwellings of Native Americans to The Kehlsteinhaus, Hitler's Eagles Nest! He's always looking for a story to tell and interesting people to meet.

Micheal Maxwell was taught the beauty and majesty of the English language by Bob Dylan, Robertson Davies, Charles Dickens, and Leonard Cohen.

Mr. Maxwell has dined with politicians, rock stars and beggars. He has rubbed shoulders with priests and murderers, surgeons and drug dealers, each one giving him a part of themselves that will live again in the pages of his books.

Micheal Maxwell has found a niche in the mystery, suspense, genre with The Cole Sage Series that gives readers an everyman hero, short on vices, long on compassion, and a sense of fair play, and the willingness to risk everything to right wrongs. The Cole Sage Series departs from the usual, heavily sexual, profanity-laced norm and gives readers character-driven stories, with twists, turns, and page-turning plot lines.

Micheal Maxwell writes from a life of love, music, film, and literature. Along with his lovely wife and travel partner, Janet, divide their time between a small town in the Sierra Nevada Mountains of California, and their lake home in Washington State.

Made in the USA
Columbia, SC
08 July 2021